Poor Kid Wealthy Kid

Lester & Edith,

Enjoy my book and best wishes to both of you!

[illegible]

Poor Kid Wealthy Kid

By
David Espinoza

E-BookTime, LLC
Montgomery, Alabama

Poor Kid Wealthy Kid

Library of Congress Control Number: 2011911461

ISBN: 978-1-60862-311-2

First Edition
Published July 2011
E-BookTime, LLC
6598 Pumpkin Road
Montgomery, AL 36108
www.e-booktime.com

Dedications

To my parents, Wences and Gabriela – thank you for always being there when times were hard, we survived the storm.

To my reader and editing partner, who happens to be my wife, Loni Espinoza – thanks for putting up with me.

To my two sons (Jake and Matt) and to my two step-daughters (Kalin and Darci) – y'all motivate me in life.

To my co-workers, Jeremy and his son (Sam), Cheryl, Terry, Shamus, Rick, Ron, Steve, Teresa, Ginger, and Paul – thanks for the names and best wishes.

To my friends and teachers in Dimmitt, Texas – the good memories live on.

To Donna French, the original Miss Sweet Home.

To Elaine Cover, a wonderful elementary teacher – you'll always be remembered.

Last Day of School in Texas

In the late spring of 1976 Carlos wakes up early for the last day of school at Dimmitt Jr. High. Carlos is finishing his eighth grade year. He comes from a large family of three brothers and two sisters.

His dad is leaving for work bright and early. A janitor is one of the few jobs he qualifies for. Pete Swavey does a very good job maintaining a grade school in Dimmitt, Texas. He somehow manages to feed his family on very little money.

Dimmitt is a small town with a few gas stations and a population of 4,371 people.

"How do I get to the library?" one might ask.

"Oh ... just take a right at the light and you'll see it on your left – you can't miss it," a friendly local will reply.

Dimmitt, Texas, sits in the north part of Texas – they call it The Panhandle. The area relies on cotton gins, feedlots, and plenty of farming. Most of the people from there are friendly and seem to know each other very well. The southern accent doesn't get any better.

Carlos is a very popular kid among his peers. He is very athletic but when it comes to books he struggles a little bit. In fact, he struggles to the point that it's quite embarrassing to him.

In Dimmitt, there is a grocery store that rewards kids with an apple for every A earned on their report cards. Carlos has never accomplished that. He did enjoy the apples vicariously through his friends though.

Carlos jumps out of bed as he hears one of his sisters open the squeaky bedroom door – *creak*! He runs as fast as he can to get to the bathroom before his sister does.

"You big jerk! I need to use the bathroom!"

"Sorry Sis you'll have to take a ticket, beauty before age."

The Swavey family does not have much money and living in a two bedroom home is not easy. Sometimes if you aren't home when everyone is eating beans and tortillas, well, you're out of luck and looking forward to breakfast the next morning.

The bathroom door pops open, "Okay Sis, it's all yours, I'm fix'n to get ready for school."

There's a line that forms with kids wanting to use the bathroom. Every morning at the Swaveys is a big challenge, but somehow they make it work with only a few arguments. One of the younger kids always ends up crying for some reason or another. Somehow they all seem to understand the poor life with their dad's minimum wage. It's tough being a single income family.

Carlos shuts the front door behind him – *slam*! He starts walking to school. He's wearing some old jeans that had been patched up over and over. Hand-me-downs are what he usually wears.

During Christmas vacations he would savor the flavor of new clothes that his parents, Pete and Isabel, would purchase using a charge card. Unfortunately Christmas is a long ways off from now.

He also wears an old white t-shirt to go along with his jeans. The t-shirt is not torn but visibly old and worn out. Carlos is a nice looking Hispanic kid with light brown complexion. He stands at 5' 10" and is very athletic. He joins one of his friends a couple of blocks down the road on his way to school.

"What's up Rudy?"

"Hey Carlos what's going on … we fix'n to have a blast today? It's the last day of school."

"You know it my main man."

They continue to walk with a few seconds of silence. Rudy looks at Carlos with a sudden change of subject.

"My dad was talking to my mom last night and he said your family might be moving to Oregon. Is that true?"

"That's news to me – haven't heard that yet. I'm always the last one to find out in my family," Carlos replies.

Rudy is a chunky kid with a medium build body, but very clever in the mind. He is one of Carlos' best friends in Dimmitt.

As they arrive at school the bell rings and it's time for the first class to start. The class happens to be Home Economics. Now why would a young boy like Carlos want to take a class like Home Economics? You got it – Carlos has a crush on a pretty girl. Her name is Cecilia. She has light red hair, her skin is white, and she has a few freckles on her cheeks below her sparkling green eyes. Cecilia is a physically fit young lady.

During class Carlos usually smiles at her and she smiles back at him. But that's about as close as things would get. He is too nervous and shy when it comes to talking to girls, especially a nice looking girl like Cecilia. Frequently after class he tries to talk to her. Somehow things just don't go well for him and this time it isn't any different. When the bell rings indicating the end of class, Carlos walks out of the classroom behind Cecilia. He nervously makes an attempt.

"Cecilia, how's your day going?"

"Not too bad I guess, but you've seen my day so far."

"Yeah, uh … uh …"

"Yes, what is it Carlos?"

"Oh, it's nothing I just wanted to say … you look very nice today."

"Thank you, that's very nice of you to say."

As she walks away she winks at him and gives him a big smile. On the last day of the school year he made huge progress. The photographic image of her smile stays with him all day long.

When school is over, Rudy and some of his friends gather at their usual spot in the hallway. It happens to be in front of the gym.

"Hey Carlos! Did you get your report card yet?" Rudy asked.

"Naw, I'm heading over there now."

"I got mine, six As and one B, yes sir!"

"Good job man! I wish I could say the same about mine," Carlos said.

It's a long walk down the hallway to the room where the report cards are picked up. As the boys approach the room to get in line, Carlos is anticipating the embarrassment of bad grades once again. He knows that the lady handing out the report cards always makes a smart-mouth remark. She's a heavyset lady wearing glasses and is in her late forties.

"Hi Carlos, six Ds and one C, you must be a jock. Maybe you should start studying more and playing fewer sports," she expressed.

"Maybe you should start wearing more deodorant and start talking less," Carlos responds.

Rudy busted out laughing, the lady gave them all a very disgusting look.

"Young man there's no reason for your rudeness – if it wasn't the last day of school I would turn you in to the principal."

"Don't listen to that old bag Carlos – she lives a lonely life at home. Let's walk over to the Dimmitt Super Market. I'll give you some of my apples. I get six of them this time."

"Alright man, sounds good. I wish they gave candy bars for Cs and donuts for Ds."

Carlos ate two apples at the park with Rudy and some other friends. This park has a playground, basketball hoops, tennis courts, and a picnic area. It has come to be the regular hangout during the evenings and summers. The park is old and beaten up. The basketball hoops have chains instead of nets. This prevents kids from stealing the nets. The grass is normally dry on an average day, but the oak trees are full of shade.

The day had come to an end and Carlos is on his way back home. He can see the sun setting on a beautiful clear day. It's about 95 degrees and a little humid during the evening. Dimmitt is a town that's surrounded by miles of flat land. There are no mountains, no rivers, but maybe a few lakes. Not much of an exciting geographical location. There is an exciting adventure but it's about sixty miles away. Palo Duro Canyon is a place that the Swaveys would travel to – that's about as exciting the vacations would get. Rodeos were fun but not quite like a vacation – there's plenty of rodeos there. The family could not afford any other kind of vacation.

Palo Duro Canyon is full of old Indian fossils, horse riding trails, and home of the famous play "Texas." The Swaveys never attended that play. It is a great tourist attraction in that part of the Texas Panhandle.

As Carlos arrives home, he is about to be shocked with a big surprise.

"What the heck is going on?" He sees the trailer and rushes in the house, a house that really needs painting. The lawn is very dry, the sidewalks are cracked, and the siding is old and broken down. When he enters their small house, he stops to listen to his dad, Pete, who is discussing an issue with his mom, Isabel.

Pete is a hard worker – he stands about 5' 9". He has dark hair and dark complexion skin – a very strong man with a medium build. Isabel stands about 5' 5" with dark hair and a big-boned body. Her skin has a very light complexion.

"I told the superintendent I have had it! I do the best I can but they want more and more! Isabel, I then looked at him, and I said ... I quit!"

"Pete, it's okay ... in Oregon there will be a lot more opportunity for you. There are plenty of farm labor jobs and factory jobs up there. My mom told me all about it. So try to relax a little."

"So it's true? We're moving to Oregon," Carlos jumps in.

"Tomorra morning bright and early," Pete said with a calm voice.

All Carlos can think about is how much he is going to miss his friends. After trying all year, he had finally made a connection with Cecilia – the girl of his dreams.

What would the coaches say? They were expecting him to play varsity football as a freshman for the Dimmitt High School Bobcats. A million things ran through his mind. He knows that the decision maker of the family is his dad, and his mom is very supportive of his dad's major decisions.

"Dad, why do we have to move to Oregon?"

"There's nothing here for me, and your mom's family is in Oregon. I think it's for the best."

Some of the kids complain and others didn't really care, but Carlos is very disappointed about the whole adventure.

So it's settled. They pack up all of their belongings or at least the most important items. They load up the trailer that's hitched to an old station wagon. Pete wants everything loaded that night so they can leave early in the morning.

There will be no time for Carlos to say goodbye to his friends or to inform the school that his family is moving to Oregon. It's just the way his dad, Pete, wants it.

On the Road to Oregon

Pete is a very responsible man and always takes care of his family. He is mechanically inclined and can repair or build just about anything. When the cars break down, he fixes them. When the house has broken down doors, he fixes them. Those are just some of the examples of what Pete does for his family. The only problem, at times, is coming up with the money for fixture parts. He needed parts to replace whatever was broken.

Bright and early the next morning, the family begins to get ready for the long trip. They are all moving slow and some had smiles on their faces, but others are dreading the unpredictable adventure.

"Maybe the next house we get will have three restrooms," explains Lydia. She is the oldest sister.

"Yeah, maybe one of them will have soundproof walls so we don't hear you," responded Mike. He is the oldest brother.

"Mom, can you tell Mike to get off my case?"

"Mike, get off of Lydia's case," Isabel said.

"It's gonna be a long ride to Oregon stuck with you people I call my family," Carlos said.

The car is loaded up and the trailer has been covered and tied down. The first stop is a nearby gas station to fill up with gas. Pete starts pumping gas into the car. A friend drives up on the other side of the pumps and steps out of the car.

"Where the devil y'all headed?"

"Oregon, we're moving out of here for good."

"Why y'all leaving?"

"It's a long story Ralph, but I'm sure we'll miss everyone here. Give my best to your family and y'all take care."

"Okay, I will. Y'all drive safely, and don't fall asleep on the road Pete."

Pete is a very private person and really doesn't like to share his family issues with anyone other than his own family.

So the adventure starts and they are heading out toward the northwest in the direction of Clovis, New Mexico, on Route 66. The station wagon is an old 1972 Ford. It has a green body with a white top. The body needs painting and also a repair done to a crashed taillight that existed when Pete bought the car. One year after a golf ball-size hailstorm, the car got banged up pretty good. Pete was able to buy it for half price. Not a pretty sight but the engine was brand new. Pete's idea was to avoid any mechanical problems in the future.

As they travel down a long highway, the kids are getting restless and need to stop for a bit. They are past Clovis. Pete pulls over to a rest area. Carlos keeps thinking, "Is this really happening? I mean, will I ever see my friends again? What will happen next year when I go out for sports in a totally different school with totally different faces?"

He finally jumps out of the car and walks into the restroom. He is the last one out of the car due to his daydreaming. The kids brought a football, a frisbee, and a basketball to play with during stops. For Carlos and everyone else, to stretch out after a cramped ride, is like heaven.

Pete and Isabel talk about plans and whether or not they have enough money to make it to Oregon. It takes about three plus days to get there based on their calculations. Most of the meals will be at fast-food places. It is quick and easy and all of the garbage can be left there.

"Okay kids! Let's get going again," Pete yells out.

"Oh man! We wanna play longer Dad!" Carlos said.

"We got a lot of miles to cover if we want to make it there in three days," Pete said.

They all load up the car and drive off once again.

They are driving down a long highway – the sight is very different than what they are used to seeing.

"Wow! Look at those mountains, I can't believe how high they go up, what a sight!" Carlos had never seen anything outside of Dimmitt, Texas. Maybe places like Amarillo, or small towns that the school team played sports against.

The excitement of being somewhere else and seeing something live that you only see on TV or school textbooks, is like a dream to him. He feels as if he's in a different world. He thinks of pinching himself to see if this is really happening.

His brothers and sisters wake up while Carlos is in awe of the Utah Mountains. The colors are amazing – a reddish shade of gravel with light brown dirt, and solid rock everywhere. In addition, there are green trees scattered around, Carlos had no clue what kind of trees they were.

Pete pulled over twelve miles south of Moab, Utah, on U.S. Highway 191. He spotted a place called, Hole N' the Rock. This is a historical tourist attraction in Utah's Canyon lands. As they slowly approach the parking ground in front of the place, Carlos opened his eyes wide.

"Hey! This looks like an awesome place. What is it?"

"It's a house that these people built inside that big rock. Pete do we have enough money to take all the kids in?" Isabel smiled.

"Well, I think we might have enough but we'll have to make sandwiches instead of fast-food on our next dinner stop."

All the kids agreed – sandwiches instead of fast-food are okay. They all made it into this amazing house built in a huge rock. This is a very unique home. It has 5,000 square feet of living space with a trading post and a gift shop that's open year-round. Fourteen rooms and a 65 ft. chimney drilled through solid sandstone. The bathtub and counters are built-in inside the big rock. It is such a miraculous sight to see.

Albert and Gladys Christensen built this home excavating 50,000 cubic feet of sandstone from the rock using dynamite and other tools. They also used a mule to haul the rocks out. When Albert died in 1957 the home was not complete, so Gladys continued to develop the home to become an attraction that fascinates people today.

"This is beyond what I could imagine anyone doing. Look at that mule stuffed, it must have been the one they used to haul the rocks out," Carlos explained to his brothers.

The clerk starts talking to the family about how the temperature remains constant inside the rock at seventy degrees year-round.

What an experience that Carlos will never forget. On the way out he noticed a sculpture of Franklin D. Roosevelt on the face of the rock.

"Look, that must be the president they really loved," Carlos said.

After an hour of observing the tourist attraction, it is time to get back into the car and hit the highway once more. The long drive is beginning to wear on the family. They had never traveled this far before. It is getting dark and another day is almost ending. In the back seat, Carlos is leaning on the door asleep – along with the rest of the clan.

The older brother, Mike, decides to get annoying. He has a feather in his hand and starts rubbing it on Carlos' ear. Carlos fidgets a little and then goes back to sleep. Mike repeats the same thing again.

Mike is Carlos' older brother who is negative about a lot of things. He is a bully type of kid and does not go out for sports. He is basically a goof-off kid at times. Mike is about as tall as Carlos. He has light brown hair and a light complexion.

"Stop it Mike!" Carlos yelled.

"I didn't do anything!" said Mike.

"Ya sorry liar, I saw ya!"

"Whatever Carlos, go back to sleep."

That's about how it went the whole trip with different kids going at it several times.

Later that night Pete is getting tired. He has done all of the driving so far. Isabel does not drive at all. She has been a stay-at-home mom for years. She took care of the kids while Pete went to work.

"Isabel, I think I'm gonna pull over to the side of the road. I don't think there's a rest area for miles."

"It's fine with me Pete, you have to get some rest so we don't get in an accident," Isabel responded.

Pete pulls over to the side of the highway, turns the car off and leans back on his seat. It's pitch black outside and the sound of quiet is evident. Now and then a car flies by.

It is very dark at 2:00 a.m. and the grounds are unfamiliar. An hour goes by and the entire family is asleep on the side of the road.

All of a sudden – *tap*! *tap*! *tap*! There's a tapping on the driver's side of the car. It is a policeman with a flashlight. He's a middle-age fellow with a dark blue uniform. He has all the police gear around his belt.

"Excuse me sir! Can you roll down the window?"

"Yes sir officer," Pete replies. His eyes are red and sleepy looking.

"Can I see your driver's license?" He shines his flashlight to the back seat while he waits for Pete to pull out his wallet. He observes all of the kids that are stirring to wake up. Pete handed the officer his license.

"We're on our way to Oregon and I pulled over to get some sleep, I didn't want to get in an accident."

"I'm going to run a check on your license, hold on for a minute I'll be right back," the officer said. He walked back to his state vehicle.

"What did they get ya for dad?" Carlos asked.

"I guess sleeping on the side of U.S. Highway 191."

After a few minutes the officer returned. He is a pretty big guy and the gun in the holster is very visible.

"Mr. Swavey, it's pretty dangerous out here in the middle of nowhere and its dark. With your lights off you could get hit by a car or a semi-truck. I'm going to let you go with a warning this time. But please don't sleep on the side of the highway again for you and your family's safety.

"Okay officer, thank you so much," Pete replies.

"Have a nice evening and enjoy the rest of your trip. There should be a rest area twenty miles up the road," the officer said.

Pete starts up the old station wagon and they drive off once again to find the next rest stop. He is tired and looks forward to a good sleep.

The next day they arrive at a junction-type town. Carlos is a very talented kid and as far as hitting a target, well, let's put it this way – Pete would bet a whole box of fruit at times when bartering with a fruit stand owner. He walks up with Carlos and starts talking to the fellow that's selling the fruit.

"I like this box of apples. How much of a discount will you give me if my son hits that sign with a rock?" Pete inquires as he points to the sign fifty yards away.

"Are you're joking me? I'll give you the whole box for free if he hits that sign, that's out there mister!"

"You got a deal. Go for it son."

Carlos picks up a large marble-size rock. He takes a couple of steps back as if he is playing quarterback. He fires the rock away – *clang*! A loud bang comes from where the sign stands.

"Oh my jumping beans! That is outstanding, where you folks from?"

"Dimmitt, Texas, but we're on our way to Oregon," Pete said.

"Well, a deal's a deal. Enjoy the apples and I look forward to seeing your son play in the NFL someday."

"Thank you sir," Pete says as he waves with his left hand and holds the box of apples with his right arm around it.

Pete would often put Carlos in a situation like that – anything to help feed the family. He'd always try to barter just to save some money anyhow he could. Carlos didn't really like being put in that situation, but he did it for his dad. The fruit does taste good, and he helps feed his family.

They found a park nearby and pulled over to eat sandwiches and apples. Pete also took a long nap – he needed the rest from driving so much. While Pete takes a rest, the kids play on an old beat up slide and some rusted swings that function pretty well, but squeak a lot. The chains on the swings had not moved much in a long while. The grass is tall from not being mowed in weeks. The air is fresh and clean with a slight breeze.

"Hey Mike! Go out for some passes! Run post patterns!" Carlos yells.

"Okay, but don't throw bullet passes, they hurt my hands!"

"You're a big wimp! The ball isn't gonna hurt ya!"

So the brothers passed the football around while the other siblings played on the playground equipment. They enjoy exercising for about two hours.

"Let's get going kids! Come on, it's getting late!" Isabel yells.

They are once again on the road traveling. By the end of the second day they arrive at the good old potato state of Idaho. Not too much there, at least not where the Swaveys drive by. It's pretty flat and dry. They did see an Air Force Base off to the side of the freeway and an amusement park on the other side. The state capital, Boise, Idaho, is the biggest city in this state. There's also Twin Falls, Idaho. Driving by Boise is an interesting sight. They see the lights at night, so many city lights.

Welcome to Oregon

By the third day of traveling they enter Oregon on the east side. More hills and mountains, but the mountains weren't as tall as the ones they saw in Utah – at least not on the east side of Oregon.

They arrive at a small town called Baker City, Oregon. Everything has gone pretty smooth with the car until now.

"I'm gonna put some gas in the car in this little town," Pete said.

So they pull over and fill the car up with regular unleaded fuel.

"Can I check the oil for you?" the attendant asked.

"Sure," Pete replies.

Pete was never one to trust anybody under the hood of his car. He was so tired from driving that this time he has them check the oil for him. When all seemed well they drive off again. A few blocks down the road the engine light came on and the car came to a dead stop.

"Dang!" Pete expressed angrily.

He gets out of the car, walks around to the front and lifts up the hood.

"What's wrong Dad?" Carlos asked.

"Y'all can get out of the car for a bit. It looks like they sliced off the fan belt. It doesn't look like a tear, it's a clean slice."

"You don't know that for a fact," Isabel informed him.

"I bet if I walk back there they'll have exactly the right size fan belt for me to buy."

Pete didn't have much money left and he was mad at himself for not checking the oil himself. He and Mike walked back while everyone else stayed in the car.

"Mom, how long is this gonna take? I'm tired of being in this crowded car," Lydia complains.

Lydia is Carlos' older sister. She has light brown skin with dark hair and brown eyes. She's a tough looking girl that usually has many opinions.

"Oh shut up Lydia, do you always have to complain about everything?"

"Mom, tell Carlos to leave me alone!"

"Stop arguing you two there's really not much we can do at this point."

After a forty-five minute wait, Pete and Mike made it back with a brand new fan belt.

"Those highway robbers, they had the exact size I needed. It cost me an arm and a leg. I hate being right."

"The good Lord works in mysterious ways. I guess we ended up paying for those apples in Utah after all," Carlos replies with a grin on his face. Isabel starts laughing and Pete storms to the front of the car to install the fan belt.

Thank God he has plenty of experience working on cars. Carlos has always been the one to help him under the car. Carlos handed him tools in most cases. It's amazing how much Carlos learned by just watching. Surprisingly, this time he asked Mike to help install the fan belt.

In two hours the Swaveys were on their way toward Interstate 84 heading in the direction of Pendleton, Oregon.

"Oregon sure has some nice country. I've never seen anything like this before," Carlos said very impressed.

"Yeah, I'd like to ride a motorcycle up that hill."

"Mike, you fool! You don't have a motorcycle!" Lydia snapped.

"Someday I will, you wait and see."

"Well, stay in school and get a good education and y'all will have nice things someday," Isabel explains.

It is getting dark once again. The freeway is starting to look as if there is no end to it. But hey, they are in Oregon and heading to grandma's house.

The Swaveys are planning on staying with Isabel's mom and dad – at least until they can catch up financially. They will then rent their own place.

"My mom and dad live in a town called Gervais," Isabel explains cheerfully.

After all it has been years since the last time she saw her parents.

Carlos' eyes opened up wide, "Do they live in a mansion?"

"Wishful thinking you moron, they live in a small dinky house. You'll probably be forced to sleep on the floor."

"Shut up Lydia! I was just hoping."

Pete pulls over to fill up the gas tank once again. As he starts to grab the gas pump, the gas station attendant came over.

"Hey! You can't pump your own gas in Oregon. I'll take care of it for you."

The attendant is a big heavyset guy with greasy hands, a dirty uniform, and long hair covered by a red cap.

"Thank you sir," Pete said.

"Where you guys going?"

"Guys? Sir, I have two girls in the car."

"Ha-ha! Here in Oregon we say *you guys*. In Texas, I'm sure you say *y'all*."

Carlos looks at Lydia, "Ha-ha! You're a guy!"

"I am not … shut up Carlos!"

They start realizing that Oregon is a lot different than Texas. The accent didn't have the southern drawl at all.

The car is finally filled up with gas. They drive away from the station toward Portland, Oregon, on I-84. Portland is the biggest city in Oregon with huge bridges and buildings. Portland also has shipping docks with large tugboats and ships. The population is about 500,000 to Dimmitt's 4,371.

Amarillo is the biggest city that Carlos had ever seen, until now. And as far as Dimmitt, well, it's just a dot compared to Portland.

As they drive up I-84 they merge into Interstate 5. Carlos can see a huge river next to the freeway, the Columbia River.

"Wow! This is amazing. I have never seen so much water in my life!" Carlos expresses with excitement.

Finally they all see a sign "Welcome to Portland." Carlos had not seen so many cars on a freeway before. Being from a small town and everything, it is a little bit of a shock. The loud noise of semi-trucks passing on the left lane, horns going off, and the monoxide smells from traffic are all too overwhelming.

Pete is trying to concentrate on the road and Isabel is helping him read the freeway signs.

"Pete, just follow the signs that say Salem. Gervais is in that direction," Isabel said in a focused manner.

"Watch out ... that car's cutting in!"

When Pete hears Isabel, he slows down and allows the person that's driving recklessly, to get in front of him into the middle lane.

"You son of a ...," Pete yells out.

"Pete, watch your language!" Isabel says.

"There are some crazy drivers in this city," Carlos thinks to himself.

"Look at those tall buildings. Man they are way up in the sky," said one of the youngest kids.

"Look at the boats, they are so beautiful," Lydia added with a huge smile.

They are driving past the riverfront in Portland. There are plenty of Portland locals hanging out near the water. It appears to be some kind of festival going on.

All of the excitement of driving through a big city is a great distraction. This helps Carlos to not think too much about leaving his friends behind in Texas. And on the last day of school he had finally connected with a precious cute girl that he really liked. That's the only thing he could not be distracted from. He still had the image of her smile as she walked away. The way she walked was flawless.

"I heard you finally talked to Cecilia on the last day of school. What did you do, pay her off?"

"I don't wanna talk about it Lydia."

"Okay, fine, whatever. I think she's gonna miss you."

Traveling on Interstate 5, south of Portland, the traffic noise has calmed down a bit. Pete is more relaxed while driving. They drive for another 35 minutes before reaching their exit. Isabel is very excited as they get off on the Woodburn, Oregon exit off of the freeway.

"Finally we're at the exit we want," Isabel said.

Now it's a matter of driving through Woodburn, a small town just three miles north of Gervais. The anxiety that Isabel is experiencing is priceless.

Grandpa Lalo and Grandma Elida are expecting the Swavey family. As they anxiously wait that evening, they finally see the old Ford station wagon turn into their driveway. Isabel is the first one out of the car. She runs over to her mom and starts hugging her. They both have tears of joy running down the sides of their cheeks. After they finish embracing they are rubbing the tears off and smiling a lot.

Carlos is trying to understand why all the tears. To him, it is like his mom being happy to see strangers. He has never met his grandpa or his grandma. In fact, he has never met any of his aunts or uncles from Oregon.

After that episode, Grandma Elida comes over to all of the kids and starts hugging them and inviting them inside.

"Oh! You must be Carlos, please come inside," she runs over to Lydia, "Lydia! Hi! Mike! You all have grown so much!"

The adults talk non-stop the rest of the evening. A joy it is for them to see relatives that they only spoke to on the phone for years. Carlos meets his aunts and uncles that live there as well. In the Hispanic culture, it is pretty normal to have more than one family living together in one house.

Pete isn't very happy about staying with Isabel's family. But he didn't have much of a choice. At least not until he finds some work to provide for his family.

First Experience Berry Picking

It is summertime. Carlos, Lydia, and Mike are about to experience berry picking with their grandfather. Getting up early the next morning isn't what they planned on. It is a big surprise for them. Pete will begin the job hunting that day.

"Get up Mike! ... Carlos! Come on y'all your grandpa is taking you berry picking. Lydia is already up. Breakfast will be waiting for you before you leave. Hurry up now!" Pete expressed.

"Why do we have to go berry picking? I don't even know how to spell berry picking," Carlos answers.

They eventually wake up, eat breakfast, and are on their way to work in the fields of an Oregon berry farm.

During the drive to the field, Grandpa Lalo, is explaining the whole procedure of berry picking.

"I'm sorry you had to get up so early. Here in Oregon, we go to work bright and early while the berries are good to pick. When you pick the berries you have to fill up your crate all the way to the top. Keep it at the end of your row and mark it with your name. When you get another crate filled, stack it on top of the first one," Lalo said.

"When do we get paid?" Lydia asked.

"What! You haven't even started working yet and you wanna get paid?"

"I'm just saying Grandpa."

"The harder you work the more money you make, they weigh the crates and they pay by the pound. Some places pay by the crate, it just depends on the farmer," Grandpa Lalo speaks with an authority voice.

He's a real get-going type of person. He wears an old hat and overalls. He was once in the military years ago. You can tell he's been a hardworking man all of his life from listening to him. Now that he's retired, Lalo still works hard in his own garden and in the berry fields for extra money. He seems to be very proud of his garden – he takes great pride in his work.

The kids didn't say much, they just listened to Grandpa – this is way out of their normal life. In Texas, they would chop weeds for farmers in 105 degree weather. Carlos worked in the fields since he was a ten-year old. In the summer, the weather is much hotter in Texas than in Oregon. The kids discovered this by freezing on the drive there.

Berry picking takes a certain skill, a skill that the Swaveys did not have. They knew how to hold a hoe and chop weeds without cutting the crop, and maybe other everyday skills to do work around the house.

"Okay, here we are. Let's go!" Grandpa Lalo said.

"Where do we get the crates ... where do we start?" Lydia asked.

"I'll show you, follow me," her grandpa replied.

Carlos closed his eyes and took a deep breath, shivering from the shocking cold of the early Oregon morning. You can hear the birds chirping and some bugs flying by – *bzzz*! There's hardly any wind early in the morning.

He starts walking at a dragging pace behind his grandpa. He is so amazed at how everything is so green in Oregon. Compared to Texas, there is much more color in the trees, flowers, bushes, and mountains. He feels like he is in a dream. Part of his life has been left behind to possibly be non-existent.

He begins to pick the berries. Carlos can smell the freshness of the berries and clean air with more sounds of birds chirping. People are talking everywhere in the field. The berries are very ripe hanging from a seven foot bush. He picks the ones that he can obviously see.

"Carlos! You're missing half the berries on that bush, go back and make sure you get them all. Look under the bush too. You don't want to get fired on your first day," Grandpa said.

"I don't think I'd be disappointed if I got fired Grandpa, I'm terrible at this."

"Hang in there, you'll pick it up in no time. It's like anything else, the more you do it the better you get."

Grandpa Lalo is the type of person that seems to be in charge at all times. He is one of the fastest pickers in the field. He makes really good money in a half-day's work.

Carlos continues to pick the best he can. Mike, his older brother, walks to the car after the first hour of picking and falls asleep. He has picked berries for only an hour and is not about to return to the field any time soon.

Lydia is having fun talking to some girls she just met in the berry field. She isn't getting much work done, but having a blast yakking away.

Carlos is working away picking berries. He wants to make some money. He is the type of kid that works hard at what he's supposed to be doing.

Someone throws a berry – it goes flying toward Carlos – *bam*! The berry hits him on the side of his arm. He turned around to see where it came from. There's a boy about his age that is laughing pretty loud.

"You're the slowest picker I've ever seen in my entire life!"

The boy is standing about twenty yards away pointing at Carlos.

"You're the ugliest boy I've ever seen in my entire life."

"Oh yeah?" the boy responds.

"Just for you sticking your nose where it doesn't belong, I'm gonna return the favor by hitting ya right on your nose."

"Ha-ha! You're very funny. Go ahead, I won't even move!"

Carlos grabs a berry and throws it with some zip – *splat*! The berry hits right on target. The boy's nose starts to bleed. Carlos rushes over to console him.

"Hey man, I'm really sorry. You okay?"

"Yeah, I'll live. You weren't kidding about hitting your target. Where did you learn how to throw like that?"

"Oh, I don't know, I used to get bored a lot, so I would go out and practice throwing the football or shooting baskets in a hoop. You know … nothing too special."

"Do you play sports for any school?" the boy asked.

"Yeah, I'm a three sport athlete – at least I was in Dimmitt, Texas."

"Dimmitt, Texas? You're a long way from home aren't you fella?"

"You could say that I guess."

"Wow, I bet you're a great athlete."

"I've had good days. I'm hoping to play somewhere in Oregon. What's your name?"

"I'm Harv," the boy answered not too flattered about his name.

"Harv? That's it?"

"Harv … as in Harvard. My dad wants me to attend Harvard and study law after I graduate high school. He's some bigwig for a law firm in Portland."

"What the heck are you doing here picking berries? Sounds to me like you should be swimming in your backyard heated pool with the nanny bringing you tea every hour," Carlos replies.

"Yeah, right – my dad has my mom bring me here three days a week. He says it builds character to do some physical labor now and then."

"Boy, I'm overloaded with character. All my past summers I've worked in the fields to help my family make it through tough times."

"Wow, that's tough. I certainly can't relate to that. What did you say your name is?"

"I didn't. But I guess I can tell ya without charging you a fee. I'm Carlos Swavey."

"It's a real pleasure to meet you Carlos," Harv reaches over to shake his hand.

The boys continue talking the rest of the morning as they try to work.

It is the end of the half-day picking session. Grandpa Lalo has picked twenty crates by himself. Carlos' aunt picked fifteen crates. Carlos came in third with a whopping four crates. Lydia came in fourth surviving two crates and making six friends. Mike came in last with half of a crate. No one knows what happened to it. He did manage to get plenty of rest though.

As they walk to the car, Carlos is dragging his feet with sweat pouring down his forehead. The day has warmed up a bit and the sun is shining bright. He raises his forearm to wipe off some of the sweat from his face. As he takes a deep breath, he sees a brand new BMW drive up.

"That car is a thing of beauty."

"Quit dreaming Carlos, you'll never have anything like that," Lydia responded.

It is Harv's mom picking him up. She is a beautiful lady in her mid-forties wearing sunglasses that look great next to her blonde hair. She reaches over and hands Harv a cold drink as he enters the passenger side.

"Carlos! Come on lets go! We'll have some water waiting for us when we get back to the house."

"Gee thanks Grandpa," Carlos says sarcastically.

On the car ride back, Carlos stays awake while everyone else in the back seat falls asleep. He couldn't help but think about why Harv didn't look very happy when he stepped into his brand new BMW with a cold drink waiting for him. Carlos is curious and he knows he will see Harv again. He looks forward to that.

After working in the fields for three weeks Carlos has improved to filling ten crates in a half-day session. He didn't make much money, but he's hoping it will be enough for some new clothes. School will be starting soon and he wants to look good entering a new school.

During the berry picking days, Carlos got to know Harv a little better, but still didn't quite feel that he knew him well enough. It was more of an acquaintance.

After a few weeks, one morning, Carlos wakes up early to get ready for work again. No one else seems to be up. He heard a door open and close – *slam*! Out of the bedroom comes Grandpa Lalo.

"Carlos, the field was completed yesterday – no more work."

"Yes … there is a God!" Carlos cheers.

During the next few weeks, Pete and Isabel landed a job at a local food processing plant in Brooks, Oregon. It is seasonal work, but enough to pay for the rent. They found an old house next to the railroad tracks in Gervais. The house is an old torn down place that had been vacant for a few years. It sits crooked as if a major stud underneath is cracked. The house has survived some strong winds and the train going by for years. The white faded paint on the house with a cracked sidewalk is very visible. Even the house they owned in Texas is better than this old ragged building.

The good news is that the rent is only $250.00 per month. Pete and Isabel can afford to feed their family and pay rent with the seasonal job. The two of them working will make it easier to pay the rent and feed the family. They will have to rely on the older kids helping out while they are at work.

A New School for Carlos in Oregon

The summer is coming to an end and school is just around the corner. Lydia has just passed her driver's test and now is a legal Oregon driver. That will be a benefit with both parents working. She can now help out by driving her brothers and sister to school, or even going on grocery store trips.

Carlos feels compelled to call his coach in Dimmitt, Texas. He dials the number from a pay telephone booth near the old rented house.

"Hello, this is Coach Durham."

"Hey coach, it's me, Carlos."

"Where in the carnations did y'all go?"

"My parents moved us up to Oregon. We're living in a small town called Gervais."

"I had no idea. Do you like it there?"

"It sure is different as far as people ... but the mountains, trees, and rivers are amazing," Carlos said.

"Sounds like nice country. We're sure gonna miss ya. We had ya selected as our first freshman ever to start on the varsity football team here in Dimmitt. It looks like the Bobcats will have to do without ya this year ... there's one other thing Carlos."

"What's that coach?"

"Try to get yourself into a big school. You have a talent that I've never seen before. You have a gift boy."

"Thanks Coach. I'm sorry I won't be there with the Bobcats this year. I'll try to get into a big school in Salem – it's not far from here. It's been good talking to ya and good luck with the Bobcats this year."

"Thanks, great talking to ya too – take care of yourself and God Bless."

The coach hangs up the phone – he looks down for a minute and shakes his head in disappointment.

"We just lost one of the best players Dimmitt has ever had – darn!" Coach Durham is very disappointed and will miss Carlos deeply.

After a day's work of moving into the old rented house, the Swavey family clean the place up and fix a few minor things. They make room assignments. Carlos will be sharing a room with Mike. The room is upstairs – an old attic that they converted into a room.

"Tomorra y'all have to get registered in school, you have to keep up your education," Isabel encouraged.

"Mom it's important that I get into a bigger school than Gervais," Carlos explains.

"Why? Gervais is only six blocks away. You can even walk there," Isabel said.

"I can drive us to a Salem school. I met a friend at the berry field last summer and she attends North Salem High School. We can try to register there," Lydia said.

"Okay, fine with me, as long as you get in school. Education is very important. You don't want to end up like your father and myself."

A deep sigh came from Carlos – the anxiety of not knowing what to expect is overwhelming. North Salem is four times bigger than Dimmitt High School. Coming in with a southern Tex-Mex accent, and not knowing anyone, is a bit scary. What would the other kids say? Would they make fun of him? But he heard what Coach Durham advised him to do. He had to give it a shot – he wanted to play for one of the biggest schools around.

The next morning Lydia and Carlos are the first ones up. They dress up with some new clothes they bought the week before. They drive to Salem to make an attempt at registering for school. Mike and the rest of the kids register to attend school in Gervais.

When Lydia and Carlos arrive at North Salem High, classes are already in session. They walk slowly down a long hallway with classrooms on both sides. You can hear the echo with each step they take as they approach the office. The hall floor is very clean and shiny – it smells like fresh floor wax. A man approaches them from behind.

"Having a little trouble finding your classroom students?"

"Oh, no sir, we'd like to register for school," Lydia replies.

"Well, you're headed in the right direction. Follow me I'll take you to the right place. I take it you're from the south somewhere – you have a little bit of an accent."

"Oh yes sir, we're from Texas," Carlos responds.

"Welcome to North Salem, here's the office you need. Good luck to you both."

"Thank you sir," Carlos smiles as he follows Lydia into the office.

The office secretary immediately jumps out of her chair and walks over to the counter.

"How can I help you?"

"We want to register for school," Lydia said.

"Okay, do you live in the North Salem district?"

"No ma'am, we live in Gervais."

"Oh darn, I'm sorry to tell you this but I'm afraid you can't register in this school. You'll have to register in Gervais where you live."

"Why can't we register here?" Lydia asks.

"Well, because you don't live in the North Salem district … like I said."

"But you don't understand! My brother needs to register in a big school."

"Young lady I am really sorry, we can't help you unless you live in the district."

As Lydia is about to make another attempt to argue Carlos steps in.

"Lydia It's okay. Let's go – I'll just register in Gervais."

Half the day is wasted and they drive back to Gervais down Highway 99E.

Gervais is located about fifteen miles north of Salem, the state capital of Oregon.

"I hope they have an offensive line that can block for me. If they don't I'll probably have to scramble a lot."

"That's if you pass all your grades. In Dimmitt, if it wasn't for the study tables, you would have flunked out," Lydia explained.

"Don't remind me. Lord knows how I'm gonna do here – I don't even know anyone."

They both continue talking for a while longer during the drive to Gervais. They finally arrive at the high school.

"Well, lets get this registration over with," Carlos gets out of the car with a bummed-out look on his face.

The office is located on the left side as they enter the building.

"Can I help you?" asked the secretary.

"Yes ma'am, we'd like to register," Lydia answers.

"Do you live in the Gervais School District?"

Lydia and Carlos looked at each other and then they both responded, "Yes."

After an hour of filling out papers and talking to a few school officials, they are ready to start school the next day. Two weeks behind is better than not starting at all. After a long day they both sit on a bench observing the school halls and pictures on the wall. This school is much smaller than Dimmitt High School. The Gervais attendance is about 600 total students.

The students are rushing out at the end of the school day. Carlos watches with a bored look on his face. Kids are yelling across the hall to their friends. The doors keep opening and slamming shut – *bam*! It's like a herd of cattle running through the gates at a feedlot. All the students stare at Carlos and Lydia as they walk by. They notice two new faces. In Gervais everyone knows each other because of the school size. Carlos definitely knows he is an outsider in this small school.

Carlos felt out of place and began to miss his old school and friends that he had gotten to know so well.

"You go ahead and go home Lydia, I'm gonna watch the football team practice for a bit. Tell Mom I'll walk home, and please tell her to save me a couple of tacos."

"Okay, see ya later," Lydia responds.

Carlos walks across the baseball field on his way to the football field, he shows very little enthusiasm. He steps up onto the old wooden bleachers that desperately need painting. He sits down three rows up on the right side of the bleachers. He is wearing an old gray t-shirt that reads, "Bobcats." His jeans are not patched up. They are brand new – thanks to the berry field work he did in the summer.

There is an assistant coach on the sidelines. He's watching the team go over plays in their white practice uniforms.

"Excuse me sir!" Carlos yelled.

The coach turns his head and looks directly at Carlos but doesn't say anything.

"Is that your freshman team?" Carlos asked.

"No, this is our varsity team. Who are you?"

"I'm your next quarterback if you'll have me. I've been watching your team."

"Oh yeah?" the coach said.

"Back in Texas, where I'm from, we have freshman as big as your varsity team."

"You don't say? You're a very humorous young boy – must be where you get that funny southern accent, from Texas."

"I don't think my accent is funny at all – y'all are the ones with funny accents."

The coach looks at Carlos, and then shakes his head.

"If you're interested in coming out for the team you'll need to practice at least two weeks. You can then play in an actual game. And that's only if you can beat out our starting quarterback or even make the team for that matter. His name is Clifford Mayberry. He only averaged 200 yards passing, and three touchdown passes per game last year. He had two interceptions all year long. He was the Capital Conference Player of the Year. Oh, and by the way … he's a senior this year. Good luck to you Mr. – what did you say your little southern name is?"

"I didn't sir but if you wanna know, my name is Carlos Swavey. I'm a freshman this year. I'm sure you won't forget it when ya see me in action tomorra. What time should I suit up for practice?" Carlos asked.

"Show up after school tomorrow, but you can't put on pads. You have to have at least a week of conditioning."

"No disrespect coach, but I run a lot during the off-season. I'm always ready to play football."

"You're talking mighty big for a freshman young man. But then again, most losers talk like that. They can't back their talk up. My name is Coach Pat McGoldrick, and I'm the assistant coach. I wish you the best of luck, you'll need it."

Carlos didn't respond, instead he steps down from the bleachers and he walks away crossing through the dry field behind the bleachers. He noticed the coach talking to the other coaches as they look his way from a distance. Carlos is not usually a kid that brags like he just did to the coach – totally out of his character. Because of the whole situation, he was taking out his anger on the coach.

After observing Clifford Mayberry, Carlos knows that he is five times better than the Gervais quarterback. He feels bad for expressing himself the way he did. Although he knows he's right about the statements he made to the coach, he should have approached the situation in a different manner.

After watching the football practice he walks home scoping out the town. There are so many old homes and very few buildings. A small grade school stands a half-mile away from the high school. It is made out of wood with old yellow siding. It resembles a huge old barn. They say it used to be the first high school in Oregon. It was turned into an elementary school when the new high school was built.

He continues walking by the grade school on his way home. When he arrives home, he has an empty feeling in his stomach. The empty feeling is not just from being hungry, but also from not knowing anyone in the area.

Carlos steps inside his rented home.

"Where's my tacos Mom?"

"Everyone ate already and there's nothing left. I'm really sorry. I have two dollars, go get yourself a burrito or something at the Gervais Market. It's right down the road."

"I can't believe you didn't save me any tacos. Dang!"

That summed up the kind of day Carlos had. He starts walking to the store with pains of hunger. He drinks some water on the way to fill his stomach up a bit. Carlos arrives at the store in no time and steps in the front door. As soon as he buys the burrito he takes a big bite. It smells really good and it is very tasty. He also buys a carton of chocolate milk. It hit the spot as he takes a big drink.

On his way back he spots an apple tree on the other side of the tracks. It's in the middle of nowhere.

"Hey, there's an apple tree. I can use some good fruit about now," Carlos runs across the railroad tracks and starts picking some apples. He fills up his grocery bag to bring some back to share with his family.

"Ha-ha-ha! I didn't have to get any As for these apples. Maybe Fs should be for free," he laughs by himself.

The next morning it's time to start a fresh day at Gervais High School. Carlos walks to school while Lydia and Mike drive there. Carlos wants to be there early to find his locker and to pick up his class list.

While he's looking at his schedule, there is a group of girls talking, but he can't make out what they're saying. He acknowledges something, "It can't be." There's a girl mixed in the group that resembles Cecilia. Practically the same build. She has light red hair and a few freckles on her white cheeks. The only difference is she has blue eyes instead of green eyes. Naturally Carlos stares at her as if he is hypnotized.

From afar she lifts her head and notices Carlos staring at her. She continues talking to her friends, and then looks in his direction again. She smiles at him. He tips his head down once to say hi to her. She did the same to acknowledge him and smiles. She then walks away to class with her friends.

"Man I've gotta find out who that is," Carlos talks to himself.

Mike appeared out of nowhere, "Her name is Liz, I found out yesterday. Forget it Carlos you don't stand a chance with her. She's in a different class. You're poor and she's rich."

"Shut up Mike! Mind your own business."

"Ha-ha! I can tell you like her bro."

"Why don't you go out for the football team so I can tackle you hard?" Carlos says.

"Ney, I don't wanna mess up my good looks. And it's too much energy to waste."

"Oh brother," Carlos sighed.

Carlos starts walking toward his first class. He stands at 5' 11" now, as a freshman, and has an athletic body. He's probably one of the tallest Hispanics at Gervais. Carlos is a handsome young man with dark hair and light brown skin color.

Three taller kids walk by heading the opposite way.

"Hey guys ... there's the loser Mexican from Texas. He thinks he's gonna replace Clifford. Ha-ha-ha!" They keep walking as they turn their heads and look at Carlos.

Carlos didn't say one word. After all he had put himself in that position after talking to the coach the way he did yesterday. That still wasn't a reason for those kids to make a harsh comment.

"I can't wait 'til practice," Carlos angrily thought to himself.

Gervais is a small school and by now everyone is talking about the new kid that transferred from Texas and what he said to the coach at practice.

The first class he walks into is Introduction to Algebra. Carlos walks to a back-row seat at the far right corner. As he walks by, the students are staring at him. Some are whispering amongst each other.

When he sits down he discovers that up in front, Liz is sitting quietly reading a book. She's waiting for the teacher to come in the room. She's not conversing with anyone.

In the middle of the class are the three boys that made fun of Carlos in the hallway. They are pretty big for freshman boys. One of them is a senior taking the class. They are the type that might play sparingly on the varsity football team.

When Carlos looks up he sees the teacher walk in the classroom. This teacher is who other than, Pat McGoldrick, the varsity football assistant coach. He is a mathematician and the algebra teacher for Gervais High School. Pat was once a successful college volleyball coach. He stepped down to teach high school kids and he became the assistant football coach. Pat is a tall man with a shade of gray starting to creep up in his hair.

He doesn't realize that Carlos is sitting in his class, but once he starts row call, it's evident. He calls out several names before calling out one that got his attention.

"Carlos," the coach called out.

"Carlos where are you? Oh, there you are way in the back. Class, let me introduce you guys to this young man from Texas. He's a transfer and I hope you guys give him a warm welcome to our wonderful school."

Carlos waits to see what the teacher will say next.

"Carlos, since you're a little behind on the first chapter I would be glad to help you catch up by assigning you some homework. It won't be too bad it's only part of a chapter you've missed."

"You don't know how much I appreciate that sir," Carlos responds sarcastically.

"Did you take an algebra class in Texas?"

"Yes sir I took a pre-algebra class."

"Then you won't mind coming up to the front of the class and solving this simple equation on the board? Its okay, everyone here has to do this today. You can start us off."

Carlos stands up slowly as if he really didn't want to do that. He walks up to the front of the class wearing some old jeans that are patched up. He had worn his new pair yesterday. One of the boys in the middle of the class started making sounds to make fun of Carlos, "Moo! Moo! Moo!"

Carlos is almost to the board. He stops and turns around facing the boy.

"You know that's pretty darn good. I have a friend in Texas that owns a cattle feedlot. He gets fifty dollars a head. He'd probably get eighty-five dollars for you."

The entire class busted out laughing including Liz, who normally doesn't laugh too much but couldn't help herself this time.

Carlos felt more comfortable and the nervousness calmed down a bit. The teacher looked at the boy that was trying to make fun of Carlos.

"Dirk, sometimes it's best if you kept your mouth shut."

After class, as Carlos is walking out, Liz follows him and catches up to him.

"Hey Carlos, that was an outstanding piece of bravery you demonstrated back there. It reminded me of David against Goliath."

"Uh … thanks," Carlos responds nervously.

"My name's Liz. It's short for Elizabeth."

"I guess you know my name already. It's a pleasure to meet you Liz," he responds more relaxed.

"I'll see you tomorrow unless you're taking some AP classes the rest of the day. I take Basic Algebra to give my brain a rest. The remaining classes are required by my parents."

"What's AP?" Carlos asked.

"Advanced Placement – I get college credit with some of them. It just puts me ahead of the game. The classes prepare me for college."

Carlos watches Liz walk away to her next class as she waves with a smile. He seemed to like everything about her. The way she walked – smooth, attractive, and very innocent. She stands at 5' 8" and is wearing a light purple v-cut fashion shirt with brand name jeans. Her clothes are the kind that you don't find in your local stores. She is definitely from an upper-class family. That's the impression Carlos has in his mind.

As Carlos walks to his next class he runs into Dirk, a troublemaker who seems to want to stir up some attention. Dirk is known for putting any type of minority down. He's a big senior kid with brown hair and green eyes. He is the type of kid that's mad at the world for no reason.

"Hey Carlos! You think you're a bad dude. Wait 'til I get you on the practice field after school today. We'll see how tough you really are."

"I look forward to it, I love football. Oh, and no offense about what I said back there. I was just playing with ya," Carlos smiles and walks away.

"You just wait 'til practice you Mexican hick."

The next class he has scheduled is an English class. Carlos walks up to the teacher, Mae McCall.

"How do I get into an AP class?"

"Well, I think anyone can get into an AP class as long as you register for it. I teach one in the afternoon. It's a good idea to have at least a 3.0 GPA."

"What's a GPA?" Carlos asked.

"It's your grade point average. Young man I would suggest that you wait a year before taking an AP class. In fact, why don't you show me your report card at the end of the semester? I would be more than happy to help you out."

"Okay, sure. Thanks."

"What's your name?"

"Carlos Swavey."

"I admire your enthusiasm to want to take an AP class, now go have a seat," Mae McCall responds.

Carlos knows that if he wants to see Liz more he has to take some AP classes. It will be a tough challenge for him. He walks to the back of the classroom and sits down. He observes the students walking in and talking to each other in a friendly way. He doesn't know anyone and he feels like an outsider from a different planet.

The English class seems to have a few more Hispanics than the algebra class. Gervais High School has about 70% Whites and 30% Hispanics enrolled. Dimmitt High School is more diverse with 60% Whites, 30% Hispanics, and 10% Blacks.

While Carlos is sitting and watching everyone, Mrs. McCall is getting out her class plans. The class starts to calm down a bit. All of a sudden a rolled-up piece of paper shaped like a little ball, flies across the room and hits his arm – *tap*! Carlos turns around to the left, and a moment of joy hits him. It's Harv, from the berry field last summer.

"You haven't learned your lesson I see?" Carlos said with a grin.

"I had no idea you were going to attend this school," Harv responded.

"I was gonna go to North Salem High but we live outside the district. It didn't work out. Do you think there's enough room for the two of us in this school?"

"Yeah, I suppose we can let a Tex-Mex in," Harv laughs.

"You going out for the football team?" Carlos asked.

"Oh yeah – I play every position."

"You do?"

"Yes sir, like I once heard a comedian say, I play every position from one side of the aluminum bench to the other side."

"You're way too funny man. I'm glad you have a sense of humor. I guess I'll be seeing ya after school. Hey, even better maybe you'd like to walk over to the Gervais Market during lunchtime? I promise I won't make your nose bleed with a paper wad."

"Ha-ha! It sounds good to me. I haven't been to the Gervais Market in ages – it'll be fun."

Carlos made a friend. The interesting thing is that he didn't see Harv as a wealthy kid with a BMW, he saw him as a good kid with a great heart.

After the next few classes, lunchtime has arrived and the two boys start walking out of the door to have lunch at the market. The little store has chicken, burritos, and other foods that the boys didn't usually get at home. On the way there they talked for a long while. There are also other kids that have the same idea – a string of kids walk to the Gervais Market for lunch. The store is pretty close, maybe a little less than a mile.

"So why is it that you don't get much playing time?" Carlos asked.

"Oh, I would love to play more but my dad doesn't really encourage sports and I don't seem to know how to get better myself. So I just accept my role by sitting the bench and helping out in practice."

"That's funny because I feel the same way about books and grades. In Texas, the only thing that motivated me to pass my grades, and what I mean by passing my grades is Cs and Ds … Aw, you don't wanna hear about all that," Carlos states sadly.

"I think I understand what you're experiencing. I feel that the only reason I make the team is because I'm taller than most of the players, and I'm a good practice target for the coaches."

Carlos and Harv made a good connection while walking to the Gervais Market. They were enjoying talking about many things. None of the athletes in Gervais had ever treated Harv the way Carlos has. Who would have thought that those two would become great friends by a berry being thrown last summer?

That night, Harv Bradford, is eating dinner with his parents and his sister.

"I met a nice kid for the second time today at school," Harv said.

"That's great Harv, who is he?" his mom asked.

"He's a transfer from Dimmitt, Texas, a small town down south. I've never seen anyone throw anything as accurate as him. At the berry field last summer he told me that he would hit my nose with a berry – I was standing far away. The impact from the berry made my nose bleed.

"What! You didn't tell us about that," Ted reacts.

"Dad, it's okay, I'm the one that started it. Anyway, like I was saying, he's a great kid and we really connected with each other on the way to lunch today. I was thinking maybe I could invite him over for dinner sometime?"

"Please don't tell me he's a Mexican," Ted said.

"He's not, he's Hispanic, born in Texas not Mexico."

"It's the same to me. I don't want you hanging around the troublemakers, and I don't want him around here. You have four years to prepare yourself to get accepted at Harvard University, and hanging around Mexicans is a big distraction."

Harv's sister knew some things but was not about to say anything that would create more of an argument.

"May I be excused to retire to my sleeping facilities?" Liz asked.

Both parents shake their heads *yes*, to indicate approval. The rest of the time it settled down to a quiet sound. Harv got up and stomped to his room upstairs.

"Ted, you are way too hard on Harv," Elaine said.

"I don't trust those Mexicans, they're always getting into trouble … and I don't want Harv mixed up in any of that."

"You don't even know the boy, Ted."

"I don't care! And I don't want to know him."

"There's talk about him going out for the football team. Harv said he's never seen anyone throw the football as well as that boy.

He said that the coaches are giving him a chance tomorrow. Today they just had him watch and learn."

"Elaine, my only focus is to try and get Harv into law school at Harvard. He isn't an athlete. All he does is warm up the bench. I don't want to discuss this any further."

"Yes Ted, I understand. I'll take care of the dishes and I'll meet you in the theater room. I think one of your favorite programs is on tonight," Elaine goes into the kitchen looking a little sad.

As she walks to the kitchen, their maid approaches her.

"Mrs. Bradford, is it okay if I go home now?"

"Of course Maria, I can take care of these dishes for tonight. I'll see you next week and thanks for the cleaning."

"Goodbye Mrs. Bradford."

The Bradfords are a very wealthy family. Their home has a three car garage. The home is 6,000 square feet with a huge backyard, tennis court, basketball court, and a swimming pool. The house is located a few miles outside of Gervais surrounded by farmland. The Bradfords lease out their farm land to farmers in the area who raise all kinds of crops. Hops are one of the main crops along with onions, and green beans. They also grow apples, cherries, and peaches. They own one thousand acres of farmland.

When Carlos makes it to his house he looks at a note his mom left for him.

"*Carlos, everyone ate already but this time I saved you a plate. Sorry about yesterday. Enjoy the tacos and vegetables. We got some free vegetables from the processing plant today ... love, Mom.*"

He felt warmth in his heart knowing that his mom cared about him.

"Hey Carlos, how'd your day go?" Lydia asked.

"It was okay I guess."

"This girl was asking about you today – in the AP Creative Writing Class."

"Who was it?"

"I don't know. It was this model-looking classy chick ... I think her name is Liz."

Carlos kept quiet and did not say anything, but it sure put a smile on his face. He is enjoying a great meal and hopes more of the same in the near future. Workouts are hard and the body requires nurturing food. If his parents can't provide healthy foods to eat, he will have to get a part-time job to buy some himself. Gervais Market food is okay, but not the kind that would help him get stronger. The other thing he will need is a form of transportation. Lydia is not going to be able to drive him around everywhere.

After dinner he walks around to the back of the old house. He spots an old rusty bike that seems to have a great body. It just needs new tires and some grease here and there. The chain looks good enough to oil – with a little maintenance he can have himself a good bike.

All of his experiences with car repairs and using all the tools paid off. His dad had done a great job teaching him how to fix things – Pete Swavey knows mechanics very well. This bike will look new after he works on it for a bit.

After a tiring day Carlos has a bowl of Cheerios before heading up to bed. The time gets to be12:00 midnight and he is sound asleep. All of a sudden the house starts shaking forcing him to wake up. He holds on to the bed frame expressing a great deal of alarm. It's a loud and everlasting sound – *hrrrrrr*!

"What the heck is that!" Mike wakes up as well. He looks at Carlos.

"I have no idea, but I know they don't have tornadoes here."

Carlos' bed starts bouncing on the floor and slides toward the wall. It hit the wall – *bam*! It stops there while still shaking. He can hear the whistling train going by.

"Oh that's great! It's a stupid train. How am I supposed to get any sleep around here? I miss Texas."

"I have no idea how we're supposed to get any sleep, but go back to sleep and stop complaining you big baby," Mike said.

"Shut up Mike!" Carlos puts the covers over his head.

The next morning it is time to rise and shine for another day at school. Carlos is looking forward to football practice on his second day. When he arrives at school his first class is Basic Algebra, the only class he has with Liz. As he walks into the class, he looks over at Liz and waves. She waves back at him putting a smile on his face.

Pat McGoldrick stops Carlos before he walks to his seat.

"You ready for a tough practice after school?"

"Yeah, I can see I'm gonna have to scramble a lot this year, your linemen need a lot of work. I won't have much blocking."

"Carlos, Clifford is a senior this year. Also, Head Coach Terry Wayne Smith, is very good to him and has a lot of confidence in him. Don't get your hopes up too high, after all, you haven't even showed us what you can do. What makes you so sure you'll take his spot?"

"I just have a gut confidence feeling."

"It'll be up to Coach Smith."

"Well, it'll depend on if Coach Smith wants to win games and make it to state. Anything else is out of my control. I'll just leave it at that."

"I can't wait to see you in action. And I like your positive persistence. If you ever need any help with algebra, you can come see me anytime, okay?"

"That sounds good coach."

During lunch, Harv and Carlos walk to the Gervais Market once again. It is a clear day with a light breeze and a bright sun shining.

"Last night, I was thinking about what we talked about earlier."

"Yeah, what about it," Harv asked.

"I was thinking, since I need help with my grades, to someday be able to take AP classes and to play sports, you can help me. In return, I can help you get better at sports so you can get more playing time. Maybe we can help each other. What do ya think?"

"It's kind of difficult for me to explain the situation at my home right now, but I really would like that. How can you help me?" Harv asked.

"I can help you with techniques I learned. For example, catching a football and running patterns. I can also help you get stronger and quicker. I think you have the potential to be a starter some day."

"You really think so?"

"Look, I can tell you love the sport and you have the height for a short-pattern receiver. It'll take time but I have confidence that you'll be playing in a few weeks."

"How can you help me with grades?" Carlos asked.

"I think I can help you by guiding you into good study habits, and practicing for tests. Not only that, but I have a sister that is a super wiz. She may be willing to help too. The most weight will fall on you – having the determination to work hard at it, just like you do at sports. It's nothing different. It's the same concept except you use your brain cells more."

"I'm looking forward to the challenge. The first thing we have to do is agree on a meeting place so we can get together and work," Carlos said.

Carlos is not about to volunteer his house. He has too much pride and would be embarrassed if Harv came over to his old rented house. His house is the complete opposite of what Harv lives in.

"My dad and mom will be away for the weekend. My dad has this important meeting in Los Angeles, California. My mom usually goes with him if it's a place they can vacation a little – sight-seeing and stuff like that. How about you come over Saturday?"

"That sounds like a plan to me," Carlos smiles.

"I'll give you the directions later."

They give each other a high-five and continue walking to the Gervais Market.

First Day of Football Practice

At the end of the school day the last bell rings. Carlos is walking through the door. He is on his way to suit up for football practice. He notices from afar, a Mercedes Benz pulling up to the front of the school. Liz is about to get in through the passenger door. She turns around and sees Carlos. She waves with her hand way up high. He waves back at her with a smile, turns around and walks away.

"Wow, they have a Mercedes and a BMW – nice," Carlos says amazed.

He finds his way to the boys' locker room where some of the players have already started suiting up for practice. Clifford looks up at Carlos and didn't say one word. Carlos tipped his head to indicate saying hi. But he didn't get a response. Instead, he got ignored by all of the senior boys. Harv follows Carlos and sits next to him.

"I see that this locker is empty, you mind if I take it?"

"I don't mind at all – I can't think of anyone I'd rather have next to me at the current time."

The coaches are talking inside a glass soundproof room. This room is located inside the locker room. This is convenient because they can talk without the players hearing what they say. They can also keep an eye on things where the players are getting suited up. High school kids horse around sometimes for no reason.

"Coach, I saw Carlos throw the football for a little bit yesterday. He's our new transfer student. He looked pretty impressive," Mr. McGoldrick said.

"He's only a freshman though. I don't think he can compete with our Player of the Year. I'll take a look at him today. Your responsibility is defense – I'll take care of the offense."

"Yes sir coach," Coach McGoldrick answers.

As Harv is putting on his shoulder pads Carlos is giving him pointers.

"I want you to give 100% on everything the coaches ask of you. At the end of practice, when it comes time for conditioning drills, stay with the person that always beats you by a small margin."

"Okay, I'll do my best," Harv said.

When the team starts warming up for practice, great memories come to Carlos. He remembers the pre-season practice days in Texas. The difference is the weather. It's a lot cooler in Oregon. He remembers practicing in 110 degree weather and having water breaks every 15 minutes.

"Okay gentlemen! Let's split up. The linemen will go with Coach McGoldrick! The running backs, quarterbacks, and receivers stay here with me!" Coach Smith yelled.

"Carlos and Clifford, I want you both to throw passes to the running backs and receivers. Do out patterns and in patterns."

Coach Wayne Smith is a very sharp person. He stands about 6' 6" and is physically in good shape. His hair is almost all gray.

The coach is watching very carefully. He watches Carlos like a hawk since he already knows what Clifford is capable of. How does the new kid hold the football? How does he take his steps back? And how is his form when he releases the football?

He studies Carlos asking all the receivers a question.

"How fast do you run the forty?" Carlos asked one of the receivers.

"Carlos! Why are you asking them how fast they run the forty?" the coach asked.

"It gives me an idea on how much I need to lead them with my bullet passes – I want to make sure I don't overthrow them."

"I see," the coach answers.

"I don't plan to do this every time. I just wanna get to know them a little bit."

"Fair enough I think that's good thinking young man," the coach replies.

Harv runs an out pattern and Carlos throws him the football. The ball bounces off his hands. It was a great pass but Harv couldn't hold on. He runs back to the receiver's line.

"Keep your eyes on the ball the whole time!" Carlos yelled.

The coach looks at Carlos while he shakes his head.

"Your wasting your time with Bradford, he's worthless."

"No he isn't coach – give me a few weeks to work with him," Carlos said.

The coach rolls his eyes and continues watching the action.

After thirty minutes of passing drills the coach grabs his tablet and looks at it.

"It's water break time! Come back in ten minutes!"

As they walk to the water fountain some of the players are talking to themselves.

"That new kid can really throw the ball."

"Yeah, he's better than Clifford."

Dirk is walking behind Harv and Carlos. He pushes Harv in the back and Harv goes down to the ground face first – *bam*!

"You're wasting your time coming out for the team Bradford," Dirk says.

Carlos didn't say anything, he charged right at Dirk spearing his helmet right into his neck – *crack*! Down goes Dirk.

"You little spec! I'm gonna kill you!" Dirk gets up and Carlos is in a defensive position.

"Hey! Hey! What's going on!" Coach McGoldrick says.

"Nothing coach, we're just having a little hitting practice," Carlos answers.

"Alright, let's break this up. You're supposed to be getting some water."

"Yes sir coach," Dirk responds.

When the players returned from the water break they worked on plays the rest of the practice time. Carlos is sent to play quarterback with the second unit. Clifford went with the first unit.

Coach McGoldrick works with Carlos and helps him execute the plays correctly. His assignment is to be the Defensive

Coordinator, but he asked Coach Smith if he could work with Carlos on the plays.

"It's very important that you learn the plays as soon as you can. You have two weeks before you can legally play in a game. You won't be playing this Friday – that's just the way the rules are."

"No problem coach, I understand, ya'll have rules like Texas," Carlos replies.

The end of practice has arrived. It is now time for conditioning drills.

"All right gents! Line up all the way across the goal-line. Run to the 50 yard line on the whistle! Then we'll come back on the whistle!"

"You mean us not you – what's this we? You're just blowing the whistle," Dirk whispered.

A few players chuckle from his humorous comment. Carlos put himself right next to Clifford, the starting quarterback from last year.

"I'll take it easy on you the first 25 yards. But after that, cover your eyes so you don't get blinded by the grass clipping," Carlos smiled as he looked at Clifford.

"You gotta be joking you little freshman punk."

"I don't usually joke in a matter like this one. Plus I want ya to go as fast as ya can when he blows the whistle. I'll even spot ya 10 yards," Carlos said.

Clifford gets in a ready position and has a serious look on his face. He appears to be focusing immensely. He really wants to prove the Texan wrong.

"Okay gentlemen! On the whistle!" Coach Smith yells.

He blows the whistle loud and clear. Carlos waits until Clifford has a 10 yard head start, then he takes off. Clifford sees that no one is next to him the first ten yards. He accelerates as fast as he can go – in hopes that Carlos will not catch him. When he reaches the 25 five yard line, he hears Carlos' cleats hitting the grass – *thump*! *thump*! *thump*! The sound keeps getting louder and louder. Clifford begins to have desperate feelings of humiliation and an agony of defeat. When he reaches the 30 yard line he sees Carlos fly by him like he is standing still. Carlos has smoked everyone in the first conditioning drill, including the starting quarterback. Second to him is one of the wide receivers on the team, J.J. The coaches look at each other and take a big swallow in disbelief.

"Coach! Stand at the 40 yard line the next time they start at the goal-line. I want you to time him in pads."

"Sure coach," Coach McGoldrick replied.

After the players ran back from the 50 yard line, the result was the same. Carlos was keeping an eye on Harv. He noticed that Dirk was beating Harv by a few yards each sprint. Carlos moved over closer to Harv and whispers a few words of encouragement.

"Harv, try to take Dirk, you can do it. You just need to push harder toward the end of the sprint."

The coach blew his whistle again. Coach McGoldrick has his stopwatch going. He clicks it as Carlos flies by the 40 yard line. He runs over to the head coach.

"Coach! This is unbelievable, 4.4 with gear on."

"That's amazing speed, wow. It's too bad we can't suit him up for the game Friday," Coach Smith said.

During that time the team ran about six wind sprints. The coach calls the boys in, gives them a pep talk, and sends them into the locker room.

As they enter the locker room, Clifford removes his helmet from his head. He then throws it at his locker – *clang*! No one said a word – the entire locker room is quiet. Carlos and Harv just look at each other and smile. They hit the showers and get out of there as soon as they can.

They both step outside of the locker room as they are heading for home.

"What did you do to Clifford?" Harv asked.

"I had a little conversation with him before the wind sprints. He'll get over it."

"I'm going to run back to the locker room I forgot my comb – I'll see you tomorrow."

"Okay Harv – good job staying with Dirk on the wind sprints."

As Carlos walks to the front of the school, he sees Liz coming out of the front door.

"Hi Carlos! Some of the cheerleaders and me have invited some students to help decorate the cafeteria on Thursday. This is for Friday's pep assembly. Would you like to come join us?"

"I'd loved to," Carlos responds.

"Okay I'll see you there. Goodbye."

Liz enters on the passenger side of her mom's Mercedes.

"Liz, who is that boy you were talking to?"

"That's Carlos. He's a really nice boy."

"You know how your father feels about you hanging around Hispanics," Elaine says in a reminding voice.

"Mom, please. I refuse to discuss that issue at the present time. I really don't understand Dad's ignorance of a good human being."

Liz slams the car door shut – *slam*! And they drive off.

Carlos starts walking home and hopes there is food to eat when he gets there. He finally arrives. When he enters the house his parents are still at work. His brothers and sisters are outside playing. He helps himself to a bowl of cereal and a half-sandwich.

Helping Harv After Practice

Carlos is thinking about going to Harv's house on Saturday. He tries to imagine what his friend's house is like. He is also anxious to start helping his friend with some football skills. He knows that Harv has potential to be a great football player. Tight end is the best position for him to play on the team. He needs encouragement and someone to help him. All of the experience that Carlos received from playing football in Texas could benefit Harv in the long run. Carlos worked very hard for years to become the great athlete he is.

Carlos feels as if he's experiencing a big dream at times. He is in a totally different environment. The people in town, teachers, friends, and coaches are all different than the ones in Texas. He has thoughts of sadness sometimes. He misses his friends down in the south. Carlos wonders how the football team in Dimmitt is doing. How did his team feel about him not being there to help them another season? Things seem to be so complicated now. All he can do is take one day at a time. That seems to keep him going.

Lydia is not involved in very many activities. She is the one that babysits while her parents are at work. Carlos helps when he can, but Lydia enjoys the job more than he does.

"Where ya going Carlos?" Lydia asked.

"I'm meeting a friend at the football field. See ya later."

Carlos spoke to Harv earlier that day at school. They agreed on meeting at the football field away from their parents. He begins to walk toward the school and in minutes he arrives.

"Good man Harv you made it."

"I wouldn't miss a chance like this for the world," Harv said.

"The first thing you need to start doing on offense is using your hands to block. As long as you don't grab the opponent you're fine. Just keep your hands opened up and push the defender away. If the defender gets by you, then you have to sacrifice your body and use a body block. That usually gives the quarterback time to throw the ball or the running back to make it to the hole."

Carlos pretends to be the defender. Time after time he shows Harv how to block better.

"Harv, you have to keep moving your feet laterally to keep me from going around you. Let's try it again," Carlos insists.

Harv works a little harder the next time they try the drill. He seems to be improving each time.

"Is that better?"

"Much better. Good job!"

The next thing they practice is on how to catch the football better. Carlos preached to Harv how important it is to keep his eyes on the ball and to catch it with his hands firmly. They worked for two hours that evening and Harv actually improved a lot.

"Okay Harv, I think we can call it a day. Do you want to meet here again tomorrow? I'm struggling with my algebra and could use some help."

"Algebra is easy, it's the same concept you just showed me. It's just learning how to solve equations by practicing over and over. I look forward to helping you, see you tomorrow," Harv said.

The interesting thing is that Harv has learned more from Carlos in two hours than from the coaches all week. Part of that reason is because the coaches have no confidence in Harv. But Carlos sees something in him that the coaches don't. He sees that Harv has a big heart and he is willing to learn if given the chance.

The next morning at school Carlos walks into algebra class. Coach McGoldrick calls him over.

"Carlos, come here for a second."

"What did I do this time?" he asked.

"Oh nothing, I was just noticing you got half of your homework incorrect. And these equations are pretty darn easy."

"Oh yeah coach, I'm working on improving my studies quite a bit. I've got it under control – I'll take care of it."

"That's good to hear," the coach responds.

As Carlos starts to walk to his seat the teacher stops him.

"One more thing, do you have any idea that your time in the 40 yard dash, with a football uniform, is the fastest anyone has ever run in our school's history? And that's including track and field."

"Naw – I didn't know that coach."

It's no big deal to Carlos. He keeps walking to the back of the classroom where his seat awaits him.

Liz heard what the coach said and is very impressed that Carlos isn't the bragging type. Carlos is walking past Dirk – Liz knows he's going to say something.

"Just 'cause you're faster than Clifford doesn't mean you have the experience that he does punk," Dirk snaps at Carlos.

"Hey Dirk, you better watch out for Harv he's gonna pass ya up by the end of the season," Carlos responds.

"You're a punk! What are you taking anyway, steroids?" He looks at Carlos.

"Yeah, they're called frijoles and tortillas." The entire class starts laughing.

Dirk turns red all over and doesn't have a response.

School is finally over and football practice is cut short due to the game the following day, which is Friday. Carlos remembers the invitation he got from Liz. He walks over to the cafeteria where the doors are closed shut. It's as if only certain people can go in to help.

Several of the football players are walking in the same direction. Harv is already inside decorating and having lots of fun with everyone else there. Shawna, the head cheerleader, walks to the door with Liz next to her. Shawna opens the door, Dirk and two other white boys from the football team walk in. Carlos is about to follow them inside when, Shawna Smith, slowly shuts the door.

"We have enough help already we don't need anymore, sorry."

"Shawna! Why can't he come in? I invited him."

"Liz, he's Hispanic … come on," Shawna whispers.

Carlos looks at Liz as he stops the door from shutting.

"It's okay Liz, I understand perfectly. I'll see ya tomorra."

"Carlos, don't listen to Shawna, you have just as much right to be here as anyone else."

Standing outside the door, looking into Shawna's eyes, brought memories to him of how cruel kids can be. He then turns and looks at Liz.

"Please go back inside and have fun Liz, I'll be okay. Don't worry about me."

Carlos walks away with his head down as he paces his walk.

"Shawna I can't believe you! When are you going to wake up and smell the roses?"

"Whatever," Shawna responds with an I-don't-care look.

Carlos had experienced discrimination in Texas, so he knew the type of people well. Shawna seemed to fit the profile. He doesn't want to stir things up since he is the new kid on the block. His friends are having fun inside and he doesn't want to spoil that for them. He walks back home feeling out of place.

The racial issues are hurtful, but there is nothing he can do about it for now. Its part of life – all he can do is focus on not being like that.

First Football Game Without Carlos

The first game of the season is against, Salem Academy, a Christian school in Salem, Oregon. Carlos is not suiting up for this game because of the rules. A player must practice a certain amount of time before playing in an actual game. Clifford is the starting quarterback for the first game.

On Friday afternoon the team bus heads south on 99E, a two-lane highway toward Salem. When they arrive, there is a small group of fans sitting on the bleachers. There's also a few of them scattered throughout the stadium. As game time gets closer the bleachers begin to fill up rapidly.

It is now game time. The excitement of the first football game of the season is indescribable. On the first play of the game Clifford throws a touchdown pass to wide receiver, John Jones. People call him J.J. He is one of the fastest players on the team. He is tall and smiles a lot. John is the only Black player on the team. The fans roar after the score and the Cougars take a 7 – 0 lead in the first quarter. That would be the only score for Gervais.

Salem Academy has a quarterback that has improved through the years. Donny Carpenter is a person overlooked by the league. On the third play of the game he fakes an out pattern to one of his receivers and runs for a touchdown. In the next sequence of plays, the Cougars are stopped in four plays. Salem Academy has the ball once again. Donny backs up on third down and throws a post pattern pass for another touchdown.

"Come on Cougars!" Carlos yells from the sidelines. He is frustrated not being able to help his team. But rules are rules – he can't play until the next game.

Clifford is starting the season on a very bad note. He had received so much attention being the Player of the Year and all, that he didn't put in the necessary work in the off-season to maintain his abilities.

At halftime it is Salem Academy leading the way, 14 – 7. In the dressing room, Coach Smith is staring at the white board.

"I have no idea what I just witnessed. We are getting spanked by a lower rated team. That proves that any team can beat us on any given night if we're not ready. And gents, you're not playing like you're ready. Clifford, you look like you just started spring training. Let's wake up fellas!"

"Coach, I'm not getting any blocking on the left side," Clifford said.

"Does that mean you have to throw the ball when there's nothing there?"

"No sir."

"Let's go out and play like we want this game more than they do."

They hustle out of the dressing room chanting and trying to get pumped up.

"Let's go Cougars we can do this!" one player yells out.

The Salem Academy Crusaders would go on to win the game, 21 – 7. Clifford threw two interceptions and fumbled the ball once.

After the game, in the locker room, the players are very quiet. Coach Smith walks in and looks at all the players. They look tired and surprised of the defeat.

"Gentlemen, let this first game be an important lesson. We cannot take any team lightly. Let's put this game behind us and prepare for next week. That's all I have to say."

Carlos felt bad that he could not help. He is anxious to get a chance to play in next week's game. He looks at Harv.

"I'm sorry you didn't get a chance to play in the game. You would have done better than some of the players out there tonight."

"I know I could have. You've taught me so much – I can't wait to get my opportunity."

Wow! What a House

Saturday morning Carlos is up bright and early, even before his parents. He goes on a jog around the town to get some kind of a workout. Not playing last night gave him extra energy in the morning. During the jog he's thinking about his big day today. He is finally going to Harv's house. He enjoys the run with the temperature being about 84 degrees. In early September the weather stays pretty warm for days before turning cooler.

Carlos returns home and gets cleaned up. It is 11:00 a.m. by this time – Carlos hops on his bike and starts riding it to Harv's living quarters. The house is located about three miles outside the city limits. He rides his bike down a two-lane highway on a sunny morning. He looks at all the green trees and hills from afar. It doesn't take long to ride three miles on a bike, especially when you have such a pretty view during the ride. He arrives in a very short amount of time. He notices a huge house on a slight uphill.

"This looks like the address he gave me," Carlos thinks to himself. The cool breeze of the wind brushes his face as he gets closer to the house. There's a fresh scent as if someone has just mowed the lawn. The clean air in the country is priceless.

He rides his bike slowly – steering the handlebars that lead him to the side of the house. He continues riding his bike down a small paved road that leads him to the back. The backyard has a heavy-duty eight foot fence all around, with some evergreen trees lined up in a row just inside. The trees make a great privacy shield. He has never experienced the smell of evergreen trees. It is a great scent, a very relaxed smell.

Carlos stops and looks through a gap between the trees. There are two girls swimming in the pool. "What an awesome backyard pool," he whispers to himself. He observes a different lifestyle – one that he has never experienced.

The girls he watches seem to be having a whole bunch of fun splashing in the water and laughing. The swimsuits they are wearing look very nice and expensive. They are like something you would buy at Rodeo Drive, in Los Angeles, California.

One of the girls steps up on to the patio that circles around the pool.

"Lorraine, this is so much fun. I'm glad you came over this morning," Liz said from the water.

"I agree with you, thanks for inviting me over Liz."

"Liz?" Carlos takes a big swallow as he leans on the fence with his two hands.

He takes a closer look at the girl that's still in the pool. Liz is the girl he knows from school. Liz has to be Harv's sister. How cool is that? Carlos rushes around to the front and finds the front door. He jumps off his bike and rings the doorbell.

Everything about the front door is high class – top of the line materials. The front porch is made of fine wood and stained. The windows are double pane lifetime warranty with a white frame that is custom designed. Anyone would describe it as amazing. Carlos keeps observing every detail while he waits for someone to answer the door. He hears footsteps coming from the inside.

"It's about time you got here, come on in. I want you to meet a couple of girls before we get started."

"Sure, that sounds good," Carlos replies.

As he follows Harv across the family room to the backyard, he is in awe of the beautiful structure.

"Wow! Your family room is bigger than my entire house."

Harv smiles and continues walking to the back where the girls are kicking back.

"Carlos, this is my sister Liz, and her friend Lorraine Fletch."

Liz jumps up from the reclining lawn chair with her eyes wide-open.

"Hi Carlos. Harv, he's the one I told you about. He stood up to Dirk like no one has before. It's really nice seeing you here," Liz smiles.

"Hi, it's nice to meet you Lorraine, and nice too see you again Liz."

"Liz has told me a lot about you," Harv said.

"She has? I hope good things." They all chuckle and Harv makes a move to retrieve the football.

Liz wraps a towel around herself to cover up most of her flesh.

"You have a very nice dream pool here," Carlos says as he follows Harv to the green fresh-cut lawn.

Liz removes the towel from her fit figure and dives into the pool. Lorraine follows her in with a scream and a laugh.

"Harv, I had no idea … Liz is your sister! She has been really nice to me at school."

"Yeah, Liz is a super sister. Her IQ is much higher than mine. Sometimes I have to look up words she speaks to me."

"Guess I better start carrying a pocket dictionary with me," Carlos said.

Harv took Carlos about twenty-five yards away from the pool area into their huge lawn. That's where they start working on football skills. They will also study later – the deal they had agreed on.

"Okay Harv, lets start out with some short distant passes just to warm up a little. That way you won't pull any muscles. It's always important to warm up before going hard.

"That makes perfect sense to me," Harv said.

Carlos grabs the football and yells, "Go!" Harv runs a short out pattern about 20 yards. They warmed up for about ten minutes before going harder.

"This time run out about 30 yards and cut inside – the ball will be coming fast right as you turn your head. Keep your eyes on the football and use both hands to catch it," Carlos explained.

"Okay I gotcha."

"Set! Hut!" Carlos signals.

Harv takes off full speed and as he turns inside, the ball is right there for his hands to catch. But it is coming so fast that it pops out of his hands – *pop*! He can't hold on to it.

"Dang! My fricking butterfinger hands!" Harv yells.

"Don't be so hard on yourself, it takes practice. That's why we're here. Let's try it again."

The boys are working hard and Harv is making progress. He is actually catching some of Carlos' bullet passes that are thrown right on the money.

Liz and Lorraine are watching from the pool.

"Liz, he's so cute, how did you meet him?"

"Oh, actually, he attends my Basic Algebra Class. He is so humorous, and the best part – he isn't afraid of the bully Dirk like most of the boys."

"I think he likes you Liz, I can tell by the way he looks at you with his dark brown eyes," Lorraine says with a smirk on her face.

"I like the way he treats people, I mean, look what he's doing with my brother. He's teaching him how to catch a football. The only thing Harv could catch before today is a cold or the flu."

"Ha-ha-ha!" Lorraine laughs. They both gradually stop laughing.

"The sad part is that my dad doesn't even know he's here today. Harv asked me not to say anything to Dad."

"Is your dad –"

"Let's not talk about that okay? Come on, I'll race you to the other side of the pool."

"Okay, go!" Lorraine yells.

After the girls swam a while longer, they lie on the lawn chairs for some girl talk. Girl talk is normally a lot. One would have to say that girls love talking more than boys on an average day.

"Hey Harv! We're firing up the barbeque grill!"

"Sounds good Liz! What are you cooking!" Harv yells from the lawn.

"Salmon is on the menu! Lorraine's making a salad to go with it!"

"Salmon? I've never had salmon. Do ya'll have burgers by any chance?" Carlos asked.

"Ha-ha! Yeah, of course. Liz! Get a burger for Carlos!" Harv yelled back.

Liz smiles and waves her hand as she steps into the house with Lorraine.

After the boys completed a lesson in football skills, Harv starts explaining algebra equations. Carlos was having problems with those in class.

"It's just like you telling me how to catch the football. It takes practice. Let's work on some equations until you get the theory."

"I've never had anyone explain algebra the way you do. This is great – I think I'm finally starting to get it."

The boys worked together to help each other in their weaknesses. They had made amazing progress in just one day.

Meanwhile, the grill is going and the salmon is cooking. The boys walk up to the backyard patio where the girls are talking. The sun is bright and the aroma of the barbeque smoke makes it an uplifting day.

"It's really nice of you ladies to cook this meal for us," Carlos said.

"Oh, I'm kind of pinch-hitting for Harv. He and Dad usually perform this task. Not to change the subject, but I have to say that Harv was tutored well today in the sports world," Liz said.

"He's actually improved quite a bit in just one week. I hope coach puts him in the game on Friday," Carlos said.

"I'll second that," Lorraine said.

"Harv, if I'm in at quarterback on Friday and coach puts you in – I wanna fill you in on a secret. The coach wouldn't even know," Carlos explains.

"What secret?" Harv asked.

"Well, whatever pass pattern I call, if you see the outside linebacker blitz on us, run a slant pattern to the middle. I'll be looking for you. I almost guarantee you'll be open."

"So even if coach tells you to run a different play?" Harv asked.

"Yes sir, coach won't say anything unless you drop the football – then it'll be you and me that get chewed out royally."

"What the heck – the worst that'll happen is me on the bench again. And that's what's happening now. I'm willing to take that gamble," Harv responds.

"Oh, don't worry you'll catch it and get twenty yards or so. The coach will see that and possibly give you more playing time."

"Can you guys stop the football talk now – what's a blitz anyway?" Lorraine asked.

"A blitz is when the defensive linebacker goes straight after the quarterback without holding back. What they normally do is watch for the pass or a running back that makes it through the line of scrimmage. The gamble for them is leaving the short pass wide open. That's why Harv will be open when that happens. My job is to get the ball to Harv before the linebacker kills me.

"Liz, this is crazy, I think I actually understand football a little. Thanks Carlos," Lorraine said.

"I've observed a few gridiron games with Dad in the past. But this makes it more interesting. Watching someone I actually know," Liz said.

"Ya'll coming to the game on Friday Liz?" Carlos asked.

"Ya'll? I love your southern accent. Of course I'll be there. I enjoy watching my brother get splinters on the bench," Liz responded.

"Ha-ha-ha!" They all start laughing except Harv.

"Harv, we're just playing with ya. But one thing for sure, when you catch the football with both hands, put your head down and run as fast as you can. And when you get hit, keep pumping your legs you'll get five extra yards."

"Okay, I'm ready," Harv raised up his hands with two fists clenched.

After they are done eating, Carlos immediately starts cleaning up and throwing things in the garbage.

"Carlos, you don't have to do that. Lorraine and I will take care of it," Liz said.

"I don't mind at all – glad I can help," Carlos smiles at Liz.

They clean up in no time and the place is in order before Carlos said his goodbyes to his new Oregon friends.

He hops on his bike and is headed back to his rental house in Gervais. When Carlos arrives back home, his mom is standing at the door waiting.

"Where on earth have you been?" she asked.

"I went over to my friend's house. His house is bigger than some of my farmer friends' houses in Texas. You wouldn't believe how huge it is. And they have a pool, a tennis court, and a basketball court in their backyard."

"Well, that's very nice but you missed dinner and there's no more left," Isabel said.

"That's okay Mom, I ate already. Harv's sister, Liz, barbe-qued for us."

"I'm glad you've made some friends. I was hoping Oregon would be an okay place for us."

"Well, so far so good," Carlos responds as he walks up to his room.

"When are we gonna get a phone? Lydia asked.

"Next month sometime, we should have enough money saved up by then," Isabel answered.

"Good, I really need to talk to my friends while I babysit the rugrats."

Carlos overhears the conversation. He looks forward to having a phone in his house. It sure would make things a lot easier as far as making plans with his friends.

The Day Before His First Game

It is Thursday, the day before the first game Carlos will play as a Gervais Cougar. He is anticipating the event and is visualizing what might happen. The colors he will wear are blue and gold – his number, 11. In Texas, he wore purple, silver, and white. The jersey number was 10, with letters written on the back, "Dimmitt Bobcats."

Carlos walks into his algebra class. The teacher starts handing out test results from the previous day.

"Carlos, I'm impressed. In one week you've raised your grade from a D to a C."

"Yeah!" Carlos jumps up with excitement.

Dirk turns around and looks at Carlos.

"You moron, why get excited about a C?"

"Correction Dirk, I was a moron last week when I got a D as in Dirk. I may get an apple this year for the first time ever."

"What? You make no sense punk," Dirk said.

"An inside Tex-Mex joke man – you wouldn't understand."

"Whatever dude. You're stupid."

Carlos is the only one that knows what he's talking about, referring to the past in Texas.

Liz is listening to the conversation and cannot wait to ask Carlos about it.

When class is over Liz anxiously waits for Carlos to come out of the classroom.

"Hey Mr. you owe me an explanation. What were you referring to when mentioning an apple?"

"Oh, it's just something between me and my old school in Texas. There's a grocery store in Dimmitt that gives apples to students for every A on their report card."

"What kind of grades did you receive in Texas?" Liz asked.

"I'm kinda embarrassed to say. If I tell ya, I'm afraid you might not want to be around me anymore."

"You don't know me very well. I know that my brother has been helping you in algebra. I would be more than glad to assist you in any other subjects if you request it."

"Really? Wow, that would be great. Thanks Liz. What kind of grades do you get?"

"Well, imagine this, if I was in Texas my backpack would be overflowing with luscious red apples," she walks away smiling.

"I'm not surprised," Carlos says to himself quietly.

After school, football practice is cut short since it is the day before the big game against the Regis Rams.

"Carlos, are we meeting at the football field today?" Harv asked.

"Not today I gotta work at the Gervais Market. I got a job there two days a week. I figure tomorra's a big game too. Get some rest tonight, you're gonna need it."

"Okay, sounds good. Sorry you have to work tonight."

"Don't worry, I'll be fine," Carlos walks away.

A young man that is too embarrassed to tell his friend that his family doesn't have much money. He needs to work to be able to buy food for the away games. Teams normally stop to eat after the games. And because Gervais is a small school with a small booster club, the players are responsible for their own food bill.

In Texas, Carlos used to sit in the bus by himself while the rest of the team members went inside to eat. When his friends offered to buy him something, he would say he wasn't hungry – too much pride in this young man. Not admitting to anyone that his family was very poor.

Carlos changed everything for his own benefit. By working in the summer and saving his money, he manages to help cover most of meal costs after games. What a great feeling that is for him. He envies kids like Harv and Liz, who have everything – all the luxuries in life. Sometimes it's difficult and he has thoughts like, "why didn't the good Lord give my family that life?" Carlos just did the best he could to live a satisfied life.

It isn't easy. He feels bad for his parents who didn't receive much education during their life. But they still manage to take care of a large family by working labor job after labor job.

At the Gervais Market, Carlos works for two hours stocking shelves, regardless of a game the next day. He walks home after dark, tired and hungry.

"There's my working son. How'd your job go? Isabel asked.

"Pretty easy, it went okay. I'm really tired though."

"I saved you some beans and tortillas."

"Thanks Mom," Carlos responds as he digs into the food.

The old rented house smells old due to the moisture coming in from the leaky windows. The house sets uneven and the aging process is very noticeable. The floor creaks as Isabel walks across the kitchen wearing her old apron that she bought at a garage sale.

Meanwhile back at the Bradfords' house, dinner is ready and the table is set just how Elaine likes it. Ted arrives from a busy day at the firm in Portland, Oregon. He walks in the door wearing a three-piece suit that shines with his brand new shoes.

"Elaine, something smells really good. What is it?"

"It's a casserole dish I found in my new recipe book. I hope you like it."

Harv and Liz are already at the table waiting for their dad to join them.

"I'll be right there kids I just have to wash my hands. I'm handling a case that's pretty dirty Ha-ha!" Ted laughs by himself.

"Very humorous Dad," Liz said sarcastically.

Ted sat down at the table with a sigh of relief from that long drive from Portland in the stressful traffic. He commutes to work everyday – sometimes it gets pretty old.

"Well son do you think you'll get some playing time in that waste-of-time game tomorrow?

"Dad, it's not a waste-of-time game. And yes I think I might get some time."

"That sounds like a fabulous miracle I cannot miss," Ted said.

"Honey, can you try to be more positive? Harv has really been working hard at improving his skills," Elaine informs.

"Well, as long as he keeps maintaining an A on his studies, I'll keep supporting and going to the games.

"Can I invite a friend over on Saturday?" Harv asked.

"It depends on what friend. I don't want any Mexicans or Hispanics around here."

Liz and Harv look at each other with eyes wide open and didn't say a thing for two minutes.

"What if this person is Hispanic? And happens to be very positive, and a great person?" Liz asked.

"I've known too many of them that have stirred up trouble. Some have stolen, vandalized, or killed people. I could go on and on – I don't want my kids around that kind."

"Dad, I really think you're being a little bit stereotypical. There are plenty of other ethnic group kids that have committed crimes as well," Liz debates.

"Let's just enjoy this wonderful meal your mom has cooked for us. I don't want to talk about this anymore," Ted begins to eat in anger – he chews his food and swallows his first bite.

"Elaine, this food is so delicious – thank you so much for preparing a fine meal."

"I'm glad you like it Ted," Elaine smiles.

Harv and Liz did not say too much while eating their meal. The food tastes so good that they clean their plates and thank their mom for the fine meal. They escape out to the pool area without saying one word to their dad.

"Do you think we should tell Dad that Carlos was over last Saturday?"

"No not yet. I think we should tell Mom first – she'll be more sensitive at this point. Maybe you can tell her when the two of you are alone, and then fill me in."

"You're probably right – I'll try talking to her when we go shopping for the supplies I need. I'm working on this cool project at school."

"That sounds like a great idea Liz. Thanks a lot for your help."

On Friday morning, Carlos walks into Coach McGoldrick's class in a fired-up mood.

"Good morning coach."

"Morning Carlos, are you ready for the big game tonight?"

"I'm always ready. Tell Coach Smith to put me in the game when Clifford throws his first interception. It'll happen in the first quarter. Regis has a kid named Jason – he'll be guarding J.J. Clifford will telegraph the out pattern and Jason will pick him for an interception and a touchdown. Jason has a 4.8 forty speed."

"Looks like you've done your homework. But I think the head coach and I will know what to do with Regis. You just focus on what you need to do in case we give you a chance," Patrick replied.

"Okay coach, I hear you. One other thing, give Harv Bradford a chance. Please put him in the game for one play when I'm in. He's not any different than anyone else on the team – he works his tail off in practice everyday. He deserves one play. I see some great things in him."

"I'll think about it Carlos. Now go sit down Mr. Confidence."

Liz heard everything that was said. Her feelings toward Carlos are getting stronger. She looks forward to seeing him everyday. And having him for the first class of the day is a great way to start the day off.

After class, Liz catches up with the Texan. She's carrying a pencil he left at his desk.

"Carlos! You forgot your pencil."

"Oh, thanks Liz, I was wondering where that went."

"I want you to know something. What you're doing for my brother is one of the nicest things anyone has ever done for him at this school. Thank you so much," Liz reaches over and puts her hand on his shoulder.

Carlos can smell the light scent of her brand name perfume. She wears just a touch of it, not heavy at all. Some females tend to overdo it by putting so much on that it makes it an uncomfortable smell.

"I hope he plays tonight. I know that would mean so much to him and my dad." She definitely captured his attention with her blue eyes and flawless smile.

"I'm so excited about the game tonight. The first touchdown pass I throw will be for you," Carlos said.

"Make it for Lorraine as well, she'll be there watching too," Liz responds.

"You got it," Carlos says.

"Can we walk over to the Gervais Market with you and Harv?"

"Of course y'all can, the more the better. See ya at lunch."

Carlos starts walking down the hallway to his next class. He notices Clifford walking the opposite way with his girlfriend, Shawna Smith – the head cheerleader.

"Hey Clifford!"

"What do you want Swavey?"

"I just wanna fill ya in on some inside info about the Regis team."

"What do you have for me?" Clifford asked.

"They have a kid named Jason, he is a defensive back. Be careful on those in-n-out patterns."

"I got it taken care of Texan, don't you worry about a thing," Clifford said.

"Sure, I understand. Good luck tonight – I hope we can get our first victory."

"I hope you're not planning on playing tonight, 'cause you might be disappointed," Shawna says rudely.

"Shawna please, he's my teammate now," Clifford responds as they walk away. Shawna has a mean look on her face. Carlos ignores Shawna's comment and he still remembers her rejection of his presence at the pep assembly last week.

Carlos has been working hard on his studies and his grades are climbing to the highest point they have ever been. He owes it all to Harv for being patient with him, especially after all those hard days of practice when they met to study. The two boys worked together day in and day out, and the improvements are showing.

After school at the Swaveys' house there is a rare moment. The entire family is sitting together eating dinner at the table.

"Is anyone going to the game tonight? Carlos asked.

"I would really love to son, but I'm so tired from working all week," Pete said.

"Good luck Carlos, I hope ya'll win," Isabel said.

"I'm going and so is Mike. He met this girl and she'll be there," Lydia responds.

"Well, at least two of my family members will be there rooting for us."

"I hope ya'll kick Regis' tail," Lydia expresses.

Carlos is used to his parents attending very few school activities. At times he feels cheated. He has all of the skills, but never has the support of his parents showing up at games. He has always been happy for the kids that have their parent's support at games. There is no doubt that Clifford, Harv, Dirk, J.J., and some of the other teammates will have their parents there cheering the team on.

"Who are you playing tonight?" Pete asked as he walks over to the living room.

"The Regis Rams. They are a private school up in Stayton, Oregon," Carlos answers.

As Carlos continues to tell his dad more about the game, he looks up and sees him starting to fall asleep on the old rocking chair they purchased at a local garage sale.

"Anyway, I think we have a chance to win. I think we can win. I say we should win," he quiets down to a whisper, realizing his dad is falling asleep uninterested.

"Carlos, your dad is very proud of you and he loves you. He just doesn't have the energy to go watch," Isabel explains.

"You don't have to explain Mom – I understand," there is a silent pause as Carlos and his mom look at each other.

"Well, I have to get going. I have to be there early – coach wants us there by five today."

Carlos makes his way outside and starts walking to the school. Ten minutes later he arrives.

Game Time!

There are a few players that have already put their uniform on. Carlos walks past the dressing room into the gym and lies down on the mats. Harv follows him and lies down next to him. There are other boys from the team whispering and visiting in the gym. It is dark – the only light shining is coming from the dressing room. The gym has that icy-hot-cream smell. Some of the athletes rub that on to loosen their muscles. Everyone is supposed to be thinking about their plays and the game plan.

"Where's the music?" Carlos asked.

"Music?" Harv questioned.

"Yeah, in Texas the coaches would usually put on some sorry country music by Hank Williams. After awhile it kinda grew on me."

"Hey hey … good looking … whatcha got cooking," Carlos begins to sing.

"Ha-ha!" Harv laughs along with some other players that pop out of their silence. The boys are having fun laughing but it comes to a stop when the coach walks in the gym.

"Keep the noise down and focus on the game tonight!"

"Yeah Carlos, keep your freshman mouth shut before I go down there and shut it for you," Dirk threatens.

"Dirk, has anyone ever called you a jerk, your head just doesn't work?" Carlos responds.

Dirk walks over to where Carlos is lying down. Carlos immediately stands up in a position to defend himself. Since the coach has already gone back to the office, it's the team alone in the gym.

"Hey! Hey! Come on guys we got an important game tonight," J.J. says as he moves between both boys who are staring each other down. They slowly went back to their spots and said nothing. They cool down eventually.

"Man Carlos, you're pretty brave, Dirk is a little bigger than you are," whispers Harv.

"I'm not afraid of him. In Texas we used to have fights regularly after school. We have a lot of punks like Dirk down south."

"You ever get into any fights in Texas?"

"Oh yeah … there's a lot of racial tension down there. I got into a few fights defending myself. The funny thing is that those punks never bothered me again. This school is much calmer than the school I used to attend. As long as Dirk doesn't pin me under, I think I can take him. I've seen him on the football field – he's not very coordinated."

Carlos is 5' 11" and weighs about 190 lbs. Dirk is 6' 2" and weighs 220 lbs. Dirk is one of the bigger linemen on the team.

"Seniors don't take it to kindly when they're threatened by a freshman. Take Clifford for example, he's threatened by you – I think he knows you're a better quarterback than he is," Harv said quietly.

"Yeah, well I look at it as what's best for our team. If we want to make it to state this year, we need to have the best quarterback on the field."

"Gervais hasn't made it to state in years, I can't remember when," Harv said.

"Well Gervais history is about to change," Carlos says as he stands up and starts walking to the locker room to suit up for the game.

It is 6:30 p.m. and the temperature is 75 degrees with a 10 mile per hour breeze. There is a wheat field next to the football stadium that was harvested earlier in the day. You can smell the light scent of hay hanging in the air.

The team is anxious to get out on the field and start warm-ups. They gather in the locker room and the coaches start delivering a pep talk.

The people are really packing in the small football stadium. The bleachers on the home side hold about two hundred people. The visitor's side holds maybe seventy-five people. There are many people standing to watch the first Gervais Cougar home game.

The *Salem Journal* newspaper had written an article about Carlos Swavey, the new transfer quarterback from Texas. They stated that he was only a freshman, but a gifted player that could possibly replace the senior quarterback, Clifford Mayberry.

The Regis Rams are the first team to run out on the field in their green and gold uniforms. The helmets are shiny and have a picture of a ram on the side. The Rams are ranked No. 2 in the Capital Conference. They have a solid line and a running back that plays both defense and offense very well.

The Gervais Cougars run out to the field next. The crowd goes wild with cheers. Liz is up on the bleachers with her parents and Lorraine. Her mom is stretching her neck trying to see if she can find Harv.

"Honey! There's Harv! He's wearing number 83. He's in the middle of the pack."

"Yes, I see. It looks like he's grown a little," Ted said.

Loraine and Liz are whispering to each other.

"Liz, I think I like your brother. That's really cool that he is helping Carlos with studies." Liz smiles and looks at Lorraine in a speechless way.

"Carlos is such a nice guy – I hope they give him a chance to play tonight. I know what he can do if they give him an opportunity. He is so amazing the way he throws the football."

Lorraine looks at Liz and acknowledges her feelings for Carlos.

"I hope we can get together again like we did a couple of Saturdays ago, remember?"

"Yes of course I remember – that was a blast," Liz whispers not wanting to continue the conversation with her dad close by.

The National Anthem begins – the school band is playing the song. Everyone is looking at the American flag. Some people have their hand across their chest to display respect for our country. The slight breeze made the flag sway up in the air. The flagpole is located behind the end zone. It is a very nice evening and the sun has just set. The song comes to an end and the crowd cheers loudly with some whistles by some people and claps by others. The ambulance pulls up to one of the far corners of the field. It's always a good idea to have the emergency service available – just in case there's an injury.

The Gervais Cougars win the coin toss and elect to receive the football. The kickoff and receiving teams run out to the field to start the game. The referee blows the whistle to signal the Regis kicker to proceed with the kickoff. The kicker pounded the football all the way to the Gervais 10 yard line. J.J. catches it and runs 15 yards before taking a brutal hit from a Regis player – *smack*!

The Cougars start the first offensive play at their own 25 yard line. Clifford is the quarterback to start the game. The team huddles up and Clifford calls the play out.

"Thirty two drive on two," he said as the huddle breaks up and the team jogs to the line of scrimmage.

"Down! Set! Hut! Hut!" The quarterback hands the football to the fullback, Jeremy Lyon, who is running to the right side of the right tackle. The fullback takes a pounding from the Regis defense – *crack*! The Cougars gain one yard on the play. Jeremy gets up slowly and jogs back to the huddle. Jeremy is one tough kid – he's stands at 5' 9" and has broad shoulders. He is a team player and never complains. He just does his job. It's now second down.

"J.J. slant right, tight end and backs, block! On three," Clifford said.

They jog to the line of scrimmage and set up again for another play.

"S-one! Hut! Hut! Hut!" J.J. takes off slanting to the middle of the field. Regis' Jason is on pursuit. The Regis gigantic line comes in strong, but Clifford gets enough protection to barely unload the football. The football goes up in the air with a nice spiral. J.J. sees it as he's moving full speed. The football is about to land in his hands, but Jason gets there just in time to slap it away.

"Dang!" J.J. yells.

"You're weak J.J! I need a challenge baby!" Jason said with a smirk on his face. J.J. gives him a dirty look as he walks back to the huddle.

It is now third down and nine yards to go for a first down.

"15 out pattern to J.J. on two!" Clifford calls out another play.

The huddle breaks and they jog down to the line of scrimmage. Carlos is watching from the sideline and anxiously waiting for his chance.

"Coach, what did you signal to Clifford?" Carlos asked.

"Out pattern to J.J."

"No! Jason will pick that, he did it time after time last Friday," Carlos said.

It's too late – the play is already under way. The bench looks to the field.

"Down! Set! Hut! Hut!" Clifford yells out.

J.J. took off for 15 yards then made a cut to the outside. Clifford fired a bullet pass. Jason reads it easily and intercepts the football running all the way back for a Regis touchdown.

"Yeah Regis! Whoo!" yelled the Regis crowd.

"Son of a ...," the coach holds back on finishing his words, "receiving team!"

The extra point is good and Regis takes a 7 – 0 lead. Clifford walks back to the sideline and looks at Carlos in a very disappointing way.

"You were right."

"It's okay man – shake it off we'll be okay," Carlos said.

Coach McGoldrick walks over to where Coach Smith is looking up at the dark sky – he's thinking of what to do next.

"Coach, give Carlos a chance. Let's see what he can do – we don't want to get in an early hole. This Regis team is tough."

"I want to give Clifford at least one more chance. If he doesn't move the ball forward, I'll put Carlos in. Sound fair?"

"Yeah, that sounds fair to me."

The head coach is very close to Clifford and his family. He has known them since Clifford's eighth grade year. He is in a tough position but he knows he has to think of the team first.

Regis kicks off again for the second time. The Cougars return it to the 30 yard line. They need seventy yards to score a touchdown. The Gervais offensive team runs out to the field with Clifford as the quarterback once again.

"Alright guys, student body left on one."

"Let's go!"All the players sound more intense and fired up.

"Down! Set! Hut!"

The center snaps the football to Clifford and he takes off to the left. He runs 10 yards to the side when he sees a linebacker charging toward him. Clifford pitches the ball to the halfback, who is running parallel to him. The defensive guard, defensive tackle, and defensive end pursue the halfback as they dodge the blocks from the Gervais offensive line. After a five yard gain the Gervais halfback is trampled by the Regis defense – *crack*!

It is now second down and five yards to go. The Cougars seem to be a little discouraged from not being able to break loose from the strong Regis defense.

The head coach signals another play from the sidelines.

"31 fake screen right on three," Clifford calls out.

"That's a smart play to call, the defense is coming in too strong," McGoldrick says to himself.

"Down! Set! Hut! Hut! Hut!"

Clifford starts his backward motion but he doesn't quite have the handle on the football. By the time he grasps the football it is too late. Here comes a Regis linebacker, who is being recruited by Oregon State University, lowering his helmet and hitting Clifford very hard. He hits him so hard that you can hear the helmets – *bang*! All the people up in the bleachers react, "Aww!" It is a sound of concern for the Gervais quarterback.

Clifford lies there motionless for a few minutes. The coaches, paramedics, and the trainer run out to the field to take a look at him. They help him up and he starts walking very slow to the sideline with assistance. All the fans started clapping, even the Regis side.

"My gosh! What a hit by the linebacker!" Ted said.

"Daddy, don't you feel bad for our quarterback?"

"Of course sweetheart, but it was an exciting hit by Regis."

After the official timeout expires it is game time once again.

"Carlos! You're in at quarterback. Run a 36 power to the right," Coach Smith demands as he grabs Carlos by the arm.

"Coach, I'm not going out there unless you put Harv Bradford in at tight end."

"What! Are you joking?"

"No sir, I've been working with him after practices. Please give him one chance, if he messes up, don't put him in again."

Carlos looks dead serious, so serious that this game is not as important as his friend Harv. Both coaches look at each other.

"Are all kids from Texas like you Swavey?"

"Not that I know of sir."

"What have we got to lose coach," Pat McGoldrick said.

There is a short silence while Coach Smith thinks.

"What the heck. Okay one chance for him. Bradford! … get in at tight end!"

"Thanks coach," Carlos smiles and runs out on the field with Harv following him.

In the huddle all of the players are looking at Carlos as he calls out the next play. They look scared and worried.

"Come on y'all, we're only seven points down – if we play like this is our last game in our career we'll do great. Coach told me to run a play that will not work. I'm gonna change it and risk getting kicked off the team. But I think it'll work. Slant to Harv"

"What the heck! Are you crazy spec?" Dirk responds.

"Dirk, please just give Harv a chance … and I'm not gonna worry about your name calling right now."

"Oh great, a freshman quarterback and an idiot tight end," mumbled another senior player.

Up in the stands Liz has her hands clamped together as if she is saying a prayer.

"Lorraine, I'm so frightened for Carlos. I hope he doesn't get hit by that big guy that took Clifford out."

"I hear you Liz. At least Harv's finally getting a chance to play."

Carlos walks up to the line of scrimmage following his team. All eyes are on him, the impressive gifted freshman that the newspaper wrote about. The concession stand workers and the security guards are even watching. As he approaches his position, behind the center, he looks at the crowd briefly and then calls his signals.

"Down! Set! Hut! Hut!" The center snaps the ball to Carlos. He backs up farther than normal to give himself some time. He's looking for Harv as he back drops to a throwing position. The Regis outside linebackers blitz and Harv cuts toward the inside. He's 30 yards down field just enough for the first down. Every Gervais fan hopes for a completion. Carlos unloads the football just the way they had been practicing the last two weeks. The football is sizzling with a perfect spiral. Harv knows it will smack him right in his hands.

"This is my chance I've got to keep my eyes on the ball the whole time," Harv thinks to himself.

Harv catches the ball with both hands! He holds on so tight that anyone would need a crowbar to take them apart. He continues running as fast as he can. By the time the safety catches him, he has gained 40 yards and a Gervais first down. The crowd goes wild! Everyone is on their feet. The Gervais players are celebrating as if they have won the game already.

"Hey! Hey! Listen! We haven't won yet!" Carlos is trying to get his team's attention. He looks at the referee, and signals for a timeout. There's three minutes left to play in the first quarter. Carlos walks over to the sideline to talk to the coach.

"Okay coach I know I didn't go with your call, I want to apologize."

"We can talk about it later. Great execution on the play you called young man," Coach Terry Smith said.

"I think we can score on the next play if we run that reverse and have the split end pitch it back to me. I know Harv will be wide open for the touchdown," Carlos explains.

"Okay, let's go with your call – if he's not open throw the ball away to avoid the sack."

"Yes sir Coach, you got it!"

The players know the play well with the exception of J.J., who will be the split end pitching the ball back to Carlos.

"Okay y'all, 33 reverse. J.J., pitch it back to me as you run by, okay?"

"What? I'm supposed to run it!" J.J. disagrees.

"Okay J.J. you run it, but if you see that linebacker that's headed to OSU coming at you, pitch it back to me. Okay?"

"Alright man … I will."

"On two y'all, let's go!"

Carlos walks up to the line of scrimmage and is looking at the defense. He observes that they've spread out with five linemen down.

"Down! Set! Hut! Hut!"

Harv takes off as hard as he can run. He runs straight to the left corner of the end zone. The Regis defense reads that the ball is being handed off to the wing, and then to the split end. The Regis defensive back drops guard on Harv, and comes after the running back thinking he is getting the ball. The running back gets the ball and hands it off to J.J. for the reverse. J.J. has no where to go and sees the big linebacker coming toward him. He pitches the ball back to Carlos. Carlos fires a bullet right to Harv. Harv is all by himself in the end zone. He catches the ball for his first touchdown pass ever!

The Gervais crowd is going wild, "Yeah! Wahoo! Go Cougars! Liz and Lorraine are jumping up and down with an overwhelming amount of excitement.

"Oh Daddy – Harv scored a touchdown," Liz expresses with a tear running down her cheek.

"Why are you crying?" her dad asked.

"You have no idea – I'm just very happy for two young men out there that I happen to know."

"Okay, so am I. I'm happy that Gervais finally scored. Wow! That young quarterback sure can throw the football. He reminds me of John Elway."

Clifford runs in to hold the ball for the extra point. As Carlos jogs to the bench for a drink, he crosses paths with Jason of Regis.

"This game ain't over yet Jason," Carlos mentions quickly.

"Who are you? Are you new to this school?"

"I'm a lucky Texan, your never-ending nightmare."

"We still have three quarters – your luck will run out."

"I know you'll be tired in the fourth quarter – in Texas we stay in shape year-round," he smiles at Jason and continues to walk to the bench while the extra point is about to be kicked.

Carlos is drenched with sweat, wearing his blue and gold uniform. He takes off his helmet, grabs a cup of water and sits for a small break. He looks up behind him and sees Liz. She looks at him and smiles while waving. Carlos smiles back and pounds his chest.

"Yes, a lot of heart," Liz says quietly.

"Is that what that means?" Lorraine asked.

"Yes that's what it means. He is such a great guy and quarterback."

"I'll second that," Loraine said.

The extra point kicked is good and the score is 7 – 7, a dead tie.

Gervais is kicking off for the first time in the game. The Gervais kicker places the football on the tee. He walks back and raises his right hand indicating to the official that he is ready. The official blows his whistle and the football is kicked to start the action. The ball goes flying straight into Jason's hands. He catches it and runs past several Gervais defenders until he is finally brought down at the Gervais 10 yard line.

On the next play Regis scores a touchdown and adds the extra point. The score is now 14 – 7 in favor of Regis. The Rams' crowd is jumping up and down with plenty of excitement. By this time, Clifford is back and lets the coach know that he is ready to go.

"Coach, I'm ready to get back in this game," Clifford said.

"Clifford, we're going with Carlos again – he's on a roll right now," the coach answers. Clifford puts his head down and walks back to the bench.

After receiving the kick from Regis, the Gervais receiver ran the ball to the Gervais 20 yard line. The team huddles up for the next play to be called.

"41 hook post to J.J. and everyone block. Harv, use your hands to push him off. If he gets by you, use the body block."

"Gotcha," Harv said.

"Okay y'all, on set."

The team looks more confident – there's a little trash talking going on amongst the linemen as they get down on all fours.

"I'm gonna kick your little behind," Dirk says.

"Let me know how the grass tastes after this play," the Regis lineman answers.

"Down! Set!"

Carlos drops back in the pocket to throw with very little time due to the weak Gervais line. J.J. runs 10 yards then hooks drawing Jason in front of him. He turns and runs as hard as he can down the field. The only player he sees is the Regis safety. Carlos throws the football right as he's about to get hit. It's a zooming pass right on the money – in front of J.J. The catch is superb and the touchdown is huge for the Cougars.

"Yes! Nice pass and great catch!" Lorraine shouts from the stands.

"I've never really watched much football, but I sure am enjoying this game!" Liz yells over the loud crowd.

The crowd starts settling down a bit, and Liz looks over to her mom.

"Mom, are we going shopping tomorrow?"

"Yes honey, I'm looking forward to it."

"I hope we win the game – it would make it a much more enjoyable shopping trip," Liz said.

She is excited about telling her mom that she knows the quarterback. Liz feels that if she tells her mom first, it will be easier to break the news to her dad.

"Do you think your dad will approve of Carlos after tonight's game?" Lorraine asked.

"I sure hope so. If we get the victory, it should help more. I'm going tell Mom tomorrow on our shopping trip – she's more open-minded than my dad."

"Great idea Liz."

The score is now, 14 – 14. The Cougars make the extra point. Clifford is the holder for the extra point and for the rest of the game he'll be part of the special teams. He keeps hoping he will get in as quarterback again, but things aren't looking too bright for him.

The Gervais defense is not very strong and Regis pulls ahead most of the game. At the end of the third quarter, the Rams pulled away, 28 – 14, after two Cougar fumbles. J.J. took a blow so hard that it popped the ball loose. The other fumble occurred when the football was stripped from the Gervais running back, Jeremy Lyon. Now it's the fourth quarter and the Cougars have the football at their own 20 yard line.

"Okay ya'll, we need to hold on to the ball. As soon as you catch it focus on holding it with both hands until you get in the open field," Carlos said.

"Sorry about that last fumble guys," Jeremy said.

"It's okay man, that's history. Shake it off. Let's run a quarterback draw – I'm running it straight down the middle. They've been collapsing to the outside – on three!"

Carlos is about to run with the ball for the first time in the game. He had been observing the Regis defense and he also knows that Jason is covering J.J. far to the outside.

"Down! Set! Hut! Hut! Hut!"

As Carlos backs up to pretend he's passing the football, he waits for the seam. He sees it and starts sprinting down the middle – he blows by the line so fast that they turn their heads and didn't even attempt to catch him.

"Oh my gosh! Look at that kid go!" Ted yelled out.

Liz is watching the game and her dad at the same time. She has a big smile on her face. She joins in with the crowd, "Go! Go! Go! Carlos!"

Regis' Jason saw Carlos out of the corner of his eye, but it's too late to catch him. Carlos goes in for the score. The score is now 28 – 21, with six minutes remaining in the game.

After scoring the touchdown, Carlos is jogging to the bench for a breather and a water break.

"Coach! Please put Clifford in at defensive end and let me play safety. Clifford is big and strong – he can apply pressure on their quarterback," Carlos insists.

"That's not a bad idea … Clifford!"

"Yes coach?"

"Go in for Hector, and bust your way into the quarterback – that's your target."

"Yes sir!"

Clifford is glad to be back in the game after a long wait, but disappointed he isn't going in as quarterback. On the first play, Regis ran for ten yards to get a first down. Their drive was eating up the clock as they got closer and closer to the goal-line. The changes that Coach Smith made slowed the Rams down a bit. It is now third down and goal.

The Regis quarterback gets the snap and drops back to pass the ball. Carlos is guarding their fastest receiver – he's not giving him any room at all. The quarterback finds his receiver wide open. He gets ready to unload the football, when all of a sudden out of nowhere appears Clifford. He hits the quarterback from his blindside – *pop*! The football is rolling on the ground. Clifford sees the football – he picks it up and runs 70 yards for a Gervais touchdown! The crowd goes wild, "Yeah! Whoo! Good job Clifford!" All of a sudden the score is 28 – 28, with three minutes left in the game.

On the next series Regis kicks a field goal for three points and pulls ahead, 31 – 28. There is fifty seconds remaining and the Regis fans are celebrating as if they have already won the game. The Rams kick and the football flies straight into J.J.'s hands. He races to the middle of the field behind the wedge made by the blockers. With the help of his team mates J.J. breaks loose for a 40 yard return before he is brought down. The Cougars take over at their own 45 yard line.

The Cougars huddle up. They are all breathing hard and sweating.

"22 slant to Harv. Remember Harv – catch the ball with two hands and hold on to it. On two y'all."

Carlos knows they have a chance. His idea of not running the football is to save as much time as he can from the game clock. He knows that Harv will be open for some huge yardage.

"Down! Set! Hut! Hut!" Harv runs the pattern and the ball comes zooming to him – *tap*! right into his hands. The clock continues to tick as he gets tackled at the Regis 40 yard line. Now there's only ten seconds left in the game.

"Timeout Ref! Timeout!" Carlos yells.

He runs over to the sideline to talk things over with the coach. The rest of the team enjoys a water break on the field.

"Coach, put Clifford in at quarterback."

"What! Are you out of your mind?"

"No, I have an idea – I'm the only one that can outrun Jason. Put me in at wide receiver and have Clifford throw it as far as he can into the end zone. I can run under his pass."

"I can't take that risk – Clifford will get sacked," Coach Smith pauses for a few seconds looking a Carlos, then he continues, "unless I have everyone block except you."

"I'll talk to Clifford and I'll tell him how to throw the ball to me – I've watched him in practice. I think this can work," Carlos explains.

"Okay, let's go for it. You got us this far." He's looking at Carlos believing in him.

Clifford goes in for J.J. – he's walking beside Carlos.

"Clifford, throw the ball deep to the right corner of the end zone. Backup fifteen yards and then throw it. I know you can throw it far – I've seen you in practice."

"Yeah, no problem, I've done it before – just catch it man."

"Oh, and one more thing … say a prayer before you throw it – I'll need it," Carlos said.

The Regis coaches are a little confused on what's happening out there in this crucial moment.

"Jason! Get on Swavey! He's the receiver now!" the Regis coach yells.

Clifford approaches the line of scrimmage behind the center.

"Down! Set! Hut! Hut!" Clifford yells out the signals.

Carlos is way out on the left side. He sprints for about 15 yards and then takes a slant heading toward the right side of the end zone. Clifford throws the football with all his might. The football is hanging in the air wobbling a little. Everyone's eyes stay on the football. Carlos is running past Jason and keeping his eyes on the football.

"Come on baby, I gotcha," Carlos thinks to himself while he's running and staring at the football up in the air. The clock is ticking 5, 4, 3, 2, 1 – Carlos catches the football with a diving motion in the end zone. The crowd goes wild! The celebration and screams go on for minutes before the extra point conversion takes place. The Gervais Cougars upset the Regis Rams, 35 – 31. They improve their record to 1 – 1.

When Carlos makes it back to the sideline, the bench players are all around him shouting with excitement and pounding on his pads and helmet to congratulate him. The coaches are amazed at the display of a talented freshman that is about to change Gervais football.

"Coach, thanks for putting Carlos in when I asked you," Patrick McGoldrick said.

"Thanks for begging me to put him in – it sure paid off," Coach Smith laughs.

The coaches look over at Carlos as he walks by. They both seem to be smiling.

"Nice job Carlos! Nice game! Nice game!"

"Thanks coaches – not bad for a Hispanic freshman from Texas," Carlos smiles.

Meanwhile up in the stands, Liz, Lorraine, and the parents are cheering. Things are definitely looking bright.

"Liz, isn't that the boy I saw you talking to in front of the school?"

"Mom, let's talk about this tomorrow, okay?"

"Sure, wow, he's quite the athlete," Elaine complimented.

"You don't know the half of it," Liz said.

"Well then, I'm really looking forward to our shopping trip tomorrow. How about we go up to Portland – maybe Clackamas Town Center?"

"That sounds great Mom! I'd love that."

The players are all walking toward the locker room hearing cheers from all sorts of Gervais fans. Clifford walks up to the coach in good spirit.

"Hey thanks for putting me in for the last play."

"I'm not the one you should be thanking, it was Carlos' idea."

Clifford stops and just stares for awhile – he didn't say anything.

After the players showered and dressed, they were all being greeted by some of the people outside of the locker room. Carlos and Harv are walking out together talking about some of the exciting plays they made.

"You sure hit me with a nice pass in the end zone – that was really nice. Thank you so much for all your help. I don't think I can compare this with what I've done for you in grades."

"Well, from six Ds and one C last year, to six Cs and one B this year – I think you've helped me more."

They look at each other and high-five each other with wide-open hands – *slap*!

A newspaper reporter walks up to Carlos and smothers him with a whole string of questions.

"Carlos, how do you feel about what you did tonight? You completely dismantled Regis single-handed," the reporter asked putting the microphone in front of Carlos.

"I give credit to all my teammates and to the coaches that made some great decisions. I was just lucky enough to be part of this great victory. Regis is a tough team and we feel very fortunate to have gotten by them," Carlos states.

Carlos is a Big Hit at Gervais

The next day, in the *Salem Journal* newspaper, the front page reads, "*Freshman Texas transfer saves Gervais football.*" This is not at all what Carlos wanted, but the press is going to print what sounds good for the people to read. There is a huge article on Carlos and where he came from. The other thing the newspaper wrote is how Carlos replaced the senior quarterback, Clifford Mayberry. That didn't go to well with Clifford and his family.

Back at the Bradfords, Harv is feeling a little sore from the game last night. He walks downstairs toward the kitchen, opens the refrigerator, and grabs the milk. He pours it into a bowl to go along with some cereal. His dad is reading the paper with a cup of coffee on the table. You can smell the coffee – it's warm.

Liz comes storming down the steps in a great mood.

"Hey, what are you guys doing?"

"What does it look like we're doing brains?" Harv replies.

"Mom's taking me shopping in Portland today. Congrats on your win last night, you played amazingly great."

"Thanks Sis. I scored my first ever touchdown, I still can't believe it … have fun shopping and bring me something."

They walk out of the front door and get into the BMW. They drive down Douglas Street toward 99E. As they drive, they come to the intersection where the Gervais Market is located. Liz spots Carlos unloading merchandise from a truck that is parked in front of the store.

"That must be tough, working after he played a tough football game last night," Liz whispers.

"What was that you said Liz?" Elaine asked.

"Oh, nothing."

They hit 99E and drive until merging with I-5 North to Portland. Mother and daughter always talk a lot. Unlike father and son, they usually talk a little. As they drive on the freeway there is a three minute silence. Liz starts a conversation.

"Ok Mom, I suppose I should fill you in on what's been happening. I don't quite know how to start."

"How about at the beginning?" Elaine asked.

"Very funny Mom," Liz gives her a sarcastic look.

"First of all, I have a great deal of respect for Dad. I'm very proud of all his successes – including what he's done for us. I love Daddy, but I don't think he's being fair to us."

"What do you mean by that Liz?" Elaine asked with concern.

"Well … not letting Harv and I spend time with a Hispanic boy that is a great person. I'm actually thinking about asking him to the Harvest Dance. You know … the dance where the girl asks the guy?"

"Yes Liz – I'm aware of the Harvest Dance," Elaine sighs, "Liz honey, do you have any idea how your father would react to that?"

"I'm afraid to say, yes, I do have an idea. But I'm willing to take that chance. If I don't ask him, some other lucky girl will, and I'll lose out," she stares at her mom and there is a long pause. Liz continues, "I guess what I'm trying to ask you is … can you please talk to Dad about this?"

"Liz, I can introduce the subject to him, but I think it's best if you talk to him. Maybe tell him what this boy is like – then ask him about the dance. What's his name anyway?"

"His name is Carlos Swavey. I guess I could talk to Dad. All he can do is say no and mess things up for me," Liz looks down.

"Why don't we try to enjoy our shopping trip, and when we get back I'll say something to your dad."

"Okay, thanks Mom."

"By the way – I think he is an outstanding athlete. What he did last night was pretty remarkable," Elaine said.

"Yeah, but I knew him before I saw him play. And he is a better person than an athlete," Liz explains.

"Ted was pretty impressed with Harv's performance. He said he'd never seen Harv do that well before. To see him play in a varsity game and score a touchdown, was what he called a miracle."

"Mom, do you know why Harv did so well?"

"No ... of course not."

"It's because of Carlos. He helped Harv everyday after practice. He gave him one-on-one lessons. And last Saturday he came over to our house when you and Dad were away. That's when I first heard all about it. I actually watched Carlos work with Harv in our backyard. I knew he was a special boy when I observed what he was doing."

"Liz, if your father finds out what you guys did, I'm afraid he'll ground you for a week or more," Elaine appears very serious.

"Please don't tell him Mom – I didn't feel right keeping this kind of information from you," Liz takes a deep sigh, "we had so much fun, and Lorraine was over as well. It wasn't like we were there alone."

"I don't think Lorraine has ever been a problem. She's not Hispanic like Carlos. What you've told me is that he is a nice kid that comes from a good family. I haven't met his family, but I bet they are nice people," Elaine continues, "does he ever talk about them?"

"Not really, he never wants a ride home from anyone. After school he always walks home."

"I think you need to get to know him a little more before you ask him to the dance."

"I can ask him!" Liz perks up with excitement.

"Assuming your father says it's okay," Elaine answers.

"Oh brother – that's like a miracle on 34th street."

"I have an idea. Let's follow him after school one day – from afar," Elaine states.

"That might not be a good idea considering the situation – what if he finds out?"

"He won't. Let me know what day would be good next week, okay?" Elaine asked.

"Okay, you talked me into it. Thank you so much Mom, I love you."

Liz smiles with a gleam in her eyes – she has such a nice smile. Anyone who saw it would have to stare for awhile at her. She is the prettiest girl at Gervais High School.

Back at the Bradfords' house, Ted and Harv are reading the paper on a sunny morning beside the backyard pool area. The clean air is refreshing with a light breeze and a scent of evergreen trees.

"Son that was a fine game you played last night. I'm so proud of you. When's the next game and where?"

"I think we play the Woodburn Bulldogs next Friday. They're ranked number one in the Capital Conference. That's going to be a big challenge for us."

"I still want you to keep in mind that Harvard Law School is your place in the near future. So football is okay for now and I am glad you are doing well."

"Yes Dad, I hear you loud and clear."

"Well, now that we have a real quarterback we might do something this year," Ted said.

Harv didn't respond to what his dad said. He just shook his head and agreed with him. He couldn't say anything about Carlos. How does he tell his Dad that he became good friends with a Hispanic boy? Instead, he got up and walked inside the house.

"I'm going to go upstairs and do some homework – glad you get a day off work Dad."

"Okay son. I'm really proud of you."

"Thanks Dad."

Ted puts the paper down, closes his eyes and leans back on the chair.

Unexpected Visit at the Bradfords

Ted is taking a small nap in the backyard deck. He is so comfortable just relaxing and passing the morning away from work, then the doorbell rings – *ding*! *ding*!

"Wonder who that can be," Ted whispers to himself.

He lifts himself up from the comfortable lawn chair and walks through the house to answer the front door. He reaches for the door knob and turns it to open the door. There stands a 5' 11" Hispanic kid.

"Hi Mr. Bradford, is Harv around?"

"Uh … we're getting ready to eat right now – I'm afraid he can't come out. Is he expecting you?"

"Oh no sir, I just got off work and thought I'd stop by to tell him what a great game he played last night."

"Thank you for that," Ted responded.

"Tell him I came by, and I'm sorry for the unexpected visit sir."

"Okay," Ted shuts the door slowly keeping an eye on Carlos. The young man hops on his bike and rides away.

While Carlos is riding back to his house some thoughts get stronger about what just happened.

"I know that kind from some of my Texas days," Carlos talks to himself.

Ted starts walking toward the backyard deck. Harv comes running downstairs.

"Dad! That was my friend! What did he want?"

"He was asking for you. I told him we were busy."

Harv looks out of the window and sees Carlos ride away in his bike. By now he is a good mile away.

"Darn, I wanted to talk to him," Harv said.

"Harv, I've told you before I don't want Hispanics around here ... or hanging out with you! You don't know a thing about that boy."

"Dad, that Hispanic kid is the reason I got some playing time yesterday, and if it wasn't for him I would have never scored a touchdown. That Hispanic kid has helped me the last two weeks. I learned more from him in two weeks than from any coach over the last two years. He has treated me better than anyone at that school. Do you have any idea what that means to me?" Harv takes a pause and then continues, "I can't believe you ran him off."

Harv stomps up to his bedroom and shuts the door – *slam*! Ted sits down on his reclining leather chair. It's a fine chair made out of the best leather with a top of the line revolving unit. He looks up at the ceiling for a long time with no words to say.

Later in the day, Liz and Elaine arrive from a long shopping trip. Ted hears the garage door open. Elaine drives the BMW inside the garage as the door shuts behind. The side door, connected to the three-car garage, opens. As Liz enters the house you can see the huge kitchen with the finest appliances and a large circular bar facing the dining room. Ted is sitting in the family room watching TV.

"Honey! We're home!" Elaine yells.

"I think Harv is pretty upset at me. How did your trip go?"

"Daddy, it was wonderful," Liz said.

"I'm glad it went well. What did you buy?" Ted asked.

"We purchased some shirts for me and some girl stuff. I also got these new shoes – aren't they pretty?"

"They sure are sweetheart. I wish I could say my day went well with Harv."

"What happened?" Elaine asked.

"One of his so-called friends, dropped by unexpectedly – I told him we were busy. He left riding an old bike that was maybe found at the junkyard. Harv is upset at me now," Ted is looking away from his wife and daughter.

Elaine and Liz looked at each other momentarily and then took a big swallow. There's a long silence.

"Why don't you go put your clothes up Liz," Elaine says.

"Okay, sure Mom."

Elaine walks over to Ted and gives him a small kiss on the cheek.

"Ted, I know who the boy is that you ran off today."

"You do?" Ted looks at Elaine.

"Why doesn't anyone tell me anything? I'm always the last one to know."

"Well honey, you're always gone. You always have a case to prepare for or a meeting to be at. You're always working. You show up late some nights when the kids are asleep. That might have something to do with it," Elaine explains.

"If it wasn't for me we wouldn't have all the things we do. Can anyone appreciate that?" Ted questions.

"Of course we can, but at what expense? You don't spend much time with your kids," Elaine stares at Ted and he looks down for a moment.

There is a long pause. Elaine realizes she just said something that hurt Ted's feelings.

"Ted, I'm sorry, I shouldn't have said that. Before I forget, Ginger called me the other day. We met for a small talk. She signed the contract to lease one of our pieces of land next year," Elaine said.

Ginger Berning is a tall lady with red hair. She is a very business-like lady that leases property to do farming. She manages the entire crop process. She also owns many horses. I guess one can say she's a cowgirl.

"That's great honey, another $50,000 for the Bradfords. Let me know if you want to donate part of it to charity, we could use the write off," Ted said.

"Anyway, back to what I was trying to say – I talked to Liz. The boy you ran off is the quarterback that played on the Gervais team last night. It sounds like he's a nice kid. But you're right we don't know anything about him. Liz tells me he is a fine young man, and I believe her."

"Elaine, can we talk about this some other time? I would really like a break from this issue."

"Sure Ted, how about tomorrow?"

"Okay tomorrow," Ted shakes his head with frustration as he grabs the remote and flips the channel on the TV.

Ted closes his eyes and reclines his chair back as far as it can go. He seems to be stressed about the whole ordeal. Listening to the TV is his favorite way to take a nap.

Dealing with Hurt

Meanwhile back in Gervais, Carlos' mom is surprised by his early return. She watches Carlos put his bike away.

"Weren't you going over to your friend's house today?" Isabel asked.

"No, I changed my mind. I decided to go in to work today. Mr. Lind said I can work today if I want to. He has plenty of shelves to stock. He's a really nice man – very supportive of me. He allows me to have a flexible schedule."

"Stock shelves?"

"Yeah, all of his stock comes in through the front door. The store is so small – there's no room in the back. I unload the merchandise truck and put all of the products in the store. Then I price the items before stocking the shelves. It's pretty easy work. He pays me minimum wage. I'm saving my money for the away games."

"Good for you Carlos, I wish we could help you more but we're barely making ends meet. Now the processing plant is talking about layoffs. It could be us."

"I hope that doesn't happen," Carlos said.

"There's a church down the street, we need to start going again. It's been a long while."

"Okay Mom, see ya later – I'm going to work."

Carlos worked about four hours. He would have rather helped Harv with some football drills. He could have used some tutoring for his classes as well. But his plan didn't work out. He cannot understand why Harv's dad is so unfair.

After work, Carlos walks home. His house is about three blocks from the store on Alder Street. As he enters through the kitchen door, which faces Alder Street, Lydia is sitting at the kitchen table eating some pie.

"Where'd you get the pie?" Carlos asked.

"I baked it. Where else would I get it?"

"You baked it? I don't think I'll try any."

"Whatever dude," Lydia replied.

"I'm just playing with you Lydia, I'm sure it's great."

"Guess what I heard today from my friend?" Lydia asked.

"Why in heaven's name would I want to guess … what did you hear?"

"She told me that there are about ten girls that want to ask you to the Harvest Dance."

"What's a Harvest Dance? Do we go out to the onion field and dance in the dirt?

"That's very funny Carlos. It's really true though – after your game, that I didn't watch, all the girls seemed to be interested in you."

"It's nice to have a selection, but there's only one girl I would go with if she asked," Carlos said.

"Who's that?"

"I'm not saying." Carlos heads up to his room and turns on some music. The song playing on the radio is, "How Deep Is Your Love" by the Bee Gees.

"Carlos! Please tell me!" Lydia is left in suspense.

The next day all of the Swavey family, except Pete, attended Church for the first time in a long while. They fill up an entire pew. All Carlos can think about is Liz. He is having a tough time paying attention to the priest. He can't wait to see her again at school, even if it's for one class and during lunch. Her pretty face with blue eyes and shiny hair keep crossing his mind. When the offering basket comes by, he is still daydreaming.

"Carlos! Pay attention," whispers his mom loudly.

"Oh … sorry."

He reaches in his pocket and pulls out two dollars to put in the basket. Isabel always encourages her kids to put whatever they can in the offering basket at church. Carlos pays attention most of the time, but the distraction of all the people around seems to lead him astray at times. They are all a little different than what he remembers back in Texas.

After church it's time to eat and then work on housecleaning and laundry. The regular routine of getting ready for the week again is pretty standard.

Monday morning has arrived once again. Carlos enters the school building and starts walking toward his locker. He opens the locker and grabs his algebra book. He is surprised by several students coming up to him.

"Great game on Friday Carlos," said one of the kids.

"Thanks," Carlos responds not knowing who they are.

"Good job Friday! You're amazing – congrats!" another kid shouted from afar.

"Thanks man," Carlos said.

That made him feel good, but he's trying to prevent the compliments from going to his head. He knows there's still a lot of work to do to prepare for the battle against the Woodburn Bulldogs. They are one of the toughest teams around – another big challenge for the Gervais Cougars.

The young quarterback walks into McGoldrick's classroom in a great mood.

"Hey coach … I know what you did for me last Friday night. Thanks a lot sir."

"It was my pleasure Carlos. You did an outstanding job for us. We're going to need the same intensity out of you this Friday night. Woodburn is a tough team. We're also thinking of playing Harv Bradford half of the game. He looked good on Friday. The head coach and I are starting to believe in miracles."

"He's worked hard the last two weeks coach."

Carlos starts walking toward his seat. He spots someone he knows out of the corner of his eye.

"Lorraine, I didn't know you were in this class."

"That's because I sit right behind Liz. You usually have your eyes set on her. By the way, you played a great game on Friday – congrats to you and the team."

"Thanks Lorraine, especially for including the team. Are you going this Friday? It'll be a barnburner."

"I wouldn't miss it for the world. I want Harv to score another touchdown."

"I'm betting he will," Carlos sits down.

Liz hustles inside the classroom – running to get to her chair. She beats the tardy bell by two seconds. She turns and looks at Carlos – she waves and smiles. Carlos waves back and shakes his head with a smile. Carlos is a handsome young man with a nice smile and straight white teeth.

"Okay class, today we are studying chapter three. We will look at parabolas." The teacher starts the lesson. It is a tough algebra session, with plenty of new theories to learn – especially for Carlos.

After class Liz catches up with Carlos in the hallway.

"Hi Carlos, how did you like class today?"

"What the heck is a parabola?"

"It's a plane curve created by a conic section taken side-by-side to an element of the intersected cone. It's the focus of points equidistant from a fixed line and a fixed point not in the line."

"I'm gonna need Harv's help on this one."

"Carlos, I don't mind helping you with algebra," Liz looks at him as if she wants to take Harv's job.

"Yeah, well I don't think that's gonna happen. I'm not allowed at your house."

"We don't have to meet at my house – how about after practice?"

"I can't I have to work, but let's figure out something – I'd love for you to help me. I'm sure Harv's okay with that," Carlos said.

"There's something else I want to ask you," Liz stares nervously.

"What's that?" Carlos responded.

"Oh … Uh … I think I'll ask you later – I have to get to my next class," she said as she runs off.

"Okay, sounds good," Carlos departs to his next class as well.

It was a long day and Liz was anxious to talk to Carlos after school. The hours could not go fast enough, but the day was finally coming to an end.

After school Liz comes running toward Carlos – he's on his way to football practice.

"Carlos! Wait a minute!"

"I have to get to practice!" he yells across the hall.

"I want you to meet someone! It'll only take a few minutes – I promise!" Liz yells back.

"Okay, but we have to hurry." They start jogging down the hallway toward the school front door. Carlos sees a black Mercedes parked in front.

"Wait, are you sure this is a good idea?" Carlos asked with his eyes wide open.

"Yes, I'm sure it's okay – don't worry."

They walk over to the driver's side of the car.

"Mom, this is Carlos. Carlos, this is my mom, Elaine."

"It's nice to finally meet you Carlos. You played a great game on Friday, and you have a real gift in the way you throw the football – Gervais is lucky to have you."

"Thank you Ma'am and nice meet'n you."

"Okay Carlos, I think it's time for your practice – see you later," Liz expresses.

"Yeah, for sure. See y'all later."

Carlos runs as fast as he can around the building to where the dressing room is located. Liz and her mom drive away as Liz is waving to Carlos.

"He's definitely from the south. I like that southern accent he has," Elaine said.

"He gets off practice about the same time Harv does, and he works until 7:00 at the Gervais Market. I think if we came back around seven and parked on Fifth Street, away from Douglas Street, we'll be able to see him from a distance," Liz said.

"We can bring our truck that has tinted windows. He wouldn't recognize the truck or be able to see us if he happened to look our way," Elaine responds.

"Mom, you're a sneaky thing," Liz chuckles.

They went home and Elaine and Maria begin to prepare dinner. Liz immediately starts her homework – she completes every assignment very quickly. She is excited to spy on Carlos with her mom. Harv walks out to the backyard and begins to work on some football drills he was shown by his friend.

When dinner is ready, they set the table and the three have dinner together. Ted is not home from work yet, so Elaine saves him a plate of food.

It is time for the mother and daughter to spy on the boy Liz is planning to ask out to the Harvest Dance. They both walk toward the front door. Harv walks in to get a drink of water.

"Hey, where you guys headed?"

Elaine and Liz stop and they both look at Harv.

"Oh we're just going to go run a few errands. Do you want us to bring back something for you? Elaine asked.

"No, I'm fine. See you guys later."

"Bye honey, have fun with your drills," his mom said.

They proceed to get into the truck and they drive off to downtown Gervais. They pull into Fifth Street and turn the lights off as it is dusk. You can still see but not too clear. Carlos is talking to Mr. Lind for a bit before heading home.

"Mom! Look … there he goes – he just crossed Douglas Street," Liz says.

Elaine starts up the truck and moves slowly turning into Douglas Street. She drives very slow as they watch Carlos walk down Alder Street. It didn't take him long to get to his house.

"Turn here Mom and drive slow," Liz said.

They start to turn on Alder Street and they see Carlos enter his house.

"Is that his house?" Elaine asked.

"It must be," Liz takes a swallow.

"Wow, I had no idea he lived in a small house like that – his parents must be poor."

"Does that really matter Mom?"

"I don't know what matters at this point, but he lives a different lifestyle than you do. You two come from different worlds, not to mention different cultures," Elaine expresses with concern.

"Well, it doesn't matter if he's poor I really like his character, and I also like how he treats Harv and I."

"Look at the kids playing in the front yard – they're having a lot of fun," Elaine observes.

"Carlos is out there now. He even throws the football to his brothers. After a day of work he finds time to play with his brothers – very interesting," Liz says with admiration.

"Well, I think we better go. I think we learned a little more about him," Elaine said.

"Yeah, I really feel bad for him and his family, I feel blessed to have what I do."

"Are you still planning on asking him to the Harvest Dance?" Elaine asked.

"I think even more so now."

"Well, just be careful Liz – I'm sure he has a lot of pride. This is probably the reason he hesitates telling you about his family and where he lives."

"I know what you mean Mom, I'll be careful."

As they drive by, Liz watches some of Carlos' family sitting on a porch bench that desperately needs painting.

The boards on the deck are broken. The lawn is dry with spots of dirt that has hardened from the kids stomping on it. The house is tilted to one side because of the main studs that are broke around the foundation. There's a train that goes by every night making a tornado-like sound – it jars the house pretty good.

Liz Gets to Know Carlos Better

The next day at school Liz is looking forward to having lunch with Carlos. She is curious and has so many things to ask him. The bell rings and it is lunchtime. The two start walking toward Gervais Market.

"Carlos, I like the burritos at Gervais Market, but I can't indulge in them. I brought my lunch. I can still purchase something to drink though."

"They have plenty of fine drinks. There's a whole section of drinks – I know, I stocked them yesterday."

"Not to change the subject, but about us getting together? I talked to Harv last night and he agreed – I should be the one to help you with algebra. He's okay with it."

"Sure, that sounds good to me," Carlos said.

"Maybe you can help me later. I plan on going out for basketball this year. It will be my first year. Girl's sports are starting to pick up because of the Title IX Amendment that passed in 1972. Our school is just now starting to implement more sports for girls."

"Basketball is one of my favorite sports, I'd be more than glad to help you."

"This will be my first year to go out for sports," Liz smiles.

"Do you have any outdoor hobbies here in Oregon?" Carlos asked.

"Well, my mom and dad have an all-day meeting with Ginger very soon. She is leasing a piece of land from us. She's a nice lady and has some amazing horses."

"Horses! I used to ride horses in Texas – at Palo Duro Canyon. My parents took us out there from time to time – it was a blast riding those trails."

"That's cool! I didn't know you could ride. We'll have to pay Ginger a visit some day to ride horses. That's what I was about to tell you," Liz smiles.

"I'm a man of many hidden talents," Carlos chuckles.

"Anyway, that's what I would say one of my outdoor hobbies is, riding horses when I can," Liz said.

"We'll definitely have to ride horses some day this summer," Carlos said.

"Why don't you come over on Saturday – but just make sure it's after 10:00 p.m."

"Why 10?" Carlos asked.

"That's usually when my parents head upstairs to get ready for bed."

"Oh, I see said the blind man."

"You're too funny. Harv said you guys can meet in our shop at the back of the house. There's an entrance on the backside of the shop – you can just ride your bike inside."

"I do need to work with Harv on his footing and catches. Okay, I'll just have to figure out how I can sneak out of my house." Carlos is thinking to himself about finding a rope and sliding down from his window at nighttime. He knows his parents would not let him stay out too late at night. If he snuck out, and then back in, they would never know.

"Where do you live?" Liz asked.

"Oh, somewhere down Alder Street. It's not our house – we're just renting it until we can find something better."

"Good answer," Liz thought to herself. She continues, "Do you have any brothers or sisters?"

Carlos takes a big sigh.

"You don't have to answer that – I'm sorry I shouldn't be too nosey," Liz said.

"No, it's okay. It's just that I have a fairly large family and I don't know how you'd feel about coming over to my house. Our house is a piece of crap compared to yours."

"That really doesn't matter to me. I think you're a great guy. And I think that what you've just told me is totally out of your control," Liz explains.

"I wish I could –" Carlos starts to say as Liz interrupts, "Your parents are doing something right – look how you turned out."

"Sometimes I wish our family could have a four bedroom house, with a double-car garage and a BMW parked in front. But I know it's a dream and nothing more." Carlos tips his head down.

"Carlos, what you and your family have is something special that many families never get. Also, you brought something to our school that no one will ever be able to match – at least not for a very long time. Keep doing what you're doing and I guarantee you someday you'll have that double-car garage," Liz said.

"You think so?"

"I know so … trust me," Liz looks at Carlos.

He's still looking downward momentarily with some deep thoughts.

"What's this Harvest Dance all about? My sister was telling me that ten girls want to ask me to go with them."

"Ten girls! You plan to dance with all of them at once?" Liz laughs.

"Yeah, they could probably dance circles around me. That would not be fun."

"How about you go with me and save the ten girls from killing each other?" Liz asked.

"Are you asking me to the Harvest Dance?"

"Well, just open this," Liz hands him a present.

"What's this?"

"Open it," Liz insists.

Carlos starts to open the present with excitement.

"*I'm going to the Harvest Dance with Liz Bradford*," Carlos reads the print on the shirt.

"Wow! This is really nice. Thanks."

The shirt is a sports blue shirt with light gold letters.

"If you say no, I'll burn it and I'll have a broken heart," Liz said.

"I don't want you to burn it and I don't wanna break your heart, so I'll say yes."

"Oh Carlos, thank you so much," Liz hugs Carlos and wipes off her tears that start running down her cheeks."

"Why are you crying?"

"I was so afraid that you wouldn't go with me. Some girls were talking and I heard them say that you wouldn't go with me."

"Well, they're wrong. Thanks for asking me."

Liz and Carlos walk into Gervais Market, buy a few things, and then sit outside of the store on a bench. They talk about many things the rest of the lunch hour. They are laughing and having a great time.

Sneaking Out of the House

Carlos didn't wait until Saturday – he called Harv that night and made some plans. At 11:00 p.m., Carlos rigs up a rope by tying it to a water pipe that's located in the attic – where his room is. He opens the window and throws the rope down. He ties a smaller rope to a nail that is sticking out of the window frame. He will use this small rope to shut the window once he's on the ground.

He looks over to be sure his brother is still sleeping. It all looks good. He slides down slowly using the side of the house for support. When he makes it all the way down he pulls the small rope to shut the window slowly – not making any noise.

Carlos hops on his bike and starts riding toward the Bradfords' house. When he arrives he sees Harv standing behind the shop with the eight foot gate opened. Harv is waving a flashlight at Carlos.

"I was wondering if you were going to make it or not."

"It took me awhile to rig up an escape from my room, but I finally did it."

"Thanks for coming down man – let's get to work," Harv said.

The boys studied and worked on pass patterns. The night light facing the backyard is just enough to be able to see the football spiral through the air.

"I heard my sister asked you to the Harvest Dance."

"Yeah, she's an amazing girl. I hope you're okay with that," Carlos said.

"Oh yeah. Not a problem. She's got you fooled though," Harv chuckles.

"I think Lorraine wants to a ask you, but she's afraid you might say no," Carlos said.

"Really? Wow, I'll have to tell Liz to give her a heads-up. That would be fun."

"When is that anyway?" Carlos asked.

"I think it's at the end of October."

"Still a ways to go I guess."

"By the way, how'd you manage to sneak out of your house without your parents hearing you?"

"Not an easy task, like I said, I rigged up something from the window and climbed down. I'm sure glad the window didn't make too much noise."

"How are you going to get back in?"

"I left a rope hanging down the side of the house. I should be able to get back up."

"Man you're brave, I couldn't do that."

"Well, the way I see it, is, we gotta do what we gotta do."

"I suppose you're right, well, let's get to work," Harv said.

The boys work all night on skills and studies. When Carlos returns home, he is able to climb up the side of the house with the rope that he left hanging. Once he gets back inside, it didn't take him long to fall asleep.

The next day Carlos is looking a little tired. Walking to school wakes him up a little bit before entering the school. He walks into his first class of the day.

"Carlos, you okay?" Mr. McGoldrick asked.

"Yeah coach, just a little tired."

"Kids these days are staying up too late – you need to get more rest. You'll need it for Friday's game. Nice shirt. I suppose Liz got that for you huh?" the coach asked smiling.

Liz has a big smile on her face when she sees that Carlos wore the shirt she gave him. She waves to him and smiles as he walks to his desk at the back of the class. She then turns around to talk to Lorraine since she sits right behind her.

"Lorraine, you should ask Harv to the Harvest Dance. I got an inside tip and it sounded positive, I'm sure he'll say yes," Liz said.

"Really?" Lorraine perks up with a smile.

"Yes, really. We can talk more later."

The days went by and Friday night has arrived. It is game day. At the end of the school day Gervais holds a pep assembly. All of the students are required to attend. During the assembly, the cheerleaders normally do some cheering and the band plays some fight songs. There is usually some kind of activity involving the students for fun– like silly races. And to conclude the assembly the coach usually says a few words.

Head coach, Terry Smith, takes the microphone in the middle of the gym. He talks about the game last week and some of their successes. After he is done with his pep speech he introduces the athlete he chooses to speak.

"And now I would like to ask a special young man to come down and say a few words. I want to introduce to you a Texas transfer. This is one of the reasons we won last Friday … Carlos Swavey!" The crowd goes crazy, "Whoo! Yeah!" Carlos is in a little bit of a shock. He did not expect this at all. In Texas he never got picked to speak in a pep assembly. He always wanted to be picked, but it was always some rich popular kid that got picked.

Carlos always wondered what that would feel like, now he gets to experience it. He begins to walk down to where the coach stands behind the microphone in the middle of the gym. Some of the students high-five him as he walks by. Carlos grabs the microphone.

"Wow, thank ya so much for the kind words coach and thank y'all out there." The crowd gives a big cheer then quiets down to a silence.

"First of all, I wanna say that last week's win was a team effort. I give credit to the front linemen – even if it was for three seconds." The students laugh, "Ha-ha-ha!" Carlos continues, "I also wanna give credit to our defense, they did a great job. The coaches did a great job communicating with the players. Thanks Clifford for throwing that touchdown pass to win the game. Coach McGoldrick, and Coach Smith, thanks for giving a freshman a chance. I'm so glad I didn't mess up the game. I'm sure there are other people that I will forget to thank. But there are two more names that I won't forget, my two best friends, Harv and Liz Bradford. They welcomed me and have helped me so much with my studies – Lord knows I needed the help. When I left Texas I felt that things weren't fair, and I had lost all my friends. But when the good Lord closes a window on us, He usually opens a door. He opened the door here at Gervais for me. Thank ya y'all. And I promise I'll do my best to cage those Bulldogs tonight!" The student body begins to chant, "Go Cougars! Yeah! Whoo!"

Battling the Woodburn Bulldogs

Friday evening at the Woodburn High School football stadium, the Cougars started out with a fumble. One of the Bulldog linebackers hit the Gervais fullback so hard that the ball popped loose. Dan Rice picked it up and ran for the score. Woodburn has some big boys and it is very noticeable they are ready for the Cougars.

In the second quarter the Cougars found themselves trailing, 14 – 0. Midway through the second quarter the Bulldogs added a field goal to make it, 17 – 0. The teams both go into the locker room for halftime.

Up in the stands Liz's family and Lorraine are a little concerned for the team.

"I just don't get it, Carlos has completed six passes for 100 yards and we are still losing at halftime," Liz said.

"It's the tough defense that Woodburn has – they have caused some turnovers. I hope we can turn it around in the second half," Ted responds.

In the Gervais locker room, the coach is not too happy with how things are going.

"J.J., you've got to hold on to that ball when you catch it! Keep your eyes on the football. Focus gentlemen. We can still win this game if you want it bad enough!"

"Coach, let's run some hook patterns. They're not giving me any room farther than 15 yards. They're also watching for the long pass," Carlos explains.

"I'm open for ideas, anyone else see anything out there?" the coach asked.

"Their linebackers are blitzing consistently – the middle is wide open," Clifford added.

"Okay, Dirk and Harv, be ready to run some slants down the middle. Listen to Carlos – I'll call the play from the sideline," Coach Smith draws up a play on the board and explains it, "Does everyone understand?"

"Yes sir!" The entire team says.

"Now let's go do something out there!" The coach shouts as the team jumps up and starts jogging to the field. One of the players shouts, "Let's go guys!" After that another player yells, "Go Cougars!" They all have something to say to get fired up for the second half of play.

At the sidelines, before the Cougars' receiving team takes the field, the coach looks at all of them as they huddle up together.

"Okay gentlemen – let's run a reverse on the kickoff return. I want either Carlos or J.J. to catch it. Make sure you hold on to the ball – don't fumble it!" Coach Smith yells out.

Woodburn kicks the football to the right side of the field. J.J. catches it and runs as fast as he can toward Carlos, but the defense thinks he's running toward the side of the field to avoid a tackle. The entire Bulldog defense is coming after J.J. Carlos gets the hand-off from J.J. and sprints to the opposite side of the field for an open range toward the goal-line.

There are only two defenders that realize a reverse is in progress. Carlos dodges one and gets by the other. They are both left in the dust once Carlos turns up the gear. The crowd is on their feet chanting an uproar. The Texas transfer displays his lightning speed scoring the Cougars' first touchdown of the night on a kickoff return.

"Touchdown! Woo! Hoo!" The Gervais crowd is going wild.

After the conversion, the score is now, 17 – 7. Gervais is kicking off and the Gervais crowd gets into the game – the intensity of football is something else.

"What are they doing? They're kicking an onside kick!" Ted expresses.

"What's an onside kick?" Liz asked.

"Just watch," Ted said.

On a kickoff, if the ball goes past 10 yards, it's a live ball – treated like a fumble.

The Gervais kicker taps the football on the top part as he kicks it – this influences the ball to roll on the ground and possibly take a quick hop. Carlos and J.J. start hustling after it. The football bounces off one of the big Woodburn front lineman! J.J. jumps on it!

"Yes! We got it!" Ted yelled.

"It's our ball?" Lorraine asked.

"Yeah! We have the football!" Liz shouted.

Elaine sits there and observes. She is enjoying watching all the action, but at the same time, a little nervous. Now that her son, Harv, is playing more and her daughter's friend, Carlos, is the quarterback, she's more attentive of the game.

Liz leans over to her mom and begins to whisper in her ear.

"Mom, I did ask Carlos to the Harvest Dance."

"What did he say?"

"Well, let's put it this way, he wore the shirt I gave him to school."

"That's great! Are you excited to tell your dad? Elaine asked.

"Very funny Mom – I will in time. I have almost a month to figure that one out."

"You'll figure out something, you're a bright girl."

"Yeah, well sometimes a 4.0 GPA is good for nothing."

While Liz and her mom are talking the next play gets underway. Carlos throws a nice pass to J.J. He runs for 20 yards before he gets hit by the Woodburn safety. Out comes the ball and Woodburn recovers.

Gervais is now trailing, 17 – 7. On the next series they stop Woodburn on third down. It's fourth and five and Woodburn elects to attempt a field goal.

"Ready! Set!" the Woodburn holder calls.

The football is snapped and the kick is shanked off to the right of the goal posts. The possession turns over to the Gervais Cougars.

The Cougar defensive team runs to the sideline and the offensive team is starting out to the field.

"Coach, I think Harv can run for some good yards on a slant if we can get Dirk to take out the linebacker," Carlos said.

"Dirk! Come here!" the coach calls.

Dirk jogs over to where the coach is standing, "Yes sir?"

"I need for you to focus on blocking the middle linebacker. If you can do that, we can gain some big yardage. Carlos doesn't have much time to throw the football. Can you do that?"

"Yes coach, I can do it," Dirk replies.

The Cougars take over the ball. The team huddles and they talk about the first play.

"Okay y'all, 31 slant to Harv, on two," Carlos calls, but not too loud.

In football, the huddle is usually 10 yards away from the defense. Quarterbacks are usually loud enough so the offensive team hears them calling the play, but not the opponent.

The Cougars jog up to the line of scrimmage. The offensive line is feeling a little tired – taking a beating from the big Woodburn line is not easy. The Bulldogs are known to be strong and very verbal. They begin to trash talk a little.

"I'm gonna make you wish you hadn't been born you little piece of turd," a Woodburn down lineman said. Some of the others joined in making some horrible comments to the Gervais offensive line. That's just football, tempers rise as the game gets more intense.

Carlos is positioned behind the center ready to make the call.

"Down! Set! Hut! Hut!" He gets the snap and steps back about seven yards as he positions himself to throw the football. The two Woodburn tackles break loose and before Carlos has a chance to scramble – *smack*! *smack*! The two tackles smashed him for a loss of 15 yards. They landed on top of him, "Take that you little punk!" one of the linemen yelled out.

Carlos gets up off the ground slowly.

"You okay Carlos?" a few of the players asked.

"Yeah, whew, there's gotta be a better way to make a living," he commented.

"I hear you – that's my fault Carlos, sorry man," Dirk said.

"No problem man, I'll live. Try using a body block next time. That'll slow him down."

Carlos takes a few seconds to regroup. He is taking a deep breath and moving his shoulders to stretch a bit from the blow he received.

"Okay, let's try the same play again. Give me at least five seconds boys. 31 slant to Harv, on three this time," Carlos calls.

He starts walking to the line of scrimmage with a small limp. He is trying to work out the hurt from the pounding he received.

"Down! Set! Hut! Hut! Hut!" Carlos drops back in the pocket and as he looks down field, he notices the defensive middle linebacker slipping and falling down. Harv is wide open. Four seconds have gone by since the snap. Carlos throws the football with an amazing velocity – a straight spiral right into the hands of Harv Bradford. Harv takes off as fast as he can go. "Go Harv!" Lorraine and Liz yell at the top of their lungs.

While the cheers from the people are getting louder, Harv runs past several yard lines. Unfortunately, while Harv is dodging one defensive back, there's a strong safety waiting for him. The safety came right at Harv putting his helmet straight into his chin – *crack*! That's an ugly sound as Harv goes down. Somehow he manages to hold on to the ball and put Gervais 20 yards away from the goal-line.

"Oh my gosh! I hope he's okay," Elaine expressed with concern.

"He'll be okay – he's just a little shook up," Ted said.

Harv gets up slowly and starts to walk toward the bench. Some of his teammates help him, one on each side holding him up as he staggers a little. The fans started clapping to give him a little support and to acknowledge his safety.

There's enough time for Carlos to make another suggestion to the coach.

"Coach, bring Clifford in as halfback – I have an idea."

"What?"

"Just trust me on this coach, please," Carlos begged.

"Alright, Cliff! … go in at halfback!"

Clifford hops up off the bench and hustles on to the field. The players get into a huddle as Carlos begins to call the play.

"Okay boys, 22 pitch to Cliff and everyone block! Cliff as soon as I pitch you the ball, I'll run toward the right corner of the end zone. Hang the pass up high for me – I'll run under it. Okay?" Carlos asked.

"Okay, gotcha." Clifford responds.

"On two! Let's go!" Carlos calls.

He then follows the team to the line of scrimmage.

"Down! Set! Hut! Hut!" Carlos drops back and turns as he pitches the football to Clifford. He than runs as fast as he can to the right corner of the end zone. The ball is thrown high. Carlos sees the football hanging up in the air with the glare of the lights bouncing off the leather. He jumps up as high as he can, reaching out for the football. He manages to grasp the pigskin with his fingers and he comes down just inside the line.

"Gervais touchdown!" the announcer in the press box yells out.

The crowd roar follows the announcer's lead. Everyone is on their feet. After the extra point the score is, 17 – 14, Woodburn is still leading.

Gervais kicks the football again. The Woodburn receiver fumbles the ball and Gervais recovers. There are two minutes left in the game. Carlos throws another touchdown pass to J.J. This makes the score 21 – 17 and Gervais gets the upset of the week. They bring down the team that was ranked number 8 in the state. The Cougars are now 2 – 1 in the Capital Conference.

Back Home and the Harvest Dance

The team is heading back home. They're all very hungry, the coach decides to stop and eat at a fast-food place. This place has good old burgers and fries. The players begin to step down off the bus one at a time. Carlos noticed Hector staying inside the bus and not joining the crowd.

"Hey Hector, aren't you gonna come inside with the team?"

"Naw, I'm not hungry."

Carlos remembers doing the same thing back in Texas. His pride was too strong – he didn't want to take any kind of charity from others. Carlos steps off the bus and walks into the burger place. He orders twice as much. The smell of the diner food is out of this world. You can hear the fries sizzling and the cooks yelling out the orders. What a wonderful sight to see after a hard football game.

"Can you put half of that order in a to-go bag?"

"Sure, you a little hungry son?" the clerk asked.

"Yeah, I'm starved – just played a tough game."

He ate quickly and headed back to the bus before any of the other players saw him. Carlos knows his plan won't work if other people are around. He approaches the bus and steps up onto the aisle. He observes that Hector is studying.

"Hey Hector," Carlos said.

"What's up man?" Hector answered.

"I'm so stuffed, ordered way too much. There's a big burger and fries in this bag," Carlos throws the bag to Hector, "I'm thinking if you don't want it you can throw it away. I didn't touch the food, they're both wrapped."

"I wouldn't wanna throw food away, thanks man," Hector smiles.

"I'll be back," Carlos heads back to the burger place to talk to his other friends.

The young Texan has money to buy food. He told himself that he was never going to go through what he went through in Texas. He understands what Hector is feeling.

After visiting with Harv and his other teammates, Carlos hurried back to the bus to talk to Hector again. Shortly after, Harv follows him to the bus.

"Hey dude, Lorraine asked me to the Harvest Dance," Harv said.

"When?" Carlos asked.

"At the game, she held up a sign."

"What did the sign say?" Carlos asked.

"Something like, *Harv will you go to the Harvest Dance with me*? It was far out!"

"What did you say?" Hector asked.

"I haven't seen her yet," Harv answered.

"That's great Harv, I'm real happy for you," Carlos added.

"My head's still ringing from that hit I took from that number 11. He's one tough dude."

"Ha-ha! Thanks for holding on to the ball stud. I have a big bruise on one of my ribs from that sack by number 90," Carlos said.

They continued talking about the game and big plays that were made. They also discussed some of the injuries they received – some good old guy talk.

The bus driver starts the bus and hits the road to Gervais. Several players are talking about bumps and bruises. But as most football players know, the injuries aren't as painful when you win a big game. And the trip back home is much shorter.

The next Monday at school, Harv arrived earlier than normal. He went over to Lorraine's locker and slipped a big note through the crack. It fell inside the locker. He then runs to the other side of the hallway and hides behind the corner. Harv stands there and waits for Lorraine to approach her locker. He's anxious to see her reaction.

Liz walks in with Lorraine – they are walking toward the locker. Lorraine opens the locker – it has a squeaking sound as the door swings open – *squeak*!

"What's this?"

"I don't know open it," Liz said.

"Oh my gosh! He said yes!"

"Wow! That's great news Lorraine!"

"Hey, maybe we can double date," Lorraine comments.

"Great idea, I'll ask Carlos and Harv today."

It sounds like both girls have a date for the Harvest Dance coming up this Saturday. The look on their faces told it all. The smiles and body language are of great joy and happiness.

"What am I gonna wear Liz?"

"Duh! We'll just have to go shopping in Portland or at the Lancaster Shopping Mall in Salem. My mom can take us on Thursday."

Carlos saved enough money to buy something nice to wear to the dance. The dance is a semi-formal kind. Some nice slacks and sports shirt will do. Harv has no need to go shopping, he has a closet full of fine jackets, shirts, and dress slacks for special occasions.

That week at school, nominations for the Harvest King and Queen are submitted. Three boys and three girls are to be finalists. On Thursday the final votes for King and Queen will be casted throughout the school day.

The anticipation of this honor for one boy and one girl has all the students talking about who it might be. The days go by with the hot topic being the King and Queen of the Harvest Dance. There are several flyers posted on each hallway wall.

On Wednesday morning, during home room, the principal announces the final candidates through the intercom system.

"For the boys, the candidates are, Dirk Newman, Clifford Mayberry, and Carlos Swavey. For the girls, the candidates are, Shawna Smith, Kalin Jensen, and Lorraine Fletch." You can hear the hollers and cheers after each name is called. In Gervais, being selected for an honor like this is a huge deal. There aren't too many students that don't want to be a part of this.

Friday finally arrives and all of the students seem to be discussing who to vote for. Carlos had never experienced anything like this. In Texas, the rich farmer kids with parents involved in school activities seemed to get the edge on any kind of nomination. Carlos is not a senior which makes it more of a surprise for him.

"Carlos, good luck – I'm voting for you my main man," Harv said.

"Yeah, I'll have one vote or maybe two if Liz votes for me. Do you really think I have a chance against these seniors?" Carlos asked.

"Well, take it from me – I know there are many voting for the underclassman."

"Hmm, well either way it'll be a fun experience and I'll cherish it forever," Carlos said sarcastically.

"Ha-ha-ha!" Harv laughs.

Liz and Lorraine walk up to the boys.

"Good luck Carlos I voted for you," Liz smiled.

"When are the results gonna be posted?" Carlos asked.

"They're supposed to announce the winners at the dance Saturday night," Liz answers.

Carlos and Liz started walking away from Harv and Lorraine.

"Liz, does your dad know about us going to the dance together?"

"Carlos please, I don't want to talk about it," Liz said.

"I don't wanna get ya in trouble – you're too important to me."

"Well, have you told your parents you're going with me?" Liz stares at Carlos.

"No, I don't know how. It's difficult for me to talk to my parents about stuff like this. I mean, I'm sure they'd be okay with it … at least I think they would."

"I'll make a deal with you, if you tell your parents I'll tell my dad. My mom already knows," Liz said.

"She does?" Carlos asked.

"Yes silly, she took me shopping for my dress and we talked."

"Nice, I bet the dress is really outta this world – you're gonna put me to shame."

"Hmm … well, do we have a deal?" Liz asked insisting a response.

"Oh what the heck, okay sure. My parents will wonder why I'm so dressed up that night … might as well tell them."

"Great! I wish you the best of luck," Liz said.

"That I'll need, and good luck to you too."

"Carlos, I will not only need luck, but prayers as well. My dad's pretty tough to convince but I'm up for the challenge."

They walk to class together as Liz pushes Carlos and laughs. The body language tells it all. The two really like each other and it's starting to show. The students around them know they are a couple.

Later that night Carlos is lying on his bed up in the attic. He is trying to figure out a way to tell his parents. He's thinking to himself, "This would have been a lot easier if we had a game – why do we have to have a stinking bye?" He gets up off the bed and walks down the steps. He stops about halfway.

"Mom, I'm going to the Harvest Dance. This girl asked me and I said yes."

"What … a girl asked you!"

"It's not what you think. This is the type of dance where the girl asks the guy."

"Oh, I see. Who is she?"

"Her name is Liz Bradford – she lives about two or three miles out of town."

"Is she a nice person?"

"She's great. Liz reminds me of Cecilia – pretty and smart."

"I remember you telling me about Cecilia back in Texas. Sounds like you really like this Liz," Isabel said.

"The only difference between Cecilia and Liz is that Liz is a lot smarter and richer. Oh, and Liz has blue eyes not green."

"Well, money isn't everything but it sure helps," Isabel said.

"Mom, it's not like that. She's a great person and has a great heart. She understands me. Can you tell Dad for me?" Carlos asked.

"Sure, he won't care."

"Thanks Mom, I love you – you're the greatest."

"Now get out of here I have to clean the kitchen," Isabel smiles.

Carlos heads back up to his room.

Meanwhile, back at the Bradfords, Liz is up against the wall. No matter how she approaches her dad, it isn't going to be good. Ted is watching TV and drinking some orange juice.

"Hi Daddy."

"Hi Liz, what are you up to?

"Oh not much, I just got done with my homework."

"That's great! Are you still maintaining a 4.0?

"Of course Daddy, getting a college scholarship is what you've always preached. I believe you also mentioned an Ivy League College as well."

"That's right, nothing but the best for the Bradfords."

"I fully agree with you Daddy," Liz smiles.

"Hey, that was a great game last week huh?"

"It was an amazing game. Would you say that Carlos Swavey is the best quarterback Gervais has ever acquired? Liz asked.

"Well, I suppose he's not too bad for a Hispanic kid."

Liz pauses for a moment and doesn't say anything, then she continues.

"Okay, hold on to your chair, I've got something I want to tell you," Liz takes a deep breath and steps back a couple of feet, "I asked that Hispanic kid to the Harvest Dance and he said yes," Liz smiles.

"What!" There is a three second silence, "Liz, he comes from a poor family what can he possible do for you!"

"You have no idea what he's all about!"

"Young lady do not raise your voice at me."

"Do you even know how hard he works or how much he helps his friends?" Liz asked.

"Why this boy? Why don't you ask someone of your own kind?"

"He treats me like a princess at school. He's caring and thoughtful. He seems to talk about people's strength more than their weaknesses. Daddy, he works after school to buy me a soda at lunchtime. For goodness sake he helped Harv get to where he is now in football – I saw it."

"Yeah, I know … Harv told me already."

"Please Daddy. I would come home immediately after the dance."

"Let me talk to your mom about this and I'll come back and give you an answer." He walks upstairs very slow with a heavy thought. Liz is sitting on the couch with both her hands over her head. She is resting her elbows on her thighs with a few tears running down her cheeks.

Elaine is upstairs talking to Ginger about hiring some farm help for next summer. Ginger is planning on two hundred acres of onions. She is looking for workers ahead of time to be prepared.

"Ginger, can I call you back later? I'll keep thinking on ideas," Elaine hangs up the phone.

"Sorry honey I don't mean to interrupt," Ted said.

"No problem it's okay Ted."

"Liz wants to go to the Harvest Dance with Carlos and I don't really approve of this."

"I've done a little research on Carlos and I've seen where he lives and where he works," Elaine said.

"What! You have?"

"Yes, Liz and I followed him one evening. We wanted to know more about him before she asked him to the dance."

"You knew about this!" Ted shouted.

"Yes, Liz talked to me about it."

"Once again I'm always the last to know!"

"Ted, calm down for heaven sake – I did tell Liz that she would have to ask you eventually," Elaine explained.

"I appreciate that, but I still wish that … well, never mind."

Elaine stares at Ted for a few seconds before she continues speaking.

"Anyway, we followed him from a distance. He works at the Gervais Market after helping Harv with football skills. After work he walks home about three blocks from the store. He lives down Alder Street – in an old rented house by the train tracks. It looks like it's about ready to fall apart."

"By the tracks?" Ted asked.

"Yes, by the tracks. They must be very poor. But he has a big heart and I've never seen anyone as talented as Carlos," Elaine notices Ted looking at her.

There's a small pause with no words said.

"Except you of course," she tells Ted.

"Hey, no one is more talented than me," he laughs.

"Ted, give him a chance with Liz – it's just a school dance," Elaine pleads.

"Was your dad acting like me when I asked you out to a dance millions of years ago?"

"Much worse and look at us now," Elaine said.

"I'll be right back," he hustles downstairs.

The stairway is a sight to kill for. The railing is smooth and made out of oak. And there's hardly a creak as Ted walks down.

"Okay Liz, here's the deal. Your mom will take you and Carlos to the dance. Then immediately after, she will pick both of you up and bring you straight home."

"Oh Daddy … really? I love you so much!" Liz gives her dad a big hug.

"The things dads have to go through," he mumbles as he walks back upstairs shaking his head.

Liz runs to Harv's room and delivers the news to him. She then gets on the phone and calls Carlos. She spent the next thirty minutes talking to her Harvest Dance date.

The next morning Carlos gets out of bed and begins working on his homework. Being around Liz and Harv inspires him to do better in the academic world. When he completes all of his school work he walks down to the Gervais Market to work a few hours.

"Carlos! You're in pretty early and in a good mood I might say," Mr. Lind said.

"Yes sir, it's a great day today."

"I don't know … they're calling for some rain tonight. You must be going to the Harvest Dance," Mr. Lind looks outside.

"Yes sir." Carlos responds.

"Who asked you to the dance?"

"Oh, some super nice girl."

"Good for you I hope the rain holds up a few days," Mr. Lind starts walking toward the back stockroom.

Carlos begins to stock the shelves with all kinds of products. He's actually getting quite good at his job. The store owner is getting to know him and the trust is beginning to grow. The work hours seem to fly by that day for the young man. Before he knows it, he is done with his work and heading back home.

Later that evening at the Swaveys, Lydia notices Carlos with his slacks and sport shirt.

"Wow! You look good my bro."

"Thanks, can you take me to the school in an hour or so?"

"No I can't, sorry. I have plans tonight," Lydia walks away to her room.

"Dad, can you take me to the school in an hour?"

"Sure son, we'll have to take the beat-up sixty-three Ford – it's been having some problems lately."

"Thanks Dad, that'll be fine."

It's getting close to time and Carlos is getting a little nervous. He has never attended anything like this before. The thought of walking in with Liz Bradford, the richest girl in town, is overwhelming. After all, he is a very poor kid.

"Dad you ready?"

"I'll be right there Carlos. I just got a new battery for the Ford but I didn't have time to put it in, so we'll just have to go without it. It should start okay."

As they start walking outside of the door, it's starts to rain.

"Oh dang! It's raining," Carlos said.

"The dance is outside?" his dad asked.

"No, but I was hoping it wouldn't rain today."

They get on Douglas Street and start driving toward the high school. They pull into the high school parking lot. There's a big line of cars. Most of the parents are dropping off their kids. Pete falls in right behind them. You can see the cafeteria through the huge window facing the parking lot. There are all kinds of streamers, balloons, and flowers – it looks really cool.

Everyone seems to be watching the new arrivals from the lobby area. The girls are especially on their toes. They are all curious of what others are wearing. The interest seems to be watching the couples walk up. Who is coming with whom?

Carlos was supposed to come with Liz, and Harv with Lorraine. Elaine was supposed to drive them all there. Carlos thought it would be better if he met them at the school to avoid any static with Ted Bradford. He didn't want to cause anymore problems for Liz.

Carlos is feeling a little embarrassed being dropped off in an old 63 Ford that is about to fall apart. At times this car would need a push to start. They pull up to the front of the school where everyone's watching.

"Hey! There's Carlos," Lorraine said.

"Oh good, he made it," Liz gasped.

Dirk, Shawna, Clifford, and some others are also watching from the lobby area. They are all curious to know more about Carlos – what kind of car does his family drive? What is he wearing?

Carlos opens the passenger door – it makes a terrible squeak – *creech*! He steps down from the car and as he shuts the door, the car dies.

"Oh no," Carlos whispers.

"I'm sorry son. Can you help me push the car out of the way?" Pete asked.

"Okay, but let's hurry – it's raining."

Carlos runs to the back of the car waving to Liz and the rest of the students. Liz waves back with a smile on her face. He begins to push the car. His dad is holding the clutch waiting for the car to arrive at the necessary speed. Pete pops the clutch and the car starts as he pressed the accelerator peddle.

"Thanks son!" Pete yells out of the window waving to Carlos.

"See ya Dad!"

Carlos starts running toward the lobby area where everyone is watching and waiting for him. Liz feels bad for him – what he just went through.

"What a loser! His car stinks it's an old beat-up Ford!" A student yelled.

"You should have asked me Liz – I would've brought you in a limo baby," Dirk says.

Carlos is running across the wet paved parking lot. He jumps on the sidewalk, his right foot lands first but his left foot catches a bump from a huge crack on the sidewalk. Carlos trips and lands on a mud puddle that's very wet – *splash*! His entire outfit including new shoes became a nightmare mess.

"Ha-ha-ha!" Several students laugh.

"That's not funny! Stop it … leave him alone!" Liz insists.

Carlos uses his arms to push himself up. The sound of the rain, and the cold mud all over him, is an uncomfortable sight. He stands up straight and pauses for a few seconds looking at some of the white kids that are laughing at him. He feels so out of place. He starts running across the parking lot toward Douglas Street. When he steps onto the main road he slows down to a walk.

"Carlos! Please come back!" Liz yelled.

She is saddened by the incident, but there is nothing she can do. After waiting for awhile she went inside with the rest of the students. She is very bothered by what happened.

Carlos is walking along the shoulder of a dark Douglas Street. Someone driving a brand new Chevy truck pulls over next to him and rolls down the passenger window.

"Hey Carlos! I'm Liz Bradford's dad – get in the truck before you get sick."

Carlos slowly inches forward to take a closer look at who this person is.

"It's okay! I have a plastic cover on the seat – water won't hurt anything!" Ted has to yell to fight the sound of the rain coming down.

"Mr Bradford. It is you."

"Yes, it's me. Let me help you – get in the truck, please."

Carlos slowly steps in the truck and shuts the door – *thunk*! The smell of a new vehicle he never forgets. The only time he experienced that was when his dad would repair a friend's new car. He would ride with his dad to test it out.

The last time Carlos saw this man was when he went to Harv's house. Things didn't go too well – he's curious of Ted.

"What size pants do you wear?" Ted asked.

"Thirty-four by thirty-three, why?"

"What size shirt do you wear?"

"Usually large," Carlos replies.

Ted presses the gas peddle to speed up once he gets on to Portland Road (99E) heading south to Salem. This city is located in the Willamette Valley of Oregon – next to the flow of the Willamette River. The city is surrounded by institutes. Salem is the home of several institutions, the state mental hospital, correctional facilities, juvenile centers, and a state prison.

Along with the bad, it does have plenty of good. Salem has a beautiful downtown area with night-life and historical sites. It is the state capital of Oregon with plenty of state offices that provide services to the people. Salem also holds the annual Marion County and Oregon State Fair that attract many people. But the best part of this city is all of its eating places – some of the best in the entire country. Salem has Seafood, Italian, Mexican, Indian, Greek, Vietnamese, and fast-food restaurants. In addition, Salem has fresh produce stands and markets during the season.

Ted has a built-in phone in his truck. He grabs the phone and begins to dial.

"Hello," the retail person answers.

"Hi Shamus. You ready to hit the mountains for some elk soon?"

Shamus is a short clean-cut kind of guy – Ted's hunting partner who owns a huge clothing outfit and two car dealerships. Ted buys all of his cars and trucks from Shamus.

"You know it, just give me a call. It might be a little tougher to get away this year – we just had our second child."

"Congrats! I'm sure the wife will understand about our hunting trip, or at least I hope she does – ha-ha!"

"Yeah, hope so man. So what can I do for you?" Shamus asked.

"Can you line me up with some of the finest slacks and sports shirts you have?"

"Sure man, what size and color are you looking for?"

"Well, they're not for me they're for my daughter's date."

"I see."

"It's a long story but he'll need a thirty-four by thirty-three in pants. He'll also need a size large for a shirt. Shamus, can you also throw in a sports jacket that matches?"

"Sure no problem."

"I'm on my way now – should be there in twenty minutes or so."

"Sounds good, I'll have them ready."

"Thanks Shamus," Ted hangs up the phone.

Carlos is in disbelief. He's not saying anything at the moment.

"Carlos, I'm sorry for what happened back there. No one should have to deal with things like that, or be treated the way those kids treated you."

"No disrespect Mr. Bradford, but they didn't treat me any different than you did."

"Maybe you're right … but you have to understand that as a father I'm very protective of my kids."

"Sir, I commend you and your wife for doing such a great job raising your two kids. They are two of the nicest kids I've ever met."

There is a long pause and Ted is touched by the compliment. The two continue talking for a while until they arrive at the department store.

"Okay, here we are – just walk in that back door. This is the Nordstrom Mall. Shamus will be waiting for you – he'll take care of you."

"I'll pay you back sir," Carlos says as he steps out of the truck.

"You don't have to do that – it's a gift for accepting my daughter's invitation."

"Thank ya so much sir … really."

"I just ask that you keep this between you and me. Okay?"

"Sure, if that's what you want."

Ted gets on his phone again and calls Shamus.

"Hello," Shamus answers.

"Shamus, he's on his way inside the back door. Just put it on my account."

"Sure thing Ted … oh, by the way, I just talked to my wife – she doesn't see a problem with our hunting trip."

"Nice, how'd you swing that?"

"Oh, she said I'd owe her big time."

"Ha-ha! Thanks man," Ted laughs.

"I'll help the kid out and send him back out with an outfit."

"Thanks Shamus, I have to bring him back to the dance really fast."

"Not a problem Ted, I appreciate your business."

When they are done, Carlos has the finest dark blue slacks on with a light blue sports shirt and a dark blue sports jacket. His two-inch heel shoes shine like the sun – they make him look like he's 6'1". He looks very handsome in his attire with a small touch of cologne – a nice fragrance.

They start driving back to Gervais High School where the dance has already begun.

"I think we can make it back for you to enjoy the last half of it."

"I'm grateful for any moment I can spend there sir."

"You just take care of my daughter – I'll have to trust you."

"No worries there sir, I think very highly of Liz."

"Okay," Ted turns and glances at him for a second.

They finally arrive and Ted turns into Douglas Street off of 99E. He works his way into the parking lot and pulls in as close as he can to the front door.

"Thanks Mr. Bradford … thanks for everything," Carlos opens the door and steps down off the truck.

"Carlos!" Ted yells out.

"Yes sir?"

"Watch out for that mud puddle!"

Carlos turns and smiles, and then he runs to the front door. Lucky for him the rain has slowed down. As he walks inside the cafeteria, where the dance is taking place, the lights are dim and many of the kids are dancing. Some are just socializing and others are drinking a beverage and eating cake.

Liz is sitting next to some of her friends, but doesn't seem to be very happy. The next tune that starts playing is a slow-dance song. Carlos walks up from behind and puts his hand on her shoulder.

"May I have this dance?"

"Oh my goodness!" She stands up and takes a hard look at him and his attire.

"What do ya think?" He holds his arms open to show off his jacket.

"How did you manage this? You look fantastic."

"Let's not worry about minor things. The important thing is that I'm here."

"It's so good to see you," Liz said.

He takes her hand and they start to dance to a song by Barry Manilow, "Looks Like We Made It," a romantic easy listening song.

"Carlos! You look sharp man!" Harv yells from a ways.

"Thanks Harv, so do you!"

They dance to every song that's played. Time is going so fast, it's like both of them didn't want the evening to end. The good feeling of being next to Liz is like a dream for Carlos. He had never experienced a moment like this – especially with a beautiful girl like Liz. She is wearing some very expensive perfume that smells very nice. Carlos will memorize that amazing scent.

When the song ends, a chaperone walks up to the stage. She grabs the microphone and the entire place comes to a silence.

"Now it's time to announce our Harvest Dance King and Queen. After that, the King and Queen will have one dance together." The entire student body begins to cheer. You can hear the hands clapping and some whistling.

"I just don't want Shawna to get it – she's such a snob," Liz said.

"Yeah, she sounded pretty confident yesterday – she probably rigged the ballots," Lorraine added.

"I'd be okay if you or Kalin Jensen got it. I just don't want Shawna to win."

The entire place starts to quiet down. You can hear whispers coming from every direction. Everyone was trying to make an early prediction.

"Let's start with the King," the announcer said, "Running a close race, the student body has selected," there's a small pause, "Carlos Swavey!"

Positive cheers from the crowd poured with some boos included in the mix. Most boos come from seniors that feel a senior should have won.

"For this year's Harvest Dance Queen … it looks like, Shawna Smith!"

Once again, there are yeahs and boos from the crowd. The boos come from Liz and all of her friends.

"Well Lorraine, it looks like the witch won."

"That's okay Liz it's no big deal."

They both walk over to where Kalin is standing.

"Hey Kalin, I'm really sorry you didn't get it. I was hoping for you or Lorraine. I can't stand Shawna Smith, she drives me crazy," Liz said.

"Oh, that's okay guys. Shawna probably rigged the ballots – she usually finds a way to cheat at everything," Kalin said as she looked down almost in tears.

The announcer is getting ready to speak once again.

"Now, the King and Queen will have one dance before everyone can join them."

"It's beginning to be a big deal to me because she's going to dance with Carlos – I can't believe this," Liz is steaming, "after the way she treated him before … now she's all cheery and gets to enjoy him looking his best in nice clothes and all."

Lorraine is watching Liz and can see that she is very jealous. The King and Queen start to dance. Shawna is smiling with a shiny silver crown on her head. She looks over at Liz and winks at her as she squeezes her arms around Carlos.

"Lorraine, I'm going to go crazy I can't believe what she just did," Liz whispers.

"Calm down Liz, it'll be over shortly."

"I can't watch this, I'm going out to the hallway," she stomps out to the hall.

"Liz!" Lorraine tries to stop her but it's no use.

Carlos keeps an eye on Liz. He watches her exit the cafeteria. The situation is one he has never experienced, and really doesn't know what to do. The dance is finally over and before Carlos can walk away Shawna stops him.

"Carlos, you're not like the average Hispanic out there, I'm beginning to like you. Where did you get those clothes?"

"Shawna, you are one piece of work. And I really don't know what you mean by the average Hispanic," Carlos walks away as the entire student body is clapping and cheering for the two.

Carlos is looking around while answering questions to the student crowd.

"Congrats Carlos!" Hector says.

"Thanks!"

He finally finds Harv and Lorraine and walks to them.

"Where's Liz?"

"She couldn't stand to watch you and Shawna, so she stormed out to the hallway," Lorraine replied.

"Okay thanks," Carlos begins to walk toward the hallway. A few of his friends give him a high-five as he walks by them.

"There you are."

"I'm sorry Carlos I just couldn't stand seeing you with Miss Slime Snob."

"Aw ... I wish it could have been you out there with me."

"Really?"

"Of course, you're my princess," Carlos leans over and kisses her on the cheek.

"I'm your princess, that's very sweet. I'm feeling much better now, we can go back inside," Liz looks into his eyes with a nice smile.

Carlos feels such a great connection with Liz but still has something hanging in his subconscious. Can the different cultures come together and work? There sure is hope after his experience tonight.

The rest of the evening at the dance, he spends the entire time with Liz. They dance the night away with some pop hits from the late 70's.

Grades and Clothes

On Monday, school is back in session and test results from the algebra class are being passed out. Harv shifts the tutoring to Liz. She helps Carlos for two weeks.

Mr. McGoldrick starts passing out the test papers. Liz gets hers – an A+. The teacher continues to pass out more papers. He steps toward Carlos' desk.

"Good job Carlos you missed a B by one point."

"A C+, wow! That's the best I've ever done in algebra!"

Carlos turns his head toward Liz and points to her. He knows that her help had a lot to do with his grade. Liz has the ability to explain the equations in a way that he understands. Carlos can apply what he learns from her immediately – that's a great situation to be in.

In his other classes the signs of improvement are comparable. For the first time he didn't have a grade lower than a C. When algebra class ends Carlos walks Liz to her locker.

"Liz, the grade I got in algebra today is the best grade I've ever received. I owe ya big time – couldn't have done it without ya."

"You did it yourself – I just guided you a little."

"What did you get, an A?" Carlos asked.

"Put a plus at the end of that sweetheart," Liz smiles. "See you at lunchtime."

"Definitely," Carlos said.

After school it's once again time for practice. All of the players seem to be dragging a bit.

"Okay gentlemen, let's put all the dance and girls behind and focus a little!" Coach Terry Smith yells.

He takes a few steps toward the players. He is wearing a blue cap with a gold sports shirt and blue sweats. They continue practicing and trying to get back into the swing of things.

In the next few weeks Gervais continues to win games. The Cougars are having one of the best seasons ever. They are playing so well that they can possibly be contenders for a playoff spot.

They get by several teams like Colton, Cascade, La Salle, and Sheridan. But the next game is a real test of what the Cougars are made out of. They start preparing for a tough challenge and the coaches are planning on what they must do based on scouting reports.

"We have a tough game ahead of us. We're tied with Regis at 6 – 1. To win the Capital Conference we need to beat Central – they are a powerhouse. Regis needs to lose also. Central's record is 5 – 2."

"Who's their quarterback?" Carlos asked.

"Sam Lyon – he's about 6'6" 210. He's being recruited by Oregon State University. Sam is one of the reasons Central has a winning record this year. We'll have our hands full with him."

They start working on plays and also run some drills. The previous week, Coach Smith had some scouts make a trip to Central. This will help prepare the Cougars for a battle and hopefully set up a game plan.

At the end of practice the coach had the entire team line up for wind sprints. They run five and they all seem to be breathing pretty hard.

"Is anyone tired?" Coach Smith asked.

"Yes!" a few players answer but not at the same time.

"Okay, we need to run another one to get you in better shape!" Coach Smith looks over at Coach McGoldrick and smiles.

They all run another wind sprint to the 50 yard line and back. The long football season along with some nagging injuries always throws the sharpness off a little. They are breathing even harder.

"Okay, is anyone tired!" Coach Smith asked again.

"No sir!" more players answered.

"We need to run one more so you get tired – good for getting in shape!" He blows the whistle to indicate the start.

"Oh brother, that's a trick," Harv said.

They all run one more sprint to the 50 yard line and back.

"Okay gents bring it in!"

The players jog toward the coach and circle around him. They are all breathing hard and sweating up a storm. Some are bent down with their hands on their thigh pads. Others have their hands on their hips and looking up while they try to catch some oxygen.

"We have a tough game on Friday. If we win we'll have a better playoff picture as far as seating."

"You mean when we win," Carlos expresses.

"I like your confidence, okay, when we win," Coach Smith smiles and the team laughs.

On the way to the locker room, Harv catches up with Carlos.

"Hey man, where are we going to meet tonight?"

"I'm riding my bike to your backyard shop – will that work?"

"Sounds good, we have to work on an essay for English class. I'm teaching you some style on essay writing."

"Lord knows I need that, I don't even know how to spell essay."

"Ha-ha! You're funny," Harv laughs.

"For my lesson to you, I thought we'd practice keeping your head down once you've caught the football. I don't think you want to catch another helmet under the chin."

"Ha-ha! Right man – that didn't feel too good the last game."

Later that night at the Bradfords' house, Elaine is talking to Liz about the dance.

"I was looking at some pictures you took. I don't understand how Carlos was able to replace his clothes with more sophisticated attire in such a short amount of time... do you?"

"Mom, I'm just as curious as you are. When I asked him that question he really didn't give me an answer. He went around my question stating he was there – that was the important thing. It sounded like he didn't want to talk about it."

"Someone must have helped him, but whom, his dad?"

"There's no way in the world Mom. He told me that his parents could possibly get laid off from the processing plant."

"What processing plant?"

"I think … Stayton Canning Company – in Brooks."

"Oh, I see. Hey, you don't think he robbed some place?"

"Not Carlos, he would never do something like that," Liz responds defensively.

"Well, I'm out of ideas. All I can suggest is that you ask him again," Elaine said.

"I think I will. I deserve to know … don't I?"

"Of course, then you can tell me," Elaine smiles.

"Let's just wait and see if he tells me, then I'll decide whether to fill you in or not," Liz smiles at her mom.

The next morning in algebra class, Liz is thinking of the best way to approach Carlos on the subject matter. She decides to wait for class to end, and to be sure no one else is around.

After class, Liz sees that Carlos is waiting for her in the hallway. She walks over to him in a firm way.

"Carlos, you need to be honest with me. Tell me how you got those nice clothes in such a short amount of time. Don't tell me you bought them. Gervais Market doesn't pay you enough to buy Armani, or Versoci."

"Liz, please, I can't tell you – I gave my word. I don't want to betray my trust to this person."

"What about trust to me?" Liz walks to her next class in a rapid way not looking back to Carlos.

"Wow, what do I do now?" Carlos thinks to himself.

At lunchtime Carlos and Harv walk to the Gervais Market, but there's no Liz or Lorraine this time. On the way there, Carlos explains his dilemma to Harv.

"I don't understand why Liz needs to know where I got the clothes. What would you do Harv?"

"That's a real tough one – that's what I think. This person must be very important. What's the worst that can happen if you tell Liz?"

"Everything will get very ugly and I will feel terrible that I didn't keep my word. And this person will never trust me again."

"Well, the way I see it is, you have two choices. See if Liz gets over it and forgets about it, or ask this person if you can leak the secret to Liz."

"That sounds like a great idea. I'll call this person tonight – that choice sounds good."

"Come on let's get something to eat," Harv said.

That evening after football practice, Carlos walks home and immediately calls the Bradfords' house. He dials the number.

"Hello," Elaine answered.

"Hi, may I talk to Mr. Bradford?"

"Sure I'll get him. You're lucky he's working on a case at home. Honey! The phone's for you," Ted picks up in his den.

"Yes, this is Mr. Bradford."

"Mr. Bradford, this is Carlos."

"Carlos? What can I do for you?"

"Well, I have a little bit of a problem with the secret you want me to keep."

"What's the problem?"

"Liz is mad at me because I won't tell her where I got the clothes last Saturday, remember? She thinks I don't trust her enough to share that with her."

Ted Bradford is laughing inside and liking that Liz is upset at Carlos. But at the same time he doesn't want all of this to haunt him later. After all, Liz is his daughter and he cares for her deeply.

"That's quite a predicament. Tell her you'll explain everything on Thanksgiving Day."

"Why Thanksgiving Day?"

"Just trust me on this one," Ted said.

"Okay, I guess I have no choice. Thanks Mr. Bradford."

"Not a problem – good luck on Friday."

"Thank you sir, we'll need it. They're a tough team – bye."

"Bye."

A few moments later the phone rings at the Bradfords.

"Hello," Elaine answers again.

"Is Liz home?" Carlos asked.

"Oh, hi Carlos, I'll get her for you – hold on."

Carlos can hear Elaine yelling for Liz. Like a young teenage girl, Liz spends time in her bedroom. She finally hears her mom and comes running down the steps to where the phone is located.

"Hello, this is Liz."

"Don't hang up, it's me, Carlos."

"I really don't want to talk to you right now."

"Come on Liz, aren't you being a little unfair?"

"I would never keep anything from you," Liz explained.

"Okay, how 'bout I tell ya everything on Thanksgiving Day?"

"Why Thanksgiving Day?"

"That's the same thing I asked her dad," Carlos thinks to himself.

Carlos is still thinking and there is a long pause.

"Hello, are you still there?" Liz asked.

"Yes I'm still here. Liz, that's the best I can do. You'll have to trust me on this one. I'll be very honest – all the details just like you girls like on Thanksgiving Day."

"Hmm … well," Liz is thinking for a few minutes.

"Come on Liz, I really don't like it when you're mad at me. I won't be able to play my best on Friday if you stay this way. It affects me in a strange way."

"Okay you turkey, gobble gobble, on Thanksgiving Day. The weirdest thing is that I like you even when I'm mad at you."

"That's a good thing. Hey, did we just have our first fight?"

"Yeah, I guess," Liz chuckles.

"Bye Liz."

"Goodbye," Liz puts the phone down.

She has a big smile on her face. She runs back upstairs to her bedroom and starts singing a song along with the radio. She's in a much better mood now.

The next day at school Liz is smiling more. Things seem to be back to normal once again. At lunchtime the four are once again walking to Gervais Market.

"Carlos, we need to do more work for writing class. You still need to improve on your essay writing," Harv said.

"I hate that class, it's too hard."

"With that attitude you'll never improve. It's like me saying the same thing about those pass patterns you taught me."

"I understand Harv. I did make a deal with you and I do want to improve my grades. It's just that I get so frustrated with studying sometimes. Being bilingual, a kid loses some English vocabulary through the years."

"What deal did you guys make?" Lorraine asked.

"Oh, it's a long story – basically he helps me in sports and I help him pick up his grades. It's actually working – I think more kids should do what we're doing."

"Harv's right. I don't see how teachers can help every kid individually," Carlos said.

"That's very true – I think that's a great idea. You guys should keep going with that strategy," Lorraine said.

"Hey Lorraine, what's your family doing for Thanksgiving?" Liz asked.

"We'll probably head down to Ashland to see my grandparents. The famous Shakespearian plays are closed for the season, but we love walking around the huge theaters in the downtown area.

"Last year we flew to California. My dad had a big lawyer meeting in Los Angeles. We had the honor of staying at Disneyland while he worked – that was so much fun! I'm not sure what the plans are this year other than the dinner," Liz said.

Carlos has heard of Disneyland but has never been anywhere more exciting than Palo Duro Canyon in Texas. And that was during an Easter vacation. How can he possibly fit in with wealthy kids? His pride is at stake. He walks along with the group and listens, but does not join in on the conversation. Carlos hopes no one asks him about Thanksgiving and what his family is doing.

"Disneyland and Universal Studious are such a blast! We've been there several times and the experience is beyond what you can imagine," Harv added.

"What kind of rides do they have and what does it cost to go there?" Carlos asked.

"I don't know what it costs because my dad pays for it all. The rides are a lot bigger than the state fair in Salem. They have huge roller coasters and water slides. The park is so huge – it's amazing!" Harv explains.

"In Dimmitt, Texas, where I'm from, we get these small carnivals that pass through in the summers. It's fun but not quite like Disneyland – I can't say I've ever been to anything like that," Carlos said.

"Harv, let's change the subject," Liz insists.

"What are you getting at the market today Carlos?" Harv asked.

"I might try a chicken with toast – I hear that's pretty tasty."

They all walk inside the Gervais Market to get a bite to eat.

Later that evening at the Bradfords, it's dinnertime and the family is sitting at the table. The place settings are light purple resting on top of the fancy white tablecloth. The china is the finest one can buy. The chairs are made out of solid oak with very expensive padding on the seats.

"Harv, I didn't think we should talk about all the places we've been to in front of Carlos. That's why I wanted to change the subject earlier. He might feel a little awkward and –"

"And what Liz?" jumped in her dad, "you're starting to realize that you two come from different worlds."

"Daddy, just because people come from different worlds doesn't mean they can't enjoy their company together."

"Well, he must have had some wealthy friends in Texas. The question is how did he deal with it?" Harv asked.

"I think he did just fine. Money isn't everything you know. I mean, the other day we started playing this game he brought up. Sitting on a bench, we threw rocks at this post. And for every three times he hit this post, I had to hit it once. It was so much fun and we didn't spend any money at all," Liz explains.

"He certainly has money to buy lunch and other things. His parents must not be able to buy much for him. He works hard, that's more than I can say for most kids," Elaine added.

"It must be tough for him, always trying to be the best he can be. Sometimes that's not enough. When a kid's growing up the parents need to be supportive in one way or another," Ted said.

"His parents do the best they can Dad, but sometimes it's not good enough. He told me that in Texas, at times, he would come home after school and there would be empty shelves in the kitchen," Liz explains sadly. "He also mentioned to me the other day, that one of his parents could get laid off from the plant. That can't be too much fun with the holiday season approaching."

"Ted, is there anything you can do to help them without hurting their pride?"

"I'll talk to Ginger, she's planning on hiring some help for her onion fields – I'm sure she needs more help to prepare. She has a lot of farm work ahead of her."

"Daddy, that's really nice of you to suggest that. What a great idea," Liz smiles.

"The only problem is that the work won't start until after Christmas. Hopefully they can find something until then," Ted said.

The night before the game against Central, Harv and Carlos stay up until midnight in the shop behind the Bradfords' house.

"Come on Carlos you can do it. You have one more problem – we're not done until you solve it."

"I'm trying but I just can't remember how you showed me," Carlos said.

"Okay, let me write another example – then I'll give you a different algebra problem."

"That sounds good."

Harv begins to write another problem and before he is done Carlos jumps up.

"Wait! I think I remember now."

"Yes … that's it … you got it. Good job!" Harv said.

"Thanks for your help Harv … and you did great today catching that football. You only dropped two out of twenty."

"Yeah, well I still need improvement. See you tomorrow – goodnight."

"See ya, goodnight."

On Friday morning, everyone is looking forward to an exciting day at school. The day will end with an exciting pep assembly to get fired up for an important game. The game will take place at Central High School in Independence, Oregon.

In Patrick McGoldrick's class, the students are taking a test covering two chapters. Carlos remembers what Liz and Harv taught him about algebra problem solving. He's doing very well. Everything seems to be coming easy because of his practice with each different kind of problem.

Liz is the first person done with the test. Carlos looks up and sees her working on a game puzzle.

"Man I wish I could already be done," Carlos thinks to himself.

He continues working for awhile longer and finally completes the test. Half of the class is done. He walks up to the teacher's desk and places his test on top of the stack.

"This was a hard test coach."

"It's only as hard as you make it Carlos."

"Yeah, I suppose. I think I did well."

"We'll see. You ready for tonight?"

"I was born ready coach," Carlos said as he walked back to his seat wearing his number 11 varsity football shirt.

All the varsity football players wear their game jerseys on game day. It's an honor to represent your school as one of the players on the football field. Varsity players, no matter what sport, seem to attract attention. They are looked at a little different than other kids in school.

Some kids get jealous because they aren't on the team. They often say negative things about the players. Anyone can be on the team if they work hard enough – it's just a matter of practice. If a kid is physically able to, he can improve just like Harv did – by working hard.

After the bell rings Carlos meets up with Liz.

"Good luck tonight, I hope you guys stomp the Panthers – gee that's cool, cats battling cats."

"I think we're gonna need all the luck we can get. Coach says Central has improved in all areas of their game."

"Carlos, I'm really proud of you. All your success on the football field, and today, handing in your test before half the class was done – that's pretty amazing," Liz said.

"I couldn't have done it without you and Harv's help."

"Thank God I didn't have to climb down my window with a rope the way you did. Have your parents discovered what you did that night?"

"Nope, I don't know if they ever will. They get pretty tired from working so much. When they hit the sack, they are out."

"When are you going to invite me to your house so I can meet them?" Liz asked.

"I'm not sure you'd feel comfortable at my house."

"Why can't I be the judge of that Mr.?"

"My house isn't as nice as yours. I think I would be embarrassed."

"Well, maybe someday you'll change your mind. I hope you do. I could ask my mom to pick me up later than normal from school. Carlos, I don't think you should be embarrassed because of where you live."

"I suppose you're right. I'll think about it."

"Great, just let me know someday."

Quarterback Sam Lyon

After school, at the pep assembly, Clifford is called up to the microphone to speak. He's been in that position several times through the years.

"This game is important to us. Not only because of the seeding in the playoffs, but also because this is the first time in years that Gervais has a winning record. We're 6 – 1 going into tonight's game and we're gonna keep it going!" All of the students and staff cheer for awhile. Coach Smith takes the microphone back and continues.

"Our players have really put in some hard work on the practice field. I feel we are ready to win tonight. Thank you for all of your support – let's go get them!" Roaring cheers are heard as the coach steps down from the stage. The assembly is the final required session to attend before school is over. All the players head to the locker room to load the equipment into the bus – uniforms, pads, and helmets.

The Gervais Cougars are heading out to Independence, Oregon, the home of the fighting Panthers – blue, white, and gold against red, white, and black.

In the evening there is a light drizzle coming down – nothing too serious. The team bus arrives at Central High School. There is a billboard that reads, "THIS IS SAM LYON COUNTRY, DON'T MESS WITH US!"

The team bus pulls into the parking lot, parks, and the Gervais team exits the bus in a single file. The players all walk into the locker room with their equipment. They all have their football jerseys with shoulder pads inside, hanging behind them like a big bag. A long line filed into the locker room where they will suit up for the game.

Fans start showing up early and before you know it, the parking lot is full with no spots left. It's a sold out crowd at Central High School. The popcorn is popping and the concession stand is open for business. The wonderful smell of the hotdogs, popcorn popping, and hot chocolate is part of the whole football atmosphere.

Carlos sits in the locker room thinking about getting a victory tonight. If they win tonight, it will mean a step closer to the state championship. He's feeling a little pressure and doesn't want to let anyone down. Harv comes over and sits next to him.

"This is it, our last regular season game. If we win we play Sweet Home, if we lose we play St. Marys of Portland."

"We have a big challenge tonight – facing Lyon and all. I hear he's a pretty sharp quarterback. But I say … we're headed to Sweet Home. If we all give one hundred percent I know we can win," Carlos said.

Coach Terry Wayne Smith walks into the locker room. He puts one foot on the bench and rests his arm on top of his knee.

"Carlos, you have to watch the defensive end, number 93. Paul Apone is the fastest defensive end we've seen yet. He averages five sacks a game. Harv, you're going to have to throw body blocks to be able to contain him. He's 6' 4" 230, and he is a very smart player."

"Remember gentlemen, whichever side Paul lines up on, we want to try and run away from that spot. We can't afford to pull a guard or a tackle to help out – Carlos will get nailed," Coach McGoldrick adds.

"Alright! Now let's go out there and kick some tail!" Coach Smith yells.

"Yeah! Let's go Cougars!" Dirk shouted.

The entire team started chanting and yelling fired up sounds as they start walking out of the locker room.

The atmosphere is amazing, the football field lights, the people in the bleachers, the sounds of the cheerleaders, the colors, the green grass, the white powdered lines, the concession stand,

and the two teams getting ready to battle. Where else would anyone want to be?

"Carlos jogs out to the field watching his teammates. They are wearing blue with gold numbers and a blue shiny helmet.

As they set up for warm-up drills, a Central assistant coach is watching them. He turns and starts talking to the head coach.

"They don't look very big at all – I don't understand why their record is so good."

"My understanding is that they have the best quarterback in the conference," Rick Alver said.

Rick Alver is a successful coach and is known for his winning record as a high school coach. He's lead Central to several state titles over the years.

"Who? ... Clifford Mayberry?" his assistant coach asked.

"No, Carlos Swavey, a freshman kid. Like I was telling you yesterday, he's only thrown three interceptions the entire season. And those were bullet passes that bounced off of his receivers and landed on the defender's hands."

"Look, they're running pass patterns," the assistant coach said.

"Let's take a look," Coach Alver said.

Carlos is throwing the ball with a nice accurate spiral. All of his warm-up passes are smooth and connecting with the receivers.

"That's a thing of beauty – look at that perfect form on his arm when he throws. Where'd you say this kid comes from?" the assistant coach asked.

"From what I've read and heard, he is a Texas Transfer. He comes from a poor family that migrated north."

"What part of Texas?"

"Dimmitt, Texas. He was supposed to play varsity down there as a freshman. They run a great football program down in Texas."

"Well, we have a defensive end that'll take care of him, and a senior quarterback with a lot more experience," the assistant said.

They both walk back to the Central Panthers' bench, not showing too much concern.

It's time to get the show on the road. The official is at mid-field with the players.

"Call it in the air home team," the official said.

The coin is tossed about five feet in the air and it hangs there for a bit.

"Heads!"

The coin lands displaying *tails*. The two captains for Gervais are Dirk and Clifford. Clifford looks at the official with a two-second pause.

"We'll take the football."

In a wet misty evening, the football will be a little slick. The ball boys will be used regularly throughout the game. The Central kicker raises his hand to signal he is ready for the kickoff. The referee blows the whistle and things get going.

The kick is long and high in the air. J.J. comes up with the catch at the Cougars' 10 yard line. He runs and gets hit by a Central Panther – *crack*! But he remains on his feet. J.J. keeps pumping his legs but another Panther hits him – *pop*! It's too much to handle – he goes down hard at the 35 yard line.

"Alright boys, watch number 93. Whichever side big Paul is on, I'm scrambling to the opposite. Okay?" Carlos asked.

"Gotcha!" some of the players responded.

"21 slot to Harv on three."

They jog up to the line of scrimmage.

"Down! Set! Hut! Hut! Hut!"

Carlos starts backing up as he sees big Apone coming at him at full throttle. No one on the Gervais team is strong enough to handle him. Apone smacks the running back down effortlessly as he continues to come at Carlos. Carlos runs to the right to avoid him. He sees Harv wide open on the slant. Here comes the football with a clean spiral right at Harv. Harv keeps his eyes on the football and puts both hands on it. The football is a little wet and slippery – it pops off his hands and lands into the hands of the Central defensive back. The Panther runs it all the way back for a touchdown.

It's Central, 7 – 0. The home crowd is going crazy, "Yeah! Panthers! Whoo!"

Carlos knows it's going to be a long night. What could they do to help the rainy situation? It's just Oregon – it rains a lot there, especially during football season. The Cougars' strongest side is their passing game.

"Carlos, come here!" Coach Smith called.

Carlos jogs over to the bench for a few seconds while the referees work on spotting the ball again.

"Yes sir?"

"Throw hook patterns. I guarantee it won't go through our receivers. It's just too wet for you to throw those bullet passes. Our players have a hard enough time catching them when it's dry."

"Okay Coach. Good idea."

That seems to work because Gervais put a drive together using hook patterns and screen passes. They made it to the end zone and tied the game at, 7 – 7. The Gervais crowd came alive, "Yeah! Let's get 'm Cougars!"

Central quarterback, Sam Lyon, is ranked at the top of the list in Oregon. He is being recruited to play for Oregon State University the following year. He's a tall quarterback at 6' 6" and weighs 210 lbs.

After the kickoff, the Central Panthers run the ball to their own 40 yard line. Sam Lyon is very visible, standing in the middle of the huddle calling a play.

"Guys, we can't let this Gervais team get the upper hand on us. Let's run a post-pattern past that weak db and sorry safety … on two!"

Sam walks behind his team to the line of scrimmage and plants himself behind the center.

"42 panther! Hut! Hut!"

Sam drops back about seven yards and launches a pretty spiral right into his receiver's hands for a gain of 40 yards. The Central crowd is fired up, "Whoohoo!"

"J.J.! … you have to do a better job of covering that wide receiver!" Coach Smith yelled out.

It's first down and 10 at the Gervais 20 yard line. On the next play, Sam once again drops back, except this time he runs a draw straight up the middle and scores a touchdown. The home crowd is enjoying watching the future Beaver at work, "That's a boy Sam … yeah!"

The score is now, 13 – 7. Sam walks to the sideline to watch the one-point conversion. The kick is good and the score is now, 14 – 7, in favor of the Panthers.

"This team is weak, we can take'm, let's go fellas!" Sam shouts out.

The rest of the Panther team join in and they start yelling fired-up phrases.

By the end of the fourth quarter both teams have battled long and hard – they seem to be evenly matched. There's two minutes left in the game. The score is Central 28, and Gervais 28. The Cougars have the ball at the 50 yard line. They are gaining small yardage running the ball and throwing short passes.

With one minute left, it's third and goal. Carlos is in the huddle calling a play.

"Let's run a fake hook and corner to J.J., on two."

The players start walking to the line of scrimmage showing they are fatigued and tired. It's a long and tough game to play in the rain. The rain starts coming down a little harder. Carlos can feel the water dripping down his helmet and landing on his face. It's cold and his hands are feeling a little numb.

"Down! Set! Hut! Hut!"

He steps back into the pocket and sees J.J. in the corner of the end zone. He starts to unload the pass with a forward motion. Number 93 comes from behind – *crack*! *slush*! Carlos gets smacked right into the wet field with spots of mud. Paul Apone, Number 93, lands on top of him putting forceful pressure as to torture him. All 230 pounds of Panther lies on top of him making it difficult for him to breathe.

"You're a sign of weakness you little shrimp," Apone said.

The clock starts to run down, 10, 9, 8, 7, 6 – "Timeout! … Timeout!" Carlos calls, lying on the ground. The referee blows his whistle giving Gervais the timeout. All of the people stood up on their feet with a sigh of concern for the young freshman quarterback. A trainer goes out to the field to look at Carlos. He helps him up slowly and they walk over to the bench.

The people start clapping realizing he could possibly be okay – they show support. Liz is up on the stands with emotions of concern.

"I hope he's okay Lorraine."

"Me too Liz."

"He's fine, he just got the wind knocked out of him for a bit," Ted said.

Coach Smith is having a talk with Carlos.

"Carlos, we have five seconds. We're too far back to try a field goal. With this weather it's almost impossible anyway. Can you still play … are you okay?"

"Yes sir, I'll live."

"Okay son. You're doing an outstanding job out there."

"Coach, the only way is to run the ball. I'll fake a slant to J.J. and I'll run it up the gut as fast as I can go."

"What do you think coach?" Smith looks at McGoldrick.

"I don't think we have a choice."

"Okay Carlos, let's go with it … and tell those guys to block!" Coach Smith yelled.

Carlos runs out to the field to call the play. It's cold – about 35 degrees.

"Okay, 22 slant keeper straight up the gut, on one... and please block y'all."

They all jog to the line of scrimmage. You can hear the shoes splashing on the swampy field.

"Down! Set! Hut!"

Carlos backs up to show he is throwing the ball. He does a pump-fake motion, puts his shoulders down, and starts running right down the middle. There is a hole big enough to drive a truck through. He sees the blocks and starts running behind them all. Carlos cuts away from the defenders as they try to tackle him.

Running toward the goal-line he sees two defensive safeties waiting for him. Carlos runs straight at them as fast as he can move on the wet field. He is approaching the goal-line. The defenders start to attack him, but as that happens, he jumps as high as he can. While he is in the air, both players hit him so hard, that they send him spinning in the air. He comes down just inches inside the goal-line for a touchdown!

"Yeah! Woohoo!" the Gervais crowd yells.

The clock expires and the Gervais Cougars beat the Central Panthers knocking them out of the playoff picture. The crowd continues to go wild! People are yelling all kinds of cheers for the Cougars. Some have noisemakers like whistles and bells.

Sam Lyon runs over to where Carlos is celebrating with his team.

"Hey Swavey, you're one heck of a quarterback – especially for a freshman. I hope to play against you in college someday."

"Thanks Sam, you're not too bad yourself. Good luck at OSU."

"Thanks … and good luck at state man, I have a feeling you'll be there," Sam says as he runs back to his team.

Lorraine and Liz hustle down to where the players are running by on their way back to the locker room. They are waiting for Carlos and Harv to run by to give them a shout out.

"Liz! Let's wait right here, they'll pass by."

"Okay Lorraine."

It takes awhile with all of the celebration amongst the players and the coaches. Carlos is still talking to the coaches. He finally starts toward the locker room – Harv is running next to him. They run by the area where Liz and Lorraine are anxiously waiting with a crowd.

"Nice game guys!"

The players are giving everyone a high five as they run by.

"Are you okay Carlos!" Liz asked.

Carlos slows down and stops to talk to Liz.

"Yeah, I'm fine … just got a little shook up tonight. I'm freezing – see ya later tonight." He runs off with the team.

"Okay, good game … I'm proud of you!" Liz yells.

Harv is hustling behind Carlos.

"Good game Harv – you were great!"

"Thanks Lorraine," Harv responds as he runs by.

The Gervais Cougars are, 7 – 1, and become the Capital Conference Champions. They win a tie breaker with the Regis Rams. Regis also wins tonight against Chemawa High School. Their record is now, 7 – 1. Regis and Gervais could possibly play against each other for the state title if they both win their remaining playoff game. But first the Cougars need to take care of business against Sweet Home. They are a tough team from a logging community.

After an exciting Friday night and plenty of celebrations with friends, Carlos finally makes it home close to midnight. The next morning, sleeping in is a must to get the well deserved rest.

"Carlos! Do you want some breakfast?" Isabel yells from the small kitchen.

"Yeah! I'll be down in a few minutes!"

The woodstove is going and he can feel the warm air rising to his bedroom in the attic. The smell of the eggs, bacon, and toast is enough to wake anyone up. Oh, and let's not forget the homemade tortillas.

It takes Carlos a while to get moving, he's feeling a little sore from the pounding he took last night at the game. He manages to come down the steps slowly.

"Mom, is there anymore tortillas?"

"No, you're too late – they're already gone."

"Okay, I'll take toast. The price I pay to be part of a big poor family," Carlos mumbles to himself.

"What did you say?" Isabel asked.

"Oh … I said … what a great family we have."

"I thought that's what you said," she points the spoon at him.

Lydia is also eating late since she helped her mom fix breakfast for everyone.

"I heard y'all won last night."

"Yeah, we're in the playoffs. We play Sweet Home next week."

"How's the girl situation?"

"What girl situation?" Carlos replied.

"You know … Miss Filthy Rich."

"Does everything have to be about money?"

"Well, it sure helps. Do you want to live like this the rest of your life?"

"Sure, if you and Mom keep fixing me breakfast, why not? I got it made."

"Why do I waste my time talking to you?" Lydia walks off to the living room.

The living room is very small with a thin green carpet. You can see the signs of aging with tears in different parts. Isabel keeps it clean and vacuumed. Despite the old house, the Swaveys are very clean people.

"Mom, can I bring Liz here to meet you next week?" Carlos asked.

"I don't see why not," she responded.

"I don't want a rich white girl coming around here!" Mike jumps into the conversation.

"Where'd that come from?" Carlos asked.

"She's just gonna use you while you're a star football player – then she'll dump you. Her parents are probably HHs."

"HHs?" Carlos asked.

"Hispanic Haters – remember Kylena in Texas?"

"She's not like that Mike – she's different," Carlos said.

"I'll be amazed if you're right – I gotta go … see ya later," he stomps out of the room.

"What's the deal with him?"

"Oh, he's probably just jealous because you're doing so well in football and he didn't go out for the team," Isabel said.

"Whatever, I don't have time to worry about Mike and he better not say anything negative to Liz when I bring her over."

"I don't think he will – he just talks big," Isabel said.

"He's probably the one that ate all the tortillas."

"Ha-ha! Carlos, everyone ate them not just Mike."

Carlos finishes eating his breakfast and walks up to his room to do some studying. This is the first year that he's focused on homework and simply just learning more. In Texas, he had friends that weren't into studying. Rudy, his friend, was the only one that studied and did well in grades.

The challenge Carlos faces is not only the grades, but also doing things with his wealthy friends. How could he compete with some of the things they did for enjoyment? His family didn't have enough money to fly to Disneyland, or go golfing. And shopping is at a different level than he could ever dream of.

Carlos sits on his bed with a book in his hand thinking.

"If I start suggesting things like riding bikes on a trail or bowling, it wouldn't cost as much and I wouldn't feel out of place."

He lies down on his bed thinking of other possibilities. The train goes by, shaking the entire house.

"Why me Lord … why must I be the one in this situation?"

The bed is clamped down to the floor to prevent it from bouncing to the wall.

"This is a real shock – the train usually doesn't come by until late at night. It would be embarrassing if this happens when Liz comes over," Carlos talks to himself.

Liz Meets the Poor Side

In mid-November, on a Monday morning, Carlos is ready to ask Liz to come meet his family. After algebra class, Liz is walking with him down the hall.

"How did you do on your test?" Liz asked.

"I got a B, can you believe it!"

"I sure can, that's great!"

"I owe it all to you and Harv – thanks."

"Well, you worked hard for it – I commend you."

"I have a question for you," Carlos expressed.

"Oh really? I'm dying of curiosity."

"How would you like to come over today after I'm done with football practice?"

"Darn! I can't today. My mom and I are getting our hair done. Is there another day that would work?"

"Sure, how 'bout tomorra?"

"Okay, that sounds good. I can't wait to meet your family and to see where you live."

"Don't expect too much," Carlos said quietly.

"What?"

"Oh, nothing – I just said, you're too much … see ya later."

"Bye. See you at lunch."

The next day, Liz asked her mom to pick her up a little later than normal. Liz is excited about the adventure and is very curious. The school day went on forever, but it finally came to an end. She hung around with some of her friends in the library to kill some time. The entire group of girls then decide to go watch the conclusion of the football practice.

After practice, Liz met up with Carlos and they walked to his house. In Gervais you can walk just about anywhere – it's a very small town. Some people say that if you drive by too fast and blink, you'll miss it.

They finally arrive at the Swaveys' house. Carlos opens the front door and Liz follows him inside.

"Mom! Where are you?"

"I'm coming!"

"Mom, this is Liz."

"Hi Liz, I've heard so many good things about you."

"It's a real pleasure to finally meet you Mrs. Swavey. You have such a talented son," Liz puts her hand on Carlos' shoulder.

"What a nice thing to say, thank you. Please come in and make yourself comfortable," Isabel said.

They walk over to sit on the only couch in the house. It's covered with a clean blanket to hide some of the holes and old stains. Liz begins to look around at the entire house. It's definitely a sight she's not used to.

"My dad's still working. He won't be home for awhile. At least you get to meet my mom and my sister. My sister should be here somewhere. Lydia!"

"What!" Lydia answered from the back of the house.

"Come here! … I want you to meet someone!"

Lydia enters the room.

"Oh hi! You must be Liz."

"Yes, it's nice to meet you. I've seen you at school before. I just didn't realize you were Carlos' sister."

"Yeah, I try to avoid my brother as much as possible. I still think I was adopted. I don't look at all like him."

"Thank God to that," Carlos said.

"You see, that's why I avoid my brother," they all chuckle.

"Lydia's okay, I don't care what everyone else says," Carlos said.

"Mom!" Lydia yells.

"Come on Carlos, be nice to your sister," Liz said.

"I'm just playing with her."

They talk for awhile. Mike took the younger kids to the grade school playground for something to do.

"Mom, is it okay if I take Liz upstairs to show her my room?"

"Sure, just leave the door open."

There is no door to the attic room. Isabel is showing her sense of humor.

"Very funny Mom," Carlos said.

They start walking up the steps. You can hear the creaks from the old boards – *creak*! *creak*! They repaired some of them to make them strong enough to last awhile.

"You'll have to excuse these old boards. I'm planning on fixing them this summer."

"It's okay Carlos … they're fine. I think they sound cool."

When they walk into his room, Liz notices the bed being clamped to the floor.

"Why do you have the bed clamped to the floor?" Liz asked.

"Oh, you wouldn't believe what happened to me the first night I slept here. To make a long story short, this keeps me from sliding to the wall when the train comes by – pretty sad huh?"

"It's an interesting scenario," Liz replies.

"You probably won't want to talk to me anymore after seeing my house and all. I figured eventually you would find out."

"Carlos, I'm surprised you would even think something like that."

"Well, I once knew someone in Texas. Her parents would go to all my games – they enjoyed watching me play. They knew me as an athlete, but once they found out their daughter was my girlfriend at school, it changed everything. They saw where I lived and that I came from a Hispanic family."

"Carlos," Liz interrupts.

"Wait, let me finish," he says.

"Okay, sure."

"Anyway, one Christmas I gave her a bracelet as a gift. It was wrapped up and I delivered it to her home."

"So what happened, did she like it?" Liz asked.

"She brought it back to school unopened and gave it back to me. I could tell she was saddened by the whole situation. She said her parents made her do that. She also said she couldn't see me anymore and apologized. I was really disappointed and started realizing that they could be HHs."

"HHs?" Liz asked.

"Hispanic Haters."

"Wow, I'm really sorry that happened. Do you want to know what I think?"

"Sure, especially if it saves me some money during Christmas."

"Well, I don't think a person should be viewed by what he or she owns as far as possessions – I don't think that way. I also don't think a person should be viewed by his or her ethnic group. I had the pleasure of getting to know you before I saw your house. It wouldn't matter to me if you lived in a one-room old house."

"So if I were to give you a gift for Christmas, your dad wouldn't make you give it back to me?" Carlos asked.

"No, in fact, I would probably get you one too."

"Wow, that's very kind of you."

Liz puts her arm around Carlos.

"I think you have a great future ahead of you. Someday you will be able to help your family. So keep working hard and don't ever give up."

Carlos shakes his head up and down and pauses momentarily.

"Well, I think we better start heading back to the school."

"Yeah, by the way, I like the way you decorated your room up here," Liz smiles.

"Thanks."

They both walk down the creaky steps.

"Mom! I'm walking Liz back to the school … be back in awhile."

"Okay! Nice meeting you Liz!" she shouts from the other room.

Battling the Sweet Home Huskies

On Friday afternoon, the Gervais Cougars are heading out to Sweet Home, Oregon. They will battle the Huskies. Sweet home has a front line that averages 230 lbs. Once again, scrambling is a must for Carlos to complete a pass.

A rooter bus is organized. Each student needs to pay one dollar to get a ride to the game. One bus has filled up so quickly that another bus is requested to take another large group of students.

No one in Gervais wants to miss this important game of the playoffs. The newspaper headlines read, "*Can a freshman lead the Cougars to a state championship*?" People everywhere are talking about the game – Gervais hadn't made it this far in a very long time. There is talk that the last time Gervais won a state title was back in 1951. It looks like Carlos was right, Gervais history is about to change.

The Bradfords are driving to the game in their BMW. Liz always invites Lorraine to come to every game with her. They are best friends and enjoy visiting with each other in the back seat. The games this year have more meaning to them because of the special players playing in the game.

"This is so exciting!" Liz said.

"I can't believe we're in the playoffs," Lorraine added.

"I hope Carlos doesn't get hit by one of those animal linemen."

"Yeah, I hope Harv stays safe too," Lorraine added.

"You two make a great couple Lorraine."

"Thanks, it's pretty amazing what those two have done for each other. I mean, Carlos getting a B on his algebra test?"

"He told me that this was his first B he had ever received," Liz said.

"Yeah, and Harv has always sat the bench, until this year. He's actually playing a lot now. Carlos helped him so much."

Ted and Elaine are listening to the girls in the back seat.

"I've been meaning to ask you about your grades Liz," Ted expresses.

"Daddy, they are really good except for one class."

"What class is that?" Ted asked.

"Honor's English – the teacher is really tough on us."

"Who's the teacher?"

"Her name is Mae McCall. She'll be at the game tonight – she loves football. In fact, she used to attend Sweet Home High School years ago."

"I may just have to talk to her if I see her," Ted said.

"Today at school, some kids were saying that she was Miss Sweet Home years ago," Liz said.

"What's Miss Sweet Home?" Elaine asked.

"When she was in high school she entered this swimsuit pageant – the winner was crowned Miss Sweet Home."

"It sounds like she was a very popular lady in her day."

"It'll be interesting to see who she roots for," Lorraine said.

"It better be Gervais," Ted added.

The Bradfords finally arrive at Sweet Home, Oregon, home of the Huskies.

"I've never seen so many people at a high school football game before," Liz said.

"That's because this is the first year you've watched Gervais football," Ted said.

"You're probably correct Daddy."

The Sweet Home Huskies are jogging out to the field in their green and yellow uniforms. Ron Sinclair, number 30, is their running back and he's been very tough to stop all season long. He's the reason Sweet Home is in the playoffs this year.

The night is clear and no sign of rain. The Gervais Cougars come out of the locker room jogging as a group. You can hear the people cheering for the Cougars as they run by and on to the football stadium.

Liz turns her head to her left and notices the English teacher, Mae McCall. She is sitting on the far left side of the bleachers. She's wearing a blue and gold coat with jeans. She is a tall medium boned lady that stands about 5' 10" with dark gray streaked hair. Mae has a very young looking face for her age. She's watching both teams warm up.

"Dad, there's my English teacher on the far left. She just stood up. You see her?"

"Yeah, I think I'm going to go over and have a talk with her."

"Please don't embarrass me Dad – I don't want her to pick on me the rest of the school year."

"Okay honey, I'll go easy," Ted said.

As he walks over to talk to Mae McCall, he says hi to a few people he knows along the way. Everyone knows who Ted Bradford is – a big shot lawyer that has a son playing on the football team.

"Hi Mrs. McCall I'm Ted Bradford – my daughter's in your class."

"I know who you are. How can I help you?"

"Well, it's about my daughter Liz."

"Aw yes, Liz Bradford. She's one of my brightest students."

"Yes, well lately we don't feel like she's one of your brightest students."

"Mr. Bradford, normally I don't do conferences during a football game, but I'll make an exception for you."

"That's very kind of you Mrs. McCall."

"First let me tell you that Liz is a very intelligent lady and she has a very bright future ahead of her."

"Thank you, that's nice of you to say. She takes after her dad," Ted smiles.

"Mr. Bradford, I'm not in a joking mood."

"Certainly Mrs. McCall, please continue."

"Your daughter is capable of writing better papers then what she's demonstrated the last two weeks. She has a B so far, in an AP class. That's pretty darn acceptable. But I understand where you're coming from. You want your daughter to do the best she can."

"I think you're right," Ted said.

"Something is distracting her – she isn't as focused as she should be. And it's not my job to find out what that is. I'm a teacher not a counselor."

"Thanks Mrs. McCall. Oh, by the way ... I found out that you were once Miss Sweet Home, congratulations."

"That was a very long time ago Mr. Bradford. Thank you. Now, if you'll excuse me I want to enjoy a game that I don't care who wins."

"Sure Mrs. McCall, and thanks for the input on my daughter," Ted starts to walk away.

"Mr. Bradford!"

"Yes Mrs. McCall?" Ted comes back for a second.

"Don't be so hard on your daughter, let her enjoy high school – she'll be fine."

"I understand. Have a nice evening," Ted said.

Ted returns to his seat and they all look at him as he sits down.

"What did she say?" Elaine asked.

"It sounds like she believes that Liz is capable of doing better than she's demonstrated in her last paper."

"Dad, I think she's being harder on me than anyone else in that class."

"She's trying to help you by challenging you, she thinks very highly of you."

"I never knew that," Liz said.

"She also thinks you've been distracted somehow. I think you've been spending too much time with a quarterback."

"Not true," Liz whispers to Lorraine.

"Liz, you bring that grade up to an A, and I'll invite that Hispanic to Thanksgiving dinner."

"You're kidding?"

"Nope, I'm serious. I want your grade up."

"You got a deal Daddy," Liz smiles.

"Now lets enjoy this game that I care who wins," Ted says.

The game is about to start as Sweet Home wins the toss. They elect to receive the football. The Gervais kicker boots it to the 20 yard line where a Husky catches it and returns it to the 40 yard line. He is hit hard by Dirk – *bam*! But he manages to hold on to the ball.

On the third play of the game, Ron Sinclair, number 30, breaks loose after receiving a handoff from the quarterback. Sweet Home takes the lead, 7 – 0.

On the next series of plays, Gervais produces a great drive with hooks and slants. But when they reach the 10 yard line, J.J. fumbles a reception. The football is picked up by Ron once again. He runs it all the way back – a 90 yard return for a touchdown. This running back is a Division I prospect and will be playing for USC next year. The Sweet Home fans are going crazy, "Whoo! Yeah!" The crowd is really into it. After all it is their home field.

The score is now, 14 – 0, Gervais is in trouble and Carlos calls a timeout. He walks over to the bench to discuss the situation with the coaches.

"Coach, let me play both ways this game. We also need Clifford and J.J. to play both ways … defense and offense."

"Both ways?" Coach Smith asked.

"Yes, otherwise we're not gonna be able to stop Ron, number 30. He's way too fast."

"I think you're right Carlos, Dirk … come here!"

"Yes coach," Dirk answers.

"I want you to key on number 30 when you're on defense. Wherever he goes you go. We have to stop him if we want a chance to win this game."

Gervais is now on offense and ready to execute more of the same pass patterns. They seem to be working for them – they just need to take care of the football.

By the end of the half the score is, Sweet Home 36 and Gervais 21. The Cougars seem to have slowed down Ron by playing their faster players both ways.

In the locker room, Coach Smith is trying to figure out how to stop the explosive offense the Huskies have.

"Gentlemen! I think from here on out your heart will determine how bad you want to win tonight. I know you're doing the best you can. All I ask of you is to take care of the football in the second half. We can't score if we don't have the football!

There's no tomorrow. Now let's go out there and fight … you can do it!"

"Yeah! Let's get this game, it's ours!" Coach McGoldrick adds.

"Let's go! Go Cougars!" Some of the players react.

In the second half Gervais receives the football after the kick. J.J. returns it to the Gervais 40 yard line. On the second play, Carlos throws a bullet pass right into the hands of Harv.

"Dang!" the Sweet Home defender yells out.

Harv took it all the way to the Sweet Home 15 yard line before being brought down by a speedy defensive back.

The Gervais team huddles up again.

"22 student body right to J.J. on one," Carlos signals the next play.

He has a good feeling this play will work. He's running it to the weak side of the defense.

"Down! Set! Hut!" Carlos calls.

All the backs and linemen block to the right side and Carlos pitches the ball to J.J. It's a thing of beauty to see the runner follow his teammates' blocks. J.J. scores a touchdown! The Gervais crowd goes crazy! They are all up on their feet.

The kicking team goes out and converts on the extra point. All of a sudden the score is, 36 – 28 in favor of Sweet Home. The score remained the same for the rest of the third quarter. In the fourth quarter both teams are battling tough. Carlos is showing a sign of tiredness – going both ways is hard on a player.

Head coach, Terry Smith, pulls Carlos out of the game to give him a breather. Clifford goes in at quarterback for a few plays. Clifford is delighted to get a chance to play quarterback. He's not too happy about being the backup to a freshman, but he realizes the coach is doing it for the team.

"Carlos, you let me know when you're ready to go back in."

"Okay coach."

After three minutes Carlos is ready to go back in. Gervais is down eight points with 3:00 minutes remaining in the game.

"Okay fellas, coach said to run this play, 34 hook turn post to J.J. I'll roll out to the right … on three," Carlos calls in the huddle.

They walk to the line of scrimmage with a little concern marked on their faces.

"Down! Set! Hut! Hut! Hut!"

J.J. takes off and is encountered with a big bump by the defensive back-*kathump*! The bump throws him off balance and he falls to the ground.

"Oh crap!" J.J. yells.

Carlos is rolling out looking for him, but sees nothing. Three defensive linemen and one linebacker come straight at him. He manages to slip away and scrambles to his left. He sees Harv all alone waving his arms. He buys enough time to throw the ball to Harv for a 50 yard reception.

The crowd is chanting with excitement. They are all yelling very load, "Yeah! Whoo!"

With 2:00 minutes left and no timeouts, Gervais needs 10 ten yards to score a touchdown. The Cougars huddle up very quickly.

"Quarterback sneak on one!" Carlos yells over the noisy crowd.

They hurry to the line of scrimmage."

"Down! Set! Hut!"

Carlos finds a seam, using his quickness he finds his way to the end zone for the score. The crowd went wild! The score is now, 36 – 34, Sweet Home.

"Coach! … should we go for two!"

"Go for it!" Coach Terry Smith agrees.

"Yeah, I don't think we have a choice," assistant Coach McColdrick said.

"If we don't get it in the end zone, we can go for the onside," Smith added.

The team huddles up and the fans settle down a bit.

"Clifford, you're at quarterback, pitch it to me and run to the far right corner. The ball will be waiting for you there. All y'all block! … on one!" Carlos called out.

Clifford walks behind the center to receive the snap.

"Down! Set! Hut!" Clifford yells.

Clifford is not used to pitching the ball. When he pitches it to Carlos he over throws it. Carlos is running after the football – a lateral is considered a live ball. As Carlos bends down to grab the football, none other than, Ron Sinclair, is running full speed right at him – *pop*! Carlos holds on to the ball, but the two-point conversion fails.

"Aw!" the Gervais crowd comes to a silence.

"Daddy! What happens now?" Liz asked.

"The only thing we can do now is kick an onside kick and hope we can get the ball."

"What's an onside kick?" Lorraine asked.

"It's when you kick the ball just past 10 yards. Once the ball goes 10 yards any player can grab it. It's a live ball – only during the kickoff though."

"Oh I see, let's kick an onside," Lorraine said.

The Gervais team is lined up and ready to kick the football. Carlos and J.J. are lined up at the end of the front line – the two fastest players on the team. The suspense of waiting for the signal from the official was very intense. This is the only chance the Cougars have to possibly win the game.

The winner of this game advances to the state championship game at Civic Stadium in Portland, Oregon. Portland is the big city that Carlos saw as his family drove by when they were traveling from Texas.

The referee blows his whistle and Gervais kicks the football. The football is bouncing everywhere at a slow pace. Carlos is running as fast as he can go – he beats the ball to the 10 yard marker but there are also a group of Sweet Home linemen in the same spot. The ball smacks one of the Huskies on his facemask – *bing*! It bounces and lands in Carlos' arms. Carlos immediately falls on the ball – three huge players stack on top of him.

Only football players know what that feels like. It's very hard to breath sometimes. Carlos manages to survive the pile up.

"Yeah! Alright! Whoo!" The crowd is really into it now. With 58 seconds on the clock, Gervais has a little time to operate. The team huddles up and you can feel the intensity of every player on the field.

"Okay boys, let's run 30 and out to J.J. on two! Y'all block for your life!"

They walk to the line of scrimmage – there's no energy to jog at this point in the game. Carlos is looking around at the defense. He gets ready to call the signals.

"Down! Set! Hut! Hut!"

J.J. is in a shoving match with the defensive back. He finally breaks loose on the out pattern. Carlos has time to pass the football since the defense is sagging back a bit. The ball comes zooming to J.J. He makes the catch and steps out-of-bounds to stop the clock.

The team huddles up again.

"31 fake hook post to Harv. J.J., you're getting double teamed. This should open up Harv … on one!" They start walking to the line of scrimmage.

"Go out-of-bounds as soon as you catch the ball," Carlos whispers to Harv.

"You got it," Harv responded.

"Down! Set! Hut!"

Harv knew what to do if the linebacker went to the right. Harv went left and Carlos connected with a beautiful spiral. Harv starts running toward the out-of-bounds line, but before he could get there, Ron Sinclair, hammers him good to bring him down – *smack*!

"Darn it!" Harv yells.

"You're not going anywhere punk … you're worthless!" Ron yells.

Ron steps on the back of Harv's helmet and shoves his head to the ground. Harv feels a little intimidated and says nothing.

Carlos calls a timeout with 10 seconds left in the game. The ball is sitting on the 20 yard line of Sweet Home.

"Come on ref, didn't ya see that?" Carlos pleads.

Carlos jogs over to the bench to talk to the coach.

"Coach, what do ya want me to run? It's our last play."

"Our kicking team is not accurate that far, especially under pressure. Fake the corner pass and run it as fast as you can go. Run it away from Sinclair – he's too quick."

"Okay Coach. I'll do the best I can."

"That's all you can do," Coach Smith said.

He walks away looking at the coaches as if all the pressure lies on him – a freshman quarterback. He also looks at all of the people up in the stands.

"They'll either love me or hate me after this play," Carlos thinks to himself.

"Okay y'all. Quarterback draw, I'll take a few steps back and fake the pass. Everyone block! J.J., you key on number 30 – take him out … on two!"

There are a few shouts from the crowd. There are also students following the cheerleaders' cheers as the team walks up to the line of scrimmage.

"We wanna we wanna … we wanna touchdown! We wanna we wanna … we wanna touchdown!" the student section cheers along.

Carlos is looking both ways at the defense as he plants himself behind the center.

"Down! Set! Hut! Hut!"

Carlos drops back as he looks for a seam.

The defenders are all watching for the pass. There are only four defensive linemen coming in for the sack. Carlos sees daylight to the right – he sprints toward the right side of the goal-line. The crowd is going wild. He runs to the 15 yard line, the 10 yard line, the five yard line. By then the safety catches up from the left side of the field. He hits Carlos from the side – *crack*! Carlos starts to fall at the two yard line, but he reaches as far as he can with one hand – hanging on to the football. He hits the ground and the ball crosses the plane.

"Touchdown!" the referee signals.

Carlos looks up at the referee, lying down on the ground. He sees the two hands straight up and is relieved that he has scored a touchdown. He doesn't have much reaction because of the exhaustion he is experiencing – a very hard game.

The entire offensive team comes over and jumps all over Carlos with excitement.

"Nice job Carlos … you did it man!" Harv yells out along with some others.

Liz and Lorraine are jumping up and down and going crazy!

"We're going to state! We're going to state!" Liz repeats several times.

She looks over at Mae McCall. Mae acknowledges and puts two thumbs up. She begins clapping for the Gervais Cougars as they defeat her alma mater.

After the extra point is kicked, it's Gervais 41, and Sweet Home 36. The Gervais Cougars are advancing to the state championship game at Civic Stadium, in Portland, Oregon. The game will be played after Thanksgiving Day.

As the players are all on the sideline congratulating each other, Ron Sinclair, from Sweet Home, runs over to where Carlos is standing.

"You played a heck of a game, I'll be at USC next year, but I'll be sure to look you up. And sorry about smashing one of your teammates – I gotta stop doing that."

"Thanks man, and good luck at USC, I'll be watching you on TV next year."

The amount of people around the players prevented Liz and Lorraine from congratulating the guys. All they can do is look from afar. They walked along with Ted and Elaine back to the car.

"I wish I could have talked to Carlos after the game," Liz said.

"Well, it's late and we still have to stop and eat somewhere. I wonder if Sweet Home has some good eating places," Ted said.

"I'm sure they do Ted – probably some good home cooking around here," Elaine said.

They managed to find a small diner downtown to grab a quick burger. After that, they were on their way back home. The two girls are in the back seat talking quietly – with the noisy road it's impossible for the front seat to hear.

"Well Liz, I would have loved to talk to Harv after the game. I agree with your earlier statement," Lorraine said.

"We should see if we can get together tomorrow."

"How is that possible?" Lorraine asked.

There is a short pause while Liz thinks.

"Daddy, do you have any plans for tomorrow?"

"Yes, your mom and I are going to Portland to start doing some Thanksgiving shopping. She saw some clothes she can't live without at the Washington Square Mall. So we're just going to get the turkey and things while we're there. Do you want to go?"

"No, that's okay I need my beauty sleep."

"I promised your mom we'd go Saturday. We should be back by three or so," Ted said.

Liz leans over toward Lorraine and whispers in her ear.

"We can get together tomorrow – I'll call you in the morning."

"Okay, not before nine though," Lorraine whispered back.

Meanwhile back at Sweet Home, the team stops to eat at a local fast-food place. They are waiting for the results of the game between Regis and Oakridge.

"Hey coach, I just heard on the radio that Regis beat Oakridge. So we'll be playing Regis for the state championship," Coach McGoldrick said.

"Okay, that'll be a tough game for us. They're going to be ready for us I can guarantee you that," responds Coach Smith.

On the other side of the restaurant, Carlos is sitting with Harv, J.J., and Hector.

"Harv, you had quite a few catches tonight," Carlos mentions.

"Yeah, you put the ball right there for me," Harv adds.

"I was so glad when you crossed that plane with the football," J.J. says looking at Carlos.

All of the players have smiles on their faces – even Dirk is smiling and joking around. The night of celebration went on for a very long time. By the time the team returned home, it was close to 1:00 a.m.

The next morning at the Swaveys, Carlos sleeps in until 11:00 a.m.

"Carlos … wake up!" Lydia yells. He didn't respond.

"Carlos … it's Liz on the phone!" Lydia yells louder.

"Okay … I'm coming down!" He steps down slowly working out all the aches from last night's game. He has a few bruises and plenty of soreness.

"Hello."

"Hi Carlos, I'm sorry I didn't get to talk to you after the game last night."

"Oh, no problem – it's okay."

"Lorraine's here. Can you come over and hang out with us for a couple of hours?"

"Can you give me about an hour?"

"Sure, we can fix breakfast for you if you want. My parents are gone for awhile."

"Okay, in that case give me a half hour."

"You did great last night, I'm proud of you – you star stud."

"See ya in a little while," he hangs up the phone smiling.

Carlos begins to head back upstairs while Mike reads the newspaper.

"Did you see the paper this morning Carlos?" He tosses the paper to Carlos.

"Freshman quarterback takes down Sweet Home, 41 – 36. That is full of crap! I wasn't the only one playing last night – reporters, what can you do?"

"Mom and Dad are actually thinking of going to the state championship game," Mike said.

"You're joking?"

"No he's not, I heard them talking about it last night," Lydia said.

"That would be a miracle on Alder Street. I gotta take a shower and go over to the rich girl's house – the one that's gonna dump me," he turns and grins at Mike.

"Ah … shut up," Mike replies.

To the Bradfords' House

It's 11:30 a.m. and the road is a little damp but not too bad. Carlos rides his bike to Harv's house where his friends are waiting for him. When he arrives, he jumps off his bike and starts walking to the front door. Liz opens the door and waves to him as he jogs closer.

"You made it."

"Yeah, what are ya up to this morning?"

"Well, first of all, let me just say that you were awesome in last night's game – congrats!"

"Thanks, I scored the last touchdown for you."

"For me? Wow! Can you do that again next week? Liz laughs.

"Sure, no problem."

"Ha-ha! You know you're bad. Want to play some air hockey? Liz asked.

"You have an air hockey table?" Carlos asked.

"And a pool table and a ping pong table," Liz said.

"I've died and gone to heaven," Carlos said.

All the teenagers play games in the Bradfords' recreation room. The room is attached to the house with a twenty foot hallway. As you walk into the room it is a sight that would make anyone relax. The light maroon walls circled the red carpet that is padded to comfort anyone's feet.

Carlos is in awe of this room. He is talented in recreational games – in Texas that was affordable to do. It didn't take much money, if any at all. Kids could play for hours – what better way to spend time with friends? He knew that this was a great blend and it would not hurt his pride.

Carlos starts to rack up the balls on the pool table.

"This used to be one of my favorite games to play back in Texas."

"Does that mean I'm in trouble?" Harv asked.

"I don't know, you own the table. I'm the one that's in trouble."

"Yeah but I don't play much on it."

"You wanna get in on the action Liz?" Carlos asked.

"No thanks. I'm just going to observe you two gentlemen."

"I'm rooting for Harv, yes!" Lorraine said.

"I'll root against my brother, yes!" Liz stares at Lorraine.

Once they begin playing, Harv is no match for the Texan. Harv gets one shot and that is it. Carlos runs the table three games in a row. This made him superior and he's beginning to feel a balance where wealthy kids look up to him with a great deal of respect.

"Okay Carlos, you ready to get beat at air hockey?" Liz expresses.

"Sure, I've never played air hockey before."

Liz is good at air hockey and she gives Carlos a good challenge. While they play you can hear the laughs from the recreation room.

"This is so much fun, thanks for coming over."

"Thanks for asking me. Maybe next time you can come over to my house. I can unbolt the bed and we can ride it when the train goes by."

"Ha-ha-ha!" Liz could not stop laughing.

Harv and Lorraine had gone to the family room to watch TV. Carlos found himself alone with Liz in the recreation room. When they are done playing air hockey they walk to the couch and sit down. The couch is next to a bar that is made out of marble. Carlos wants to somehow find a way to kiss Liz. He didn't want to do anything that might turn her off – it's very nerve racking to him.

"Liz, is it okay if I kiss you?" He puts his arm around her.

"Uh... Uh … sure I guess it's okay," she starts to blush a little.

Carlos slowly moves toward her beautiful red lips. As he moves closer he smells an amazing fragrance. When his lips touch hers he experiences a great feeling throughout his entire body. Liz reaches over and puts her arm around his neck and presses him closer to her. She feels love and a moment she has been waiting for.

They separate slowly and look at each other with blazing eyes.

"Wow, that was very nice," Carlos said.

"Yes, very nice," Liz responded.

It was the first romantic experience for both of them. They enjoy talking for a long time about many things.

Meanwhile, in the TV room, Harv and Lorraine start walking toward the recreation room. Carlos and Liz hear the footsteps and immediately get up and grab the ping pong paddles.

"Good game Liz!" Carlos shouts.

"That's an understatement," Liz replies.

"What are you two up to?" Lorraine asked.

"What are we up to? More like what are you two up to?" Liz responds.

"We were just watching TV," Harv added.

"Oh no … it's 2:50, Mom and Dad should be home any minute! Carlos, you need to leave through the back," Liz expressed with worry.

"What about my bike? It's in the front."

"I'll bring it around for you in case they drive up."

"Okay," Carlos said.

Liz hustled to the front, grabbed the bike and started riding it toward the back of the house. Ted and Elaine turn into the driveway.

"Hey … where did you get that piece of junk!" Ted yelled from the opened car window.

"It's Lorraines. I'm bringing it to the back for her!"

Ted and Elaine looked at each other in a puzzling way.

"Lorraine's parents have enough money to get her a nicer bike than that," Elaine said.

Liz rides the bike around to the back where Carlos is waiting for her.

"They're here. I'll see you at school on Monday." She leans over and gives him a kiss on the check.

"For sure, bye Liz," Carlos jumps on his bike and takes off as fast as he can through the backside of the house.

When Carlos arrives at his house, Pete is standing at the door waiting for him.

"Where you been?" Pete asked.

"I was at a friend's house."

"That's nice, but I need your help."

Pete takes a drink from the can of beer he holds in his hand.

"Want me to help you drink beer?"

"No smartmouth."

"Dad, I'm kinda tired. Can we do this later?"

"No, I need to replace the water pump in the car, and I can't do it myself. I need you to hand me the tools."

"I played a tough game last night, why can't Mike help?"

"Why don't you quit football? You're wasting your time playing that useless game."

"The coach tells me I can get a scholarship to play college ball. That'll pay for my education."

"That's hog-wash! You're gonna get hurt! All they care about is what's in it for them."

"Dad, you don't understand. That's the reason we live in this piece of crap house! You never got an education! Your parents never got an education! Why can't ya support what I'm trying to do?"

"Carlos, get the heck out of here! Go in the house and rest."

There is a long silence as Pete starts looking under the car hood.

"Dad, I'm sorry."

"Just go, I don't need your help."

Carlos starts to walk slowly to the front door. He opens it and the hinges break off – *slam*! The door falls to the ground as he moves away. He turns around and looks at his dad, who is very angry by this time.

"I suppose you want me to fix that too!" Pete shouts.

"No, I'll fix it. Better get used to doing labor jobs myself," Carlos mumbles.

"What did you say?"

"Oh nothing, I just said I should do more labor jobs for you."

Isabel is inside close to the door, listening.

"Carlos, don't listen to your dad, education is very important. You're right. You don't want to end up like us. You have to follow your heart and your dream. Your dad's just frustrated right now."

"Thanks Mom. I'm gonna go to the store to buy some hinges for the door. I better fix it before Dad gets a heart attack," he looks at his mom while she laughs.

Back at the Bradford's house, Harv, Liz, and Lorraine are eating dinner. Liz is feeling a little envious because her brother is spending more time with Lorraine.

"How are your folks doing Lorraine?" Ted asked.

"They're great – my dad just bought a new Jaguar. He really loves it."

"I don't like the body style, but they're great performance cars."

"Yeah, I didn't like it either but my dad sure does."

"How are you doing on your grades Harv?" Ted asked.

"Straight As Dad. And I'm even helping Carlos with his grades."

"That's only because you're not taking AP classes," Liz said.

"I will next year."

"I'll believe it when I see it."

"Kids! We're eating and we have a guest," Elaine interrupts.

"Don't take your anger out on Harv," Ted directs the comment at Liz.

"It's not fair that I can't invite Carlos over to eat with us."

"Harv has straight As. When your grade in Mrs. McCall's class comes up to an A, the Hispanic kid can join us for Thanksgiving. You have my word."

"I'll do better than that, I'll even do extra credit," Liz replied.

When dinner is over, Lorraine's mom shows up. She drives up in a new Lexus four door sedan. It's a silver car that shines with the lights reflecting on the body. A slender lady with blonde hair and green eyes walks up to the front door.

Elaine walks to the door and opens it quickly with a smile.

"Hi Laura."

"Hi Elaine, is Lorraine ready?"

"Yeah, she's getting her coat."

"She speaks very highly of your son – I think they make a great little couple," Laura said.

"I'd say that's pretty accurate," Elaine agreed.

"We have to keep the money in the families you know?"

"Laura, what does money have to do with any of this?"

"I wouldn't want my daughter hooking up with a poor kid. Think of the future she would have struggling all the time."

"They're still pretty young to have a thought like that," Elaine stares at Laura.

"It's never too early to think like that."

Lorraine walks into the room with her coat on.

"Okay Mom, I'm ready."

"Lorraine, it's always a pleasure seeing you. Goodbye," Elaine smiles.

"Bye Mrs. Bradford, thanks for the dinner. See you in school Harv and Liz."

On Monday Liz talks to Mrs. McCall and works out a plan on how she can bring her grade up to an A. She shows up early at Honor's English to plead her case.

"Hi Mrs. McCall."

"Well Hi Liz."

"What exactly are you requesting of me to escalate my grade to an A?"

"Liz, you are a very bright young lady. You're capable of writing much better papers."

They both look at each other for a few seconds. The teacher walks to her desk. Liz is following her. She sits down and continues talking.

"Your dad must have had a talk with you. I talked with him at the game."

"I'm very aware of that conversation," Liz said.

"Okay, try writing with more conviction. You have to write what you feel. Be more descriptive in all of your topics – more than the average person. You're capable."

"Will I know before Thanksgiving if my grade is up to an A?

"You'll know in three days – that's when the next paper will be graded."

"Thanks Mrs. McCall, I really need to bring my grade up, I promise I'll work very hard."

"Liz, let me give you a few words of advice. You can take it or you can leave it."

"Sure, I'd love to hear."

"When I was a young girl someone once told me that I was a talented writer. I was passed around from one foster home to another. Another person told me the same thing. I didn't listen to them until later in life. I wish I could take that moment back. Don't make the same mistake I did as a youngster. You are a very talented writer, put more energy into the talent you've been given."

"Thanks Mrs. McCall, I plan to do that. And you're right I have been slacking off a little."

"Good luck sweetheart, I look forward to reading your next paper."

Liz walks to her desk and the English teacher starts getting ready for class. By the time their talk concludes the rest of the students start pouring into the classroom.

It's Wednesday and the end of the day. Mae McCall had graded the papers that were completed and turned in the day before. She starts passing them out. Liz is sitting on her chair anxiously waiting for hers. She worked very hard the last couple of days. She worked late every night writing and rewriting. She edited over and over until she felt it was close to perfect. The teacher finds her way to Liz's desk.

"Here's your paper Liz," Mrs. McCall smiles as she hands her the paper.

"Oh my gosh! An A+." Liz's mouth and eyes are opened wide.

It looks like Carlos is going to the Bradfords for Thanksgiving dinner on Thursday evening. Liz has such a smile on her face – you'd think she'd died and gone to heaven.

"Why are you smiling? You always get good grades," Shawna Smith asked.

"Oh … it's a long story Shawna," Liz replied.

"Whatever, you're spacing out chick."

"Shawna, the only space I see is in your brain."

After class Liz runs to find Carlos.

"Hey … slow down! No running in the hall!" a teacher yells.

"Sorry, I'll slow down," Liz replies.

She spots Carlos walking down the hall with Harv and J.J.

"Carlos!"

"Hi Liz. What ya been up to girl?"

"Guess what?"

"What?"

"How would you like to come to Thanksgiving dinner at our house on Thursday night?" Liz looks at him with a smile.

"I'd love to, but I think your dad might have a different idea."

"Nope, my dad approves this time. You can also tell me what you promised. Remember?"

"Oh yeah … I need to explain to you how I magically came up with my attire during the Harvest Dance."

"I'm glad you remember. I'll see you on Thanksgiving night," Liz said as she walks to the next class.

"I'll be there. I'll have my limo pick me up!" Carlos yells from afar.

Liz turns around and looks at his smile from a distance.

It's settled, Carlos will experience a family dinner at the Bradfords' house on Thanksgiving Day. That works out great for him since his family always celebrates during the day.

The Swavey family usually has turkey, mashed potatoes, corn, tortillas, and refried beans. For dessert it was usually apple pie, or a new invention by Isabel. This year money is very tight for the poor family – Carlos doesn't know what to expect. They normally enjoy Thanksgiving with their immediate family. Relatives stop later in the day and visit for awhile. Carlos enjoys company, but it's the alcohol drinking that bothers him. Alcohol makes people different when they've had too much. The kids always find a game to play outside. In Carlos' culture it is rare that the adults play games with the kids – normally it's segregated.

The Bradfords celebrate differently. They usually go all out and invite aunts, uncles, and grandparents. They cater the dinner and hire servants to cook, serve the food, and clean up. The hired help are all related to Maria, their maid. They focus on visiting and having fun with family. After dinner they play games in the recreation room. Others play board games and watch sporting events on TV. Ted Bradford would rather be hunting somewhere in Eastern Oregon, places like Wallowa County.

That's how both families normally celebrate Thanksgiving Day. This year will be different for the Swaveys. They don't really know the relatives here in Oregon as well as they did in Texas. In Texas, after the big meal, Pete Swavey, was used to getting together with his brother and some friends outside the house. They would sit in the car and play guitar and accordion. They would try singing songs while drinking beer – basically hanging out. This year would be different for him. His brother is miles away. Isabel hated that part of the celebration anyway. She would clean up and be angry at Pete for drinking and playing music outside their house.

Liz and Carlos are two high school kids with different cultures – can they make this work? Anything's possible if both sides truly want it to work.

It's Thanksgiving Day morning with the beautiful sun shining. The leaves from the trees are full of yellows and oranges. Some lay on the ground and some are barely hanging on the trees. There's something about Thanksgiving morning. Before the actual meal takes place, everyone seems to be in a great mood anticipating a good meal. The best part is that there's no school or work – a good majority of people don't work that day.

Carlos wakes up with the smell of a turkey cooking in the oven. The woodstove is on to keep the house warm – the temperature outside is 40 degrees. He walks down the steps from the attic.

"What's that great smell coming from the oven?"

"Duh! It's what I should call you," Lydia said.

"I guess a turkey does smell good," Carlos answered.

"Oh brother," Lydia rolls her eyes.

"Can you bring some more chairs from the living room?" Isabel asked.

"Sure Mom," Carlos grabs a couple of chairs.

Isabel bought some old chairs at a garage sale a few weeks ago. Some are falling apart.

"Mom I can fix these chairs. I can put some screws in them so they don't fall apart."

"That would be great Carlos, thanks."

He walks to a small room where his dad keeps the tools. He grabs the drill, some screws, and a screwdriver. He begins to repair the broken chairs.

"Mom, I forgot to ask you something. Is it okay if I go to my friend's house for Thanksgiving dinner this evening?"

"What friend?"

"Harv Bradford. He's Liz's brother. He plays on the football team with me."

"Well, I would ask your father. It's okay with me as long as you didn't invite yourself."

"Not the case, I was invited yesterday."

Carlos finally completes the task of fixing the chairs. He walks over close to the entryway where his dad is putting together a carburetor.

"Dad, Mom said I could go to my friend's house for Thanksgiving dinner tonight. Is it okay with ya?"

"I don't care. After we eat here in a bit I don't think there will be much left for later – you might as well eat there tonight."

"Thanks Dad. I'm sure they'll have plenty of food."

Time went by and before you know it, the whole Swavey family is at the table ready to eat. Pete was never one to say grace – it was rare that he attended church with the family. Isabel was very religious and usually the one that said grace.

"Lord, thanks for this food and for our family being together on this Thanksgiving Day. Amen."

"Amen," everyone else responds.

"Let's eat now!" Mike yells out.

They all start feasting and talking. The younger kids start fighting over the rolls. Lydia starts joking around making funny comments. They seem to be one big happy family. In fifteen minutes the food is all gone and dessert is next.

There's nothing like a family spending time together during a big holiday. It's like an escape from the normal everyday life. It doesn't take much money for the Swaveys to spend time together.

As the dessert is being dished up for some of the kids by Isabel, the kids are talking amongst themselves.

"Carlos," Lydia says.

"What?"

"I know why you're going to the Bradfords tonight."

"Why Lydia?"

"I'm guessing to see your rich girlfriend."

"You're right, she is rich, but she's also a very nice person and she has a name. How would you like it if someone called you poor girl?"

"Mike says that the only reason she likes you is because you're a good quarterback on the team and you're popular at school."

"You keep listening to Mike and someday you'll end up in a mental hospital. In fact, Salem has one on Center Street – they'll be waiting for you."

"Shut up!" Lydia grabs some dishes and stomps to the kitchen.

"You wait and see Carlos, after the season I bet she dumps you," Mike said.

"Mike, you surprise me. I thought the only meaning of dump for you, was going to the bathroom."

"Hey boys! It's Thanksgiving ... Lydia why is it that you start these nice talks all the time?" Isabel looks at her.

"Sorry Mom."

"I'll take some more turkey, I mean Mike," Carlos said.

Mike grabs a roll and throws it at Carlos. Carlos sees it coming and catches it.

"Thanks Mike, I was just about to ask you to pass a roll."

"Punk!" Mike continues eating.

Pete shakes his head and keeps eating. It is nothing new to him.

"Regis has a new quarterback. He's a transfer from Corvallis. You better bring your A game on Saturday," Mike said.

"I know, he's played the last five games with Regis – he's tough," Carlos responded.

"What's his name?"

"Rick Toby. The word is that he wasn't very happy with the program in Corvallis, so his family moved to Stayton. And now he's leading the team. Regis is a tough team with Jason. Now they have a tough quarterback," Carlos shakes his head.

"Even though you're a punk, I still hope y'all kick their butt," Mike said.

"I think we have a good chance, we'll have to wait and see."

The day is relaxing and everyone seems to be content with a satisfied stomach. There wasn't enough food to fill everyone completely, but close enough. The day passed by slowly and the evening is approaching. Carlos put on his nice slacks and sporty shirt. He looks very handsome and official for a formal dinner.

"Why are you getting all dressed up?" Pete asked.

"You wouldn't understand Dad."

"Try me."

"Well, these people are not like us. They have a huge house and they drive classy cars like BMWs and Mercedes. I don't wanna go to their house and be the only one wearing a t-shirt and jeans."

"Where did you get the nice clothes?" Pete asked.

"That's another thing you wouldn't understand – it's a long story."

"Okay, whatever. Have fun tonight," Pete said.

"Thanks Dad. Have fun working on the car."

"Want me to give you a ride there?" Lydia asked.

"That'd be great. Thanks."

"See, I am nice to you occasionally."

"Very true Lydia."

They both walk out through the front door and hop into the car and drive off.

On the way there, Lydia is anxious to see where Liz lives. She's heard so much about her that this will be an exciting treat.

"I think Liz is the hottest looking girl at Gervais High School."

"You think so?"

"Oh yeah, for sure. She looks a little bit like Cecilia in Texas."

There is a long silence as they get closer to Harv's house.

"It's right here, start slowing down. Turn on that driveway."

"Oh my gosh! That is a beautiful home. That's where she lives?"

"Yes, this is it."

"Wow … okay bro, have fun. You are one lucky dude."

"We'll see ya later," Carlos says as he shuts the door.

Lydia continues to stare with her mouth wide open as she drives away.

Thanksgiving with the Bradfords

Carlos walks to the front door as he notices all of the cars parked on the side of the Bradfords' house. He looks around and stares for a few minutes.

"That must be all of the relatives," he thinks to himself.

He starts feeling a little nervous. Never had he been in this situation. The young man steps up to the front deck – it's a light blue house with white trimming and a stained deck in front to match the back deck. He walks to the front door and pushes the button to the doorbell. Liz opens the door and steps out to greet him with a big hug.

"You made it and you look very nice."

"Wow, so do you."

Liz is wearing a light purple blouse – very shiny. Her pants are made out of black expensive material. She walks around introducing Carlos to all of her relatives.

"Is this the star quarterback I've been hearing about?" one of her uncles asked.

"Yes it is Uncle Bob," Liz smiled.

The table looks amazing, with colors coordinated. There is a huge plate of turkey and ham in the center of the table. The plates are all new – as if they've never been used before. The plates shine displaying a reflection from the chandelier lights above. The silverware is wrapped in cloths.

Carlos is used to eating with his hands. How would he hold the fork, or cut the meat? Would the people watch him? He felt out of place – very uncomfortable. He is the only Hispanic at the table. The only other Hispanics there are the workers Ted hired.

"Maria, we're ready for the drinks."

"Yes Mrs. Bradford."

Out come the soda, juice, milk, and wine – a variety of drinks to keep everyone happy. Carlos is amazed at all of the trouble and money this family goes through to make the holiday a special one. He has many thoughts going through his mind and plenty of opportunities to observe and listen to everyone else.

When you care about someone, I guess you go through the discomfort of a different culture. You make an effort to experience the differences of upbringing.

"Carlos, you can sit next to me – right here," Liz said.

They both sit down. Elaine stands up at one end of the table and everyone comes to a complete silence.

"Thank you all once again for joining us in a delightful meal that Maria and her staff have prepared for us. Enjoy the evening and eat plenty of food."

Everyone starts to clap and cheer a bit.

"Do your folks ever say grace?" Carlos asked.

"Not usually," Liz said as she grabs a plate.

Carlos is prepared to watch Liz – he has to see how she eats. He wants to use the knife and fork the way she does to not be embarrassed. You can see the questions in his eyes. The turkey plate is being passed around. When it comes around to Carlos, he takes several pieces of turkey and places them on his plate. The mashed potatoes, gravy and other foods are also passed around.

His plate is now full and without thinking he grabs a piece of turkey with his hands and starts eating. The young Hispanic is chewing his food and notices that everyone is staring at him, including Liz. They all look away and continue eating.

"Do you ever use a fork?" Liz whispers.

"Not usually with meat, but with mashed potatoes and corn I do. I did wash my hands. Should I start using a fork?"

"Oh I don't care, I was just curious," Liz said.

"Your family is definitely different than mine when it comes to eating."

"Oh yeah, how so?"

"Well, we use our hands more."

"Very interesting."

"I wanna ask you something, but not now," Carlos says.

"I can imagine that your culture is a little different than mine. But that's okay – so what?"

"Yeah, I agree with you."

When dinner is over Carlos observes the Hispanic workers cleaning up. They look at him and he looks at them, but neither says anything. The workers do their job and see Carlos as privileged. Deep down Carlos knows that he is just like them. He feels bad for them and never wants to end up like that when he's that old – cleaning up for someone else for money to survive.

"Carlos, you okay?"

"Oh yeah, I'm fine … just thinking a bit."

Some finish eating sooner than others. Some talk the entire time and haven't touched their plate. Everyone does their own thing.

"Come on, let's go play some games," Liz suggested to Carlos.

"Sure, that sounds like fun."

They walk to the recreation room and talk to a few people on the way. When they get a few minutes to themselves Carlos is curious about some things.

"Okay Liz, now I can ask you what I wanted to earlier. How much do ya pay the workers that cater the food?"

"I have no idea – Daddy takes care of those details. You sure like to analyze a lot of things. I've never met anyone quite like you before."

"Oh yeah? I hope that's a good thing."

"Yeah, it is – come on, let's go play some games," Liz smiles.

They play games the rest of the night. Some of the adults join in but it's mostly a younger crowd of cousins in the recreation room. Carlos is having fun since he's winning most of the games and displays an exceptional talent.

Ted comes in and pulls Liz over to the side.

"It's time to take Carlos home."

"Why? No one else is leaving," Liz said.

"He's been here long enough."

"That's not fair!" Liz runs out to the back to not cause a scene.

Carlos sees her and walks outside after her. She's leaning on the rail with a few tears running down her face. It's a clear night and the moon is shining. Carlos walks up and leans on the rail next to her.

"What's wrong Liz?"

"My dad says we have to take you home now."

"He must have his reasons – don't be so hard on your dad."

"Why aren't you upset? It's you he wants to get rid of. I want you to stay longer."

"It's Thanksgiving. I told you I would tell you how I got the clothes I was wearing the night of the dance. Do you remember?"

"Yes, I do remember. Where did you get them?" She wipes her tears.

"I was walking home after being laughed at. I had mud all over myself and I was soaking wet. A truck pulled over next to me. He opened the door with much concern."

"Who was he? Please tell me."

Carlos pauses for a moment as Liz looks into his eyes.

"It was your dad. He helped me. He took me in to town and bought the finest clothes I have ever seen. He asked me to promise not to tell anyone. That's why I couldn't tell you. I called him up when you insisted I tell you. He suggested I wait until Thanksgiving Day.

"Oh Carlos, I'm so sorry I put you through that. That was so nice of my dad to do that. I would have never guessed he'd do something like that for you."

"I think he's gotten to know who I am a little. I think he's had a change of heart on how he views Hispanics. Not all of us are like his first impression of a bad experience he might have once had with Hispanics."

"I feel bad that I yelled at him," Liz said.

"Your dad wanted to gain my trust. I honored that. I also knew you would understand once I explained it to ya. But it was no fun seeing ya angry at me."

"I'm so sorry Carlos," she reaches over and hugs him.

"You are forgiven. Let's go back inside so y'all can take me home."

"Okay," Liz smiles.

They enter the house and Liz is smiling again. She walks over to her dad and puts her arm around him.

"Daddy I love you. I'm sorry for what I said to you."

"I love you too sweetheart. You can go with your mom when she drives Carlos home."

"Okay."

"I hope it wasn't too much of a culture shock for you tonight," Ted said as he looks at Carlos.

"Not at all Mr. Bradford. Thanks for having me over."

"Good luck on the game Saturday, we'll be watching."

"Thank ya sir. Goodnight."

Liz takes Carlos around to say goodbye to the relatives.

On the way back to Carlos' house, Elaine and Liz are in the front seats and Carlos is in the back seat.

"Wow, this is a nice car Mrs. Bradford."

"Thank you. Ted bought it for me as a Christmas present last year."

"Carlos you were really something else in the rec room. Where did you learn how to play those games so well?" Liz asked.

"Back in a small Texas town there really isn't too much to do. We played a lot of pool, foosball, ping-pong – you know."

"Well, no matter how much I practiced I could never be better than you."

They drive up on Alder Street and find the house. Elaine pulls over to the side of the road.

"Well, here's my mansion. Thanks for the ride," Carlos said quietly.

"Mom can I walk him to the door?"

"Sure honey, but don't be too long."

They both carefully step out of the car – Carlos opens the door for Liz.

"Be careful Liz there's a big puddle right here." He grabs her hand and leads her.

"Thanks for coming over Carlos. I know it must have been a difficult experience for you – especially the dinner part."

"The important thing is that I had fun tonight and I learned a lot about you. See ya at the game Saturday."

They hug each other, but no kiss with Liz's mom there watching. Liz walks back to the car dodging the puddles again.

Carlos tries to open the front door but it seems to be locked. He knocks on it a few times but no one seems to be opening it. He knocks a bit harder – *bam*! *bam*! *bam*! Lydia finally comes to answer the door.

"About time you got home. Everyone's asleep."

He steps into the house and stands there for a minute. He looks at the ceiling and the walls. The maintenance needed is unbearable. He thinks about how opposite his house and family are compared to Liz's house and family.

Carlos walks up to the attic, changes his clothes, and goes to bed with mixed emotions. Could he continue this friendship with two wealthy kids? What could he ever give Liz that she doesn't already have? He likes her a lot and he loves spending time with her. Carlos falls asleep thinking about those things.

Gervais Makes it to State

It's finally Saturday night and the state championship game between the Gervais Cougars and the Regis Rams is about to unfold.

The Cougars are warming up on the field at Civic Stadium. The Rams come running toward the artificial turf – it looks very nice and green. The Regis crowd goes crazy, "Yeah! Go Regis!"

"I hope we can pull a victory tonight," Lorraine said.

"You and me both," Liz responds. She seems very nervous.

"It's going to be tough. Regis has a new quarterback that transferred from Corvallis a few weeks ago."

"Who is he?" Elaine asked.

"Rick Toby. He has a heck of an arm and he's tall – about 6' 3" 210," Ted said.

"Harv was out practicing with Carlos yesterday to get ready for this game," Liz said.

"Yeah, they probably worked off that turkey from Thanksgiving dinner," Lorraine chuckles.

The night is cold and all of the people are wrapped up in blankets and heavy coats. The good news is, it's not raining or snowing. The players are all cold and by the time warm-ups are done, they begin to feel a little numb.

Regis wins the coin toss and elects to receive the football. Clifford and Dirk, the captains, start running back to the sideline. The referees signal that Gervais is kicking.

"Hey Carlos! Rick Toby said to tell you good luck," Dirk yells out.

"He sounds like a good sport," Carlos replies.

The kicking team runs out to the field. They all line up a step behind where the ball is placed. There are five players to the left of the kicker and five to the right of the kicker. The Gervais kicker is ready and signals to the official by raising his right hand. The whistle blows and the kicker puts his foot into the football.

The Regis receiver catches the ball and returns it to the Regis 30 yard line. J.J. is defending Jason. The coach wants to save Carlos for offense – at least through the first half.

Rick walks behind his team to the line of scrimmage and positions himself behind the center.

"45! 45! Hut one! Hut two!" He drops back into the pocket. Rick has a great offensive line to block for him. He passes the ball to Jason on a slant – a nice spiral with some great zip to it. The ball is caught by Jason and he wastes no time – he scores the first touchdown of the game on the very first play.

The Regis fans are on their feet screaming, "Go! Regis! Yeah! Whoo!"

It's like a huge train passing by. The noise is so loud you can hear it for miles in downtown Portland. The score starts out, 7 – 0, Regis.

"Carlos, it looks like you have a challenge. That Rick kid can really throw the ball well. You need to focus on what you've been doing all year," Coach Smith said.

"Yes sir! I'm ready," he turns to watch the receiving team as he anxiously awaits his turn to get into action.

Regis kicks the ball and J.J. is the player that catches it and runs it all the way to the 20 yard line.

"Okay offense … let's go!" Coach Smith yells.

Carlos runs out to the field and huddles up the team.

"Okay boys, this is it. We're starting with a slant to Harv. Twenty-two slant to Harv on one."

"Let's go!" They all chant before jogging to the line of scrimmage.

"You're going down this time Swavey!" yells a Regis defensive lineman.

Carlos heard him well, but refused to reply to his comment. Deep inside he's thinking otherwise. He is about to show Regis what he's made of.

"Down! Set! Hut!"

Carlos drops back into the pocket – he sees Harv cut to the opposite side of the outside linebacker's direction. He fires a pass right into Harv's hands. They pick up 15 yards on the play. His hands are numb and the motion seems to be a step slower because of the temperature.

It's first down and ten – the Cougars fire another pass, this time to J.J. on a post pattern. He's brought down hard with a solid hit – *bam*! J. J. gets up very slowly. Jason of Regis is looking at him, "Take two aspirin in the morning, you'll feel better."

Gervais is at the Regis 40 yard line. The next two passes are incomplete. The ball bounces out of Harv's hands in one play. In another play, the ball hit J.J. on his facemask. He turns right as Carlos rifled the ball at him. His reaction was not fast enough.

It's third down and 10 yards to go for a first down.

"Come on y'all those are good passes – I can't catch it for you," Carlos said.

"My hands are numb – I'm freezing," J.J. said.

"Let's try a hook to J.J. 31 hook to J.J. on two."

They walk up to the line of scrimmage. You can see their breaths creating a white steam because of the cold weather.

"Down! Set! Hut! Hut!"

Carlos drops back and as he turns to throw the ball he catches a defender coming right at him. He puts his head down and runs forward to avoid the sack. He scrambles to the left and sees J.J. on the hook pattern. He zooms it right at his stomach. J.J. makes the reception at the Regis 10 yard line. The Gervais crowd goes crazy!

"Whoo! Alright! Go Cougars!"

The Cougars line up again. With only two receivers going out for a pass, everyone else stays to block. Carlos put the football on the right corner of the end zone. Harv reaches out with his two hands and snatches the football as he falls out-of-bounds. One foot lands inbounds. The Cougars score a touchdown! The crowd is jumping up and down and a loud noise is heard all over Civic Stadium.

The game is now tied at 7 – 7. By halftime the score is Regis 21, and Gervais 7. Carlos threw his fourth interception of the year. On one play he was getting ready to unload the ball to Harv on an out pattern. He got blindsided by the defensive end while his arm was in a forward motion. The ball popped up into the hands of a Regis defender.

Both teams start for the locker room – a nice warm place to get out of the cold for a bit. The fans are cuddling next to each other with blankets. Some are walking over to the concession stand to buy some hot chocolate. One thing about a football game in the cold weather is that the hotdogs, chocolate, and coffee taste better than ever.

The Gervais football team is looking a little down in the dressing room. It's very quiet in there. You can hear a few coughs and sniffles. Some of the players that get more playing time are still breathing hard. Carlos, Dirk, Harv, Hector, and J.J. are sitting together on one of the benches.

"We gotta win this guys!" Dirk said.

"Yeah, come on, we can do it," Harv adds.

Carlos turns to look at them for a few minutes, and then he shakes his head up and down. Coach Terry Smith walks in after meeting with his coaching staff.

"Gentlemen, we're fourteen points down. How bad you want this game is entirely up to you. I know it's cold, but they're just as cold as you are. Clifford, I'm putting you at wide receiver. J.J. needs the break – we'll alternate you two. Carlos, let's go with short quick passes. We're not giving you enough time to throw the ball."

The coach went over some plays and continues talking to them about some of the things they can do to have a better second half. When he concludes his talk, he stands up from where he is sitting.

"Let's go out there and give one hundred percent!"

"Yes sir!" the team replies.

"Let's go Cougars," some cheer.

The second half is going to be a battle. There's no choice but to have Carlos play both ways – defense and offense. He's the only one that can stay with Jason. It's a long second half once the game gets going. Some players are coming out of the game because of injuries or just to warm up their hands. There are more punts because of the tough defenses – both teams seem to be evenly matched.

The Cougars manage to narrow the gap, 21 – 14, with two minutes remaining in the game.

"Timeout!" Carlos yells.

Gervais is sitting at the 50 yard line. It's third down and five yards to go for a first down.

"Carlos, listen carefully. Pull the guard and the tackle on the left side. Run a 32 veer. Okay?"

"Got it coach."

Carlos calls the play in the huddle and they march to the line of scrimmage.

"Down! Set! Hut! Hut! Hut!"

Jeremy, the fullback, gets the ball with four linemen blocking for him. They drive toward the weak side of the Regis defense. He gets eight yards – enough for a Gervais first down. Once again the Gervais crowd goes wild. The clock is ticking with 59 seconds left in the game.

They line up quickly. Carlos waits until his team is all set before signaling the play. They are running a hurry-up offense.

"Down! Set!"

J.J. runs an in-and-out pattern as he heads to the left sideline. Carlos fires a bullet pass. Despite his numb hand, J.J. stumbles a bit but manages to catch the ball as he runs out-of-bounds. He's able to stop the clock with 30 seconds left in the game.

"I can't watch, this is too intense," Elaine says up in the stands.

"I know what you mean. Come on Carlos!" Liz yells.

"Yeah, let's go Cougars!" Lorraine adds.

"42 yards to go for a touchdown. – you can do it!" Ted yells.

Carlos gets to huddle-up his team because of the clock stopping on the out-of-bounds play.

"29 reverse on two!" Carlos yells due to the crowd noise.

"Down! Set! Hut! Hut!"

Carlos hands the ball to the halfback. The halfback runs to the left. Clifford runs the opposite way – to the right. Clifford gets the handoff from the halfback and sprints to a little daylight. A shocking surprise appears in Clifford's vision. Jason, from Regis, spears him hard – *pop*! His helmet flies off and blood starts running out of his nose. He made it to the Regis eight yard line – first and goal with six seconds showing on the clock.

"Timeout! Timeout!" Carlos yells.

The clock runs down to three seconds before the officials signal a timeout.

"Come on Ref! Give us three seconds back – you're a little late!" Coach Smith argues. The officials just smile and shake their heads.

Clifford gets up slowly and runs to the sideline so the trainer can take a look at him. He took a pretty hard hit and is shaken up. Carlos runs over to the sideline to talk it over with the coach.

"Run a draw, if it's not there, find the hole and run it in as hard as you can. My advice to you is pass it quick if you see someone, otherwise, run for it."

"Okay coach," Carlos runs back to the huddle.

"Alright y'all, right draw on one."

The fans are all up on their feet cheering for the Cougars as the offensive team walks to the line of scrimmage. The freshman quarterback is under a lot of pressure.

"Down! Set! Hut!"

Carlos drops back about eight steps to prepare for the draw play. Regis has more than five linemen coming in on the rush. He looks for a hole but there's nothing there. He looks at the end zone. Harv is standing there just inside the goal-line. Carlos throws the football just as he gets clobbered by the linebacker and two defensive tackles. He doesn't see what happens, smothered under three Regis players. He can hear the roar coming from the Gervais side. Harv catches the ball for a touchdown! He did just what Carlos taught him in the backyard – keep your eyes on the football.

The score is now, 20 – 21, Gervais is down one point. The coach uses his last timeout. Pat McGoldrick is consulting with Coach Smith.

"Let's go for it coach. I think Carlos can either run it in on the rollout or pass it for a score," McGoldrick said.

Carlos makes his way to the sideline very slowly after getting pounded.

"That's risky, I don't know. I'd feel safer with overtime," Coach Smith said.

"If we go into overtime, I'd hate to see Regis get the ball. We can put the game away here on the conversion," McGoldrick insists.

Terry Smith is thinking with his hand under his chin and his head tipped down."

"Okay, let's go for it! Carlos, you okay?"

"Yeah, I'll live, what do you want me to do?"

"Roll out to the left and send J.J. to the right corner. Get it to him, he'll be open."

"I'll try my best coach." Carlos is tired and is gasping for air.

He runs back out to the field and huddles up with the team.

"Okay, let's go for the win. Roll out left J.J. slant right on two."

This is it, one final play for the win. Gervais will either be state champions, or runner up.

"Down! Set! Hut! Hut!"

Carlos rolls out to the left with a trail of Regis defenders that break through the offensive shield. He plants himself, turns, and sees J.J. all alone. Peripheral vision sometimes doesn't help, he sees Jason of Regis coming at him hard. Carlos unloads the football as quick as he can toward the right corner of the end zone. J.J. is running and turning his head waiting for the ball. The ball is soaring through the air with a beautiful spiral. J.J. knows he needs to jump to catch it. They had practiced this play over and over all week long.

J.J. jumps up high and as the ball lands in his hands the defensive back hits him hard – *whack*! The ball gets knocked out of his hands. J.J. lands on his back but lady luck couldn't have come at a better time. The ball landed on him without touching the ground! It's a touchdown for Gervais! They connected on a two-point conversion and Gervais wins! 22 – 21. The crowd goes wild – the Gervais Cougars are the Oregon State Champions! Carlos runs over to J.J. and the entire team follows to congratulate him on a great catch.

Liz and Lorraine are jumping up and down with excitement. Ted and Elaine are smiling and taking in all of the excitement.

Never had they been in this position before – having a son and a good friend playing in a big-time game.

The coaches are smiling and celebrating. Coach Smith looks over at McGoldrick.

"Coach, thanks for the suggestion to go for it – nice call," he shakes his hand.

"I'm glad it worked out. I might have been out of a job next year if it didn't."

Carlos looks up at the stands as he walks back to the locker room with the team. He is trying to find Liz, but with so many people it's very difficult. Just to get one look at her and maybe a wave would make his evening. Civic Stadium is huge, plenty larger than a high school football stadium.

"Carlos! … Carlos!" Liz yells as loud as she can.

He finally sees her waving to him. He waves back with a smile on his face. His shiny white teeth are visible as his smile gets bigger. There's something about the water in Texas that makes teeth nice and strong – perhaps the minerals or something.

"Mom I wish I could get down there to give him a big hug," Liz said.

"Well, I don't think we can make it down there with all of the people in the way."

"Yeah, it's a long way down there," Lorraine said.

"Harv!" Lorraine tries to get Harv's attention.

"Let's just go down there, they'll wait for us," Ted said.

The entire football team is hanging out on the north end of the football field as people come down to congratulate them. Carlos and Harv notice Liz and Lorraine making their way down to the field.

After a long while, they finally make it through the crowd. Liz runs to Carlos and gives him the biggest hug ever.

"I'm so proud of you. You were great!"

"Thanks Liz, it feels really great to win a title."

Ted and Elaine are talking to Harv for awhile. They show all the signs of being proud happy parents. After that, they walk over to congratulate Carlos on a fine job.

"Congratulations Carlos, you played a heck of a game."

"Thanks Mr. Bradford. Not bad for a Hispanic kid from Texas huh?"

"Not at all," Ted chuckles.

"Dad! I owe this all to Carlos. He helped me all season long."

"What do you mean?" Ted asked.

"We got together after school, during practice, and in our backyard at midnight."

"You're kidding me?"

"Nope, it's no joke."

"Is that true Carlos?" Ted looks at him in a surprised way.

"Yes sir, it's true. You have a hardworking son that wants to win."

"I'm proud of you son. You two should have come to me sooner, I could have made it easier for you."

"It's okay Dad. It all worked out fine. It was kind of fun sneaking around too," he smiles.

Liz starts walking next to Carlos as he heads toward the tunnel leading to the locker rooms.

"My birthday's coming up next week, want to come?" Liz asked.

"I'll check my schedule, I'm sure it's open."

"Very funny. It's Sunday at 2 p.m. – don't be late Mr.," Liz said.

"Okay Miss I won't."

After talking to some other people that were congratulating him he comes back to Liz and looks at her for a moment.

"I wanna thank ya for all your support. The help you gave me in algebra was amazing, plus coming to all my games. That meant a lot to me."

"I enjoyed every minute of the adventure. I'm really sorry your parents didn't make it to the game," Liz looks at him in a sad way.

"That's okay, I'm used to it. They get really tired from work and all – I think they look forward to getting the rest."

"I feel bad that your family struggles financially. It's not fair. I don't understand life sometimes. But just understand that I view you for how you treat me, and not by how much money you have. I hope you feel the same about me," Liz said.

"Yeah, well I gotta get in the locker room before coach hunts me down. I'll see ya later."

Carlos hustles through the tunnel and makes his way to the locker room. He opens the door and is surprised by his teammates.

"Carlos! Carlos! Carlos!" The entire team chants his name.

"Okay! Okay! Settle down gentlemen!" Coach Smith shouts out.

He takes a moment and looks at all of the players.

"I know that we acquired a special young man this year. But don't forget that you all played as a team this year. I love all of you guys. I can't remember the last time Gervais football won a state title, but today we are the state champions!"

"Yeah!" The entire team shouts.

Harv walks over to Carlos and shakes his hand.

"Hey man, thanks for your help. If it wasn't for you I'd still be sitting the bench. I don't know how I can ever repay you."

"You already have. My grade point average is about a 3.0 – I couldn't have done it without your help. Thanks."

Clifford, Dirk, J.J., Hector, and some of the other players join Carlos and Harv. They start talking about some of the exciting plays of the game. It is pretty late before they all get showered and dressed. They are all moving slow carrying their gear into the bus. They head out of Portland onto I-5 South. The freeway is not so busy late at night.

When they arrive at Gervais High School, they are surprised by a pack of people waiting to greet them. It's unbelievable – this night will be a night that the entire team will remember forever.

After a long night, Carlos makes it home at 12:30 a.m. He walks to the front door of his house. It's locked and everyone is asleep. He starts knocking. Pete comes to the door rubbing his eyes. He looks sleepy but continues to walk slowly toward the door.

"Did you win?" Pete asked.

"Yeah we did. It was a great game."

"State champs huh?"

"I'm tired Dad, goodnight."

"Goodnight son."

Carlos can not figure out why his parents never seemed to get involved with his school activities. Were his parents uncomfortable to be around people? Did they feel embarrassed because they were very poor? He wanted them to be proud of him for his accomplishments. It didn't matter how many times he invited them to come watch his games. They always had something more important to do, or needed the rest.

He finally accepted the fact that his parent's culture is a little different than most white people. And he had been around a lot of white people in his days.

Carlos knows that he wants to get an education to not end up like his parents. He doesn't understand why they never got a decent education. Was it because of their parents and how they were influenced? Were they too caught up on labor jobs and never realized they could have landed a better job with a better education? He didn't know the answer and his parents never talked about it. He fell asleep thinking about all those possibilities.

The woodstove is on most of the night, it helps keep the house warm. Pete does a good job keeping it going all night with the wood he chops. He gets scraps from factories that toss the wood in the back alleys. He hauls the wood with the trailer he hooks up to the car.

Lydia and Mike are out later than Carlos. They went to the game to support their brother, who was the big star of the night. He racked up 300 yards passing including the winning touchdown pass to J.J. that put Gervais in a position to win the game. They didn't go down to the field after the game and Carlos did not see them before falling asleep that night.

Birthday Party

Monday has arrived once again. The algebra class is about to start. Carlos, Dirk, and Harv are walking a little slow – it's due to the hard game they played. The bruises a football player gets normally take a few days to heal. In the championship game, Carlos took a very hard hit from a big guy. He'll be sore for a week.

"Congratulations on a great game Saturday," the teacher said.

"Thanks coach," Carlos replied.

"What are you going to do next? Do you play basketball?"

"It's one of my favorite sports," Carlos said.

"That's great. Good luck with it, and remember keep your grades up."

"I definitely will, thanks."

Liz looks at Carlos across the classroom and smiles at him. He returns the smile. After a long class session, and sometimes classes in high school can be long and boring, they meet in the hall. They walk together elbow-to-elbow.

In the school hallway Liz is talking about her event coming up. She has a great big smile on her face and a striking gleam in her eyes.

"I can't wait until Saturday," Liz said.

"Oh yeah? Big birthday party at the Bradfords huh?" Carlos responds.

"If you want, come over earlier. Lorraine will be there early too. My dad will be okay with that."

"Sounds like a plan to me," Carlos responds.

Harv catches up with Carlos.

"Hey Carlos, are you going out for basketball?"
"Does my name start with a C?"
"Sounds like a yes to me."
"It's one of my favorite sports, friend," Carlos smiles.
"What position do you play?" Harv asked.
"No positions on the wooden bench."
"Ha-ha!" Harv laughs.
"I play the point, the number one position."
"That doesn't surprise me," Harv said.
"When are tryouts?"
"Next week."
"I'll be ready. I'm helping your sister – she wants to tryout for the girl's team."
"She's always wanted to play but never really had the encouragement," Harv said.
"I'll do the best I can to help her out."
"She'll appreciate that even if she doesn't make the team," Harv said.
"She'll make the team, I have confidence in her."
Later that day, on a Monday evening, Harv is discussing what Liz would like for her birthday with his dad.
"I think she wants a car since she just got her driver's license."
"Does she talk of any specific kind or model," Ted asked.
"I know she's always liked the Corvettes," Harv replied.
"Do you know what year and color she likes?"
"That's easy, a 1961 light blue and white. She likes the older models."
I think I know where I can get one. It'll need painting. I'll also have the engine rebuilt."
"She'll flip Dad."
"Well, I'm proud of her – she has a 4.0 GPA and has done many things that would make any parent proud."
"Ted, don't you think that's a little too much for a sixteen year-old girl?" Elaine asked.
"Not for my little girl. I think she's shown me how responsible she can be."
"How's that going to make Carlos feel?" Elaine is concerned.

"Look Elaine, I'm not responsible for Carlos' feelings … and I can't help that he isn't as fortunate as Liz."

"Okay, I'm just putting my two cents in – I don't think it's a good idea. But you do what you think is best," Elaine said.

"Good, then it's settled. Not a word to Liz about this, I want it to be a surprise."

Ted immediately gets on the phone and calls his friend Shamus. His friend has all kinds of connections with car dealers and mechanics. He can get this car, have it painted and purring like a kitten in no time. The Corvette will basically be a brand new car with an old body style.

Elaine isn't too thrilled about the idea, but she knows her husband is determined to do this and nothing is going to change his mind.

Liz is at Lorraine's house when her birthday present is being discussed and has no clue. It is definitely going to be a shock and a surprise at the same time.

Carlos is sitting at home thinking of what he can possibly get Liz for her birthday. Mr. Lind has music boxes at the Gervais Market. He thought maybe he could get a discount on one of them.

The next day after school, he walks to the Gervais Market. He's scheduled to work for two hours stocking shelves. During his break, he stops at the shelf that displays music boxes.

"Which one do you like?" Mr. Lind asked.

"It's not for me," Carlos smiled.

"I figured that – you getting it as a gift for someone?"

"Yes sir."

"Well, I'll tell you what I can do. I can sell it to you at cost if you'd like."

"Really?"

"Yeah, you've done a great job for me. Just pick the one you want."

Carlos takes a moment, then selects one off the shelf.

"Now get back to work." He winks at Carlos and walks to the back of the store.

The music box he picks is a very beautiful pink piece. It's about six inches long, three inches wide, and three inches high.

Carlos opens it and he hears a tune. The tune is from a song by the Bee Gees called, "How Deep Is Your Love." The lyrics to that song are the perfect fit to his relationship with Liz.

He closes the music box and walks to the back room.

"Mr. Lind?"

"Yes Carlos."

"How much is that music box gonna cost me?"

"You work for me an extra hour tonight and it'll be yours at no cost. I'm a little behind on stocking today."

"I'll do it. Thanks a lot, I'll make sure all the merchandise is stocked before I leave." He returns to stocking shelves.

After work, Carlos walks home carrying the music box in a sack. He enters his house. Lydia and Mike are looking at him and naturally become curious of what he has in the store bag. When a family is poor and someone walks in with a store bag, naturally everyone will be very curious.

"What'd you buy?" Lydia asked.

"Yeah, what's in the sack?" Mike asked.

"You probably bought Liz a birthday present," Lydia said.

"How'd you know?" Carlos said.

"Oh, talk at school. I heard she's only inviting her special friends," Lydia said.

"Why do you even spend money on that white girl? It's people like you that give Hispanics a bad name," Mike jumps in.

"Mike, I wish you would get off my case. Her name is Liz, not white girl. If anyone's giving Hispanics a bad name, it's you."

"Whatever dude," Mike starts to leave the room.

"There ya go, you're not even bright enough to remember my name."

Mike comes back and is headed straight to Carlos with his fists.

"Hey! Hey! Y'all are brothers – calm down," Lydia steps between them."

"Punk! You need a girl to protect you," Mike says as he leaves.

"Don't listen to Mike. I think that's sweet that you're buying her a gift. What'd you get her?"

Carlos takes the music box out of the bag and hands it to Lydia.

"A music box, that's very nice. She'll love it. Girls like music boxes."

"I hope so. And thanks for stepping in front of Mike and me – he owes you a thank you," Carlos responds.

"How much did it cost?"

"My boss gave it to me for an extra hour of work, so I guess an hour of work."

"Music boxes like this cost about twenty-five dollars or so – very nice."

"Really?" His eyes open wide.

"Yes, really. Oh my gosh! There's a huge scratch on it!" Lydia says.

"Oh no!"

"Just kidding," Lydia starts laughing.

"Thanks a lot," Carlos rolls his eyes.

She hands it back to him and he runs up the steps to his bedroom in the attic. Carlos turns the light on and gets ready for bed while observing the music box a little more.

It's Friday, the day before Liz's birthday. Her birthday falls on December, 6th. The weather is cool with a clear sky and a light breeze. The forecast shows that the pattern will continue through the weekend.

In the school hallway there's a group of girls around Liz and Lorraine.

"What kind of things do you have planned for your birthday on Saturday?" Lorraine asked.

"I'm thinking … um … desserts and plenty of games. I'm having my birthday party in the recreation room," Liz said.

"That sounds pretty stupid and boring to me," Shawna looks at Liz.

"Shawna, that's a really nice dress you have on – too bad they didn't have your size."

"Ha-ha-ha!" Kalin busted out laughing.

"You just wait Bradford … and you, Kalin, you sound like a laughing hyena," Shawna walks away as the girls laugh.

"I don't know why Shawna is so rude. That sounds like a lot of fun Liz," Kalin said.

"I'd like to come over tonight to help decorate," Lorraine insisted.

"That would be great – ask your mom if you can stay over tonight," Liz said.

"Okay, I'm sure it'll be fine. Kalin, you're welcome to come as well."

"Count me in – I'll be there," Kalin said as she walks off to class.

Liz and Harv are fraternal twins, but they usually celebrated on different weekends to make it special for both of them. Harv is mostly interested in going somewhere for his birthday. One year his parents took the family to Disneyland to celebrate his birthday. Another year they went to a Seattle Seahawk's football game.

Meanwhile back at the Swaveys, on a Saturday morning, things get a little depressing.

"What's for breakfast?" Carlos asked as he walks down the attic steps.

"Eggs and toast – enjoy it because that's all you get," Isabel said.

"Why so sad Mom?"

"Oh, I just found out that I'm being laid off at the plant."

"I'm real sorry to hear that Mom."

"Your dad has a job for awhile longer. We just don't know how much longer."

Carlos can see the disappointment on her face. She's almost in tears.

"We're gonna have to be careful about where we spend our money. I'm worried about Christmas. This might be our first Christmas without presents," Isabel said.

"Mom, it's okay. It'll all work out," Carlos said.

"I'll just have to pray that it does, money's tight right now."

Carlos immediately changes the subject to avoid his mom from getting too down.

"Mom, I'm going to a birthday party – it starts at two."

"Whose birthday is it?"

"Liz's."

"Wish her a happy birthday for me and make sure your dad knows too."

"Okay."

"I need to talk to Mike about his negative attitude toward Liz … just because she's white."

"Yeah, please. That would really be nice," Carlos agrees.

"Liz and her brother, Harv, seem like nice kids," Isabel said.

"They both helped me bring my grades up in school. Countless hours those two spent with me hitting the books. I owe them so much."

"Carlos, why don't you tell people about things like that? We had no idea."

"Well, it's a deal that Harv and I worked out before I played my first game here at Gervais. I helped him with football skills and he helped me with my studies – brought my grades way up."

"What! That's great! Good grades are very important."

"Yeah, and my coach thinks I have a chance for a college scholarship."

"Did you tell your dad?"

"I tried, but he doesn't understand. He thinks I'm wasting my time."

"Well, he's wrong. Keep going with that – your education is very important."

Isabel grabs a few dishes and walks to the kitchen to wash them. Carlos walks back up to his room for some cleaning and then listens to some good old 70's music. He begins to work on his homework to get that done as well.

The time has come for Carlos to hop on his bike and ride over to the big birthday party. He's wearing jeans with a t-shirt that reads, "Gervais Football." He looks very handsome and clean cut. He wants to look his best for the girl of his dreams. The bottom part of one leg has a thick rubber band wrapped around it – to prevent the chain from snagging his pants.

When he arrives at the Bradford's house, Liz is at the door waiting for him.

"Hey girl, happy birthday!" he shouts as he rides to the door.

Carlos hops off his bike and hands her the gift, which is wrapped up in some nice bright pink paper.

"Wow! Thank you. You didn't have to get me anything," Liz said.

"That's not my style. I hope you like it," Carlos said.

"I can't wait to open it."

The parents are preparing all of the desserts. They have soda, punch, fruits, cookies, and cake. The kids are all having fun in the recreation room.

Lorraine and some of the other girls from school are there. Harv invited some of his friends from the football team as well. Some of the kids are playing pool and some are playing ping-pong. There's also social people who are just talking the whole time. Everyone is smiling and enjoying the Bradfords' house.

As the party starts to wind down, Elaine comes into the recreation room.

"It's time to sing Happy Birthday to the birthday girl!"

Liz starts blushing as they sing to her. Being in that position is kind of strange to some people, but some people relish the moment. Liz is a little embarrassed, but living up the moment.

After she blows the candles out from the huge cake, everyone claps and whistles. The kids line up to get a piece of cake while Liz gets ready to open her presents.

"Open your presents Liz!" Lorraine says.

"Wait a minute, I will," Liz smiles.

She starts out by opening Carlos' gift to her.

"Oh my goodness! This is so special – I love this tune. Thank you so much Carlos," Liz hugs him and demonstrates a big smile.

She continues opening presents for the next thirty minutes. When she's done, Ted looks at her.

"Liz, are you ready for one more from your mom and I?"

"Yes! Where is it?"

"Okay, let's go outside," Ted said.

She follows him outside. Behind them is a line of her friends following.

Liz steps out to the front of the house.

"Where is it?"

"Walk around the house and you'll see your present. I couldn't get enough wrapping paper," Ted said.

Liz walks around the side of the house and her friends follow. Carlos is right behind her.

"Oh wow! I must be dreaming."

She stood there speechless for a few seconds. She turns and looks at her parents.

"Mom and Dad, how can I ever thank you. This is more than I can ever imagine. Thank you so much I love you both."

"Just remember, the keys can be taken away just as easy. We trust that you'll be a very responsible lady," Ted said.

Carlos is not surprised at the gift she got. Observing how excited and full of joy she is made him feel great.

"Can I take it for a drive Dad?"

"Of course, it's all yours," he replies.

"Carlos, you want to come?"

"Yeah, I'd love to."

"Don't stay too long," Elaine said.

"Okay we'll be right back Mom."

She starts up the car. The engine has a perfect hum. The shiny paint reflects the light rays coming from the house. She starts backing up and turns the wheel, then shifts into drive and hops onto the highway. On a clear night the ride is full of pleasure, and to have someone like Carlos sharing that experience makes Liz very happy.

"Liz, I'm so happy for you. It's really nice to see you smile so much."

"Everything is great for me right now, but without you here it wouldn't be as great," she turns and looks at Carlos momentarily.

"That's really nice of you to say that."

"Thank you for the music box. I'll cherish it forever and ever."

"You are very welcome. Wow … a 1961 Corvette!"

Carlos is looking at Liz while she keeps her eyes on the road – her light red hair with blue eyes. He feels very lucky that a girl like Liz has any kind of interest in a poor Hispanic kid like him. "Bless her heart," he thinks to himself.

The Kidnapping

While Liz and Carlos are out taking the Corvette for a ride, Lorraine's mom stops by for a bit to drop off a gift. She is also picking up Lorraine.

"Where's Liz?" Lorraine's mom, Laura Fletch asked?

"Oh, she took her birthday present for a drive," Elaine said.

"By herself?"

"No, she took Carlos with her."

"Is she still hanging around that Mexican kid?"

"Laura, he's a nice boy and he's not from Mexico – he's from Texas."

"It's all the same to me, he's got brown skin."

"If you got to know him you'd think different."

"No thanks, keep me away from those Mexicans. I don't want to have anything to do with them. Come on Lorraine let's go. Be sure to tell Liz I said happy birthday."

"Sure thing Laura, and thanks for coming Lorraine," Elaine said.

"Bye Mrs. Bradford, tell Liz I'll see her tomorrow."

"Okay, we'll do. Bye." Elaine shuts the door and returns to the cleanup party.

They drive off in their fully loaded car.

Lorraine has her hand pressed against her head. Her arm is resting on the side of the door. She looks very disappointed.

"What's a matter with you Lorraine?"

Lorraine does not answer – she's ignoring her mom.

"Do you want a car too?" her mom asked.

"No ... I just think it's very rude of you to say mean things about Carlos. Do you realize I got invited to Liz's birthday party?"

"Now you listen to me you spoiled little brat! Just because that kid has the Bradfords fooled, doesn't mean he has me fooled."

"Why are you like that?"

"Like what?"

"Why do you hate a nice boy like Carlos?"

"Don't talk to me like that. I'm protecting you from getting mixed up in trouble!" She looks at Lorraine for second.

"Stop the car and drop me off! I'd like to walk the last mile!" Lorraine yells. "Fine! ... go ahead!" Laura stops the car in the middle of nowhere. Lorraine steps off and swings the door shut – *slam*! She starts walking to her house in the dark. You can see her house from a far distance. The outside lights are all on.

Her mom steps on the gas and drives fast toward the house.

"She wants to walk, she can walk," Laura talks to herself.

After an hour of waiting for Lorraine to arrive, Laura begins to worry.

"It shouldn't take her an hour to walk one mile," she thinks to herself.

Laura is pacing back and forth in the living room, looking out of the front window. She sees nothing. There is no sign of Lorraine. Her heart is pounding and she's beginning to feel very nervous.

Laura decides to get back in her car and go look for her. She's driving down the road looking everywhere. She has a flashlight to shine toward the sides. She opens her window.

"Lorraine! ... Lorraine! ... where are you? I'm sorry I didn't mean it!"

After shouting for awhile, she returns home and tells her husband, Silas Fletch, about the whole incident.

"I'll go drive around – see if I can find her. You call the Bradfords – she might have gone back there," Silas said.

Silas is a tall man that owns a business. He is very successful and he drives a brand new Toyota Four Wheel Drive.

Liz and the group of friends have just finished cleaning up the house. The phone rings at the Bradfords.

"Hello," Elaine answers the phone.

"Elaine, this is Laura."

"Hi Laura."

"Is Lorraine there?"

"No, I haven't seen here since she left with you."

"We got into an argument and she got out of the car and started walking."

"Oh my gosh! I'll ask the kids if they've heard from her. I'll call you back if I find out anything."

"Thank you so much Elaine."

"I'll get right to that, Bye."

She runs over to the recreation room where Harv, Liz, and Carlos are playing air hockey.

"Hey kids, we have an emergency."

They all stop for a moment, and the attention is all focused on Elaine.

"Lorraine is missing."

"What!" Liz said.

"Has she called here?" Elaine asked.

"No, we've been here the whole time," Harv said.

Elaine explains the situation to the three.

"Let's go look for her," Carlos said.

"Good idea, but be careful out there," Elaine said.

The three run out of the front door and hop into the Corvette. They drive off to start the hunt. Ted and Elaine take the truck and head out as well.

Back at the Fletchs' house, Laura is thinking to a strain. She seems very worried.

"I think we should call the police, it's just not like her to disappear like that."

"That wouldn't hurt. I'm afraid they would say that we need at least twenty-four hours before they can start a search."

"I'm calling anyway," Laura said.

The phone rings at the police station.

"This is the Gervais Police Department, how can I help you?"

"Our daughter's missing, we need your help."

"Calm down, whom am I talking to?"

"This is Laura Fletch, and my daughter's name is Lorraine."

"When was the last time you saw her?"

"Officer, we had an argument. She decided to get off of the car and walk to our house. It's been an hour and a half."

"Well, I'm afraid we can't really start a search until twenty-four hours from now. She'll probably call you or turn up soon. I'll send an officer out there to look in the mean time."

"Officer, you don't understand – this is my daughter we're talking about."

"That's usually what they all say Mrs. Fletch. I wish I could do more for you. Call us back in twenty-two and a half hours. If she doesn't show up we'll get the search crew together."

"Okay, thanks for nothing."

"Talk to you later Mrs. Fletch," the officer hangs up the phone.

"Can you believe that Silas?"

"I told you that's what they'd say. Now let's go look for her – time is crucial."

"Silas, I'm not in a mood for, I told you so."

"Let's just go Laura, we can argue later."

Meanwhile, Liz is driving pretty fast stopping at every house. They are asking every neighbor down the road for clues. Carlos steps out of the car to ask another home owner. He knocks on the door firmly. An old man opens the door.

"What can I do for you?"

"Hi sir, we're looking for a girl. She's about 5' 6", medium build, with blonde hair. Have ya seen her or noticed anything that might help us?"

"Well, I did see something about an hour and a half ago. I heard a scream that came from that direction over there."

"Did you see the kind of car it was?" Carlos asked.

"A yellow old beat-up truck – it peeled off. I thought it was the same young kids that race from time to time. I'm afraid that's all I can tell you."

"Did you see which direction they went?"

"Yeah, it turned on the road up the hill – where the evergreens are bunched up. I thought that was strange – never seen that before."

"Thank you sir, you've been a big help."

"Good luck!" yelled the old man as Carlos runs back to the car.

"Let's go! The old man said he heard a scream awhile back. He saw a yellow old beat-up truck go up that hill – over there," Carlos points in the direction.

"Did he say anything else?" Harv asked while Liz steps on the pedal.

"Yeah, he said he heard a scream," Carlos replied.

"Man I hope Lorraine's okay," Harv said.

Liz is a great driver. She has years of practice around the farm roads. She turns into the small dirt road that leads up to the hill. The forest surrounding them is pitch-black. The only lights they have are the car lights.

"Maybe we should go call the police," Liz said.

"Based on my experiences, the police will come too late... probably need at least twenty-four hours before they do anything," Carlos said.

"That's true we can't wait for them," Harv added.

"Look! … way up there. It's a small house with a dull light. Pull over and turn the car off," Carlos said.

Liz pulls over to the side of the small dirt road and turns the car off. They get out of the car. Carlos walks to the backside of the car.

"Liz, hand me your keys so I can open the trunk." Liz walks over to him with the keys.

"There's gotta be a flashlight somewhere," Carlos said as he looks in the trunk.

"Look in that bag under the tire," Liz said.

"Yes, a small travel flashlight and it works." He turns the flashlight on.

The flashlight is light blue with white lines to match the car color.

"Okay, I'll take this crowbar in case we need it – lock the car," Carlos said.

"What are you going to do with the crowbar?" Liz asked.

"I'm gonna bust the punk up – whoever it is."

"How did you know to look in the trunk for a flashlight?

"Oh, I guess being around my dad. He taught me a few things about cars and stuff."

"Let's stay together. Carlos, you lead since you have the flashlight," Harv said.

"Okay, sounds good. Be careful – don't step in any holes or traps on the ground. Let's go," Carlos said.

The young Texan has never experienced being in the dark woods. In Texas, he read forest and wildlife stories in the classroom. But he had never seen a real forest.

"This isn't the kind of hiking I had in mind in Oregon," Carlos said.

They move slowly on the trail that leads up to the small house – a very eerie feeling on unfamiliar territory.

"I'm getting a little scared," Liz said.

"Do you wanna go back? Harv and I can go up there."

"No, I want to help Lorraine." Liz looks worried.

The ground is damp and there is fog settling all around them. It's quiet with a few animal noises now and then.

"How much farther do you think we have to climb," Liz said as she follows.

"About another hundred yards or so, but I'd much rather be traveling that in a football field," Harv said.

"I hear you," Carlos agreed.

"This is so scary," Liz said as she holds on to Carlos' shirt from behind.

After walking up the forest hill for a half hour or so, they start hiding behind huge rocks and trees. They get closer to the old house. All three come together behind a big rock. The rock is wet from the moisture of the fog.

"Look!" Liz whispers loudly.

"Oh my goodness," Harv said.

Liz starts to get emotional – what she sees is very hurtful. Her best friend is tied up by her ankles with a big rope. Her hands are tied up behind her. She is hanging head down five feet up from the ground. There are chopped logs under her with big rocks around them – like a huge campfire being prepared. Lorraine seems to be on the menu.

"Some sick person in that cabin," Carlos said.

"What are we going to do?" Harv asked.

"Let's see who it is. Let's wait for a bit," Carlos said.

"Wait? That's Lorraine we're talking about," Harv is upset.

"Trust me on this. I need a baseball-size rock – help me look for one quick," Carlos insists.

"I'll help you Carlos," Liz answers.

"Harv, keep an eye out – let me know if anyone comes out of the cabin."

"Okay, but hurry – this is nerve-racking."

"Carlos, it's so dark. I can hardly see anything," Liz said.

"Here use the flashlight, I'll try to see out of the light ya shine," Carlos said.

They are searching everywhere, but everything seems to be too small or too large. They finally come to a batch of rocks of all sizes. They are scattered all over an old campfire someone left days ago.

"How about this one?" Liz turns and shows Carlos.

"That's too small. It has to be at least baseball size – that wouldn't hurt a flea."

"What do you envision doing?" Liz asked.

"I'm gonna throw it and hopefully hit this person on the head – just enough to stun the sorry idiot. I'm hoping this'll give us time to finish this freak-animal off."

"Can you guys hurry!" Harv whispers loudly in a worrying voice.

"I found one … look!" Liz whispers with excitement.

"That's it … perfect – good job Liz," Carlos puts his arm around her and takes the rock.

They return to where Harv is waiting behind the huge rock. It's very difficult for Harv to see his girlfriend hanging upside down and not moving much. He can tell she's crying with aching sounds now and then. Her clothes are smothered in dirt and mud from being dragged on the ground. Her face has red marks – she's a big mess.

"Have you seen anything Harv?" Liz asked.

"Yes, it's Crazy Lady Teresa. Remember that huge lady that escaped from the Oregon State Mental Hospital on Center Street?"

"Oh yeah, I remember reading about that," Liz said.

"She's gonna have a lot more mental problems when I get through with her," Carlos said angrily.

"She has a shotgun with her. I don't know about this," Harv said.

"Liz found a nice rock for me. Here's the plan, you take this crowbar. I'm gonna get a little closer. I need to be at least forty yards to get a good shot at her head or neck. I once won a box of apples hitting a sign fifty yards away," Carlos said.

"You what?" Harv and Liz both said at the same time.

"It's a long story … some other time."

"Yeah, well the way I've seen you throw the football gives me hope," Harv said.

"This is a little different. When I hit her, she'll go down hopefully. Then you run as fast as you can and smack her a few times on the body. Don't kill her but mess her up enough that we can tie her up."

"What do I do?" Liz asked.

"You run as fast as you can – untie Lorraine. I'll help Harv with Crazy Lady Teresa, and then we'll help you get Lorraine down."

"Shh! There she is," Harv said.

They can hear Crazy Teresa from afar. She mumbles to herself throwing more wood on top of the stack she already has.

"Please let me go!" Lorraine pleads as she hangs down in tears.

"It'll just be a matter of time until supper's ready you sweet little thing," Crazy Teresa said.

"Why are you doing this to me?" Lorraine asked.

"They think I'm crazy. They never listen to me. Well, now who's crazy?"

"What? What do you want?" Maybe I can help."

"No one can help me. But I can help myself to a nice home cooked meal. Ha-ha-ha!" The crazy lady looks at Lorraine.

Carlos and Harv are waiting and listening. Harv is waiting for Carlos to throw the rock.

"When are you going to throw it?"

"The angle is not quite right yet," Carlos observes.

"What do you mean?"

"Well, she needs to move a little farther from Lorraine and I'd like to be sure she's not gonna move suddenly."

"I see," Harv said.

Teresa starts to pour gasoline on the wood. She gets a match and strikes it against the matchbox to ignite the fire. She reaches down to light the soaked wood. The fire begins – *poof*! Crazy Teresa sits down on a stump to watch the fire under Lorraine.

"No! No! Help!" Lorraine is frightened.

Carlos sees that the opportunity won't be at a better time. He stretches his arm a bit to loosen it up. He's in focus with the target and visualizes where the rock will go when he throws it. He knows it has to be a direct hit the first time – it isn't just a wide receiver he is throwing to this time. A life is at stake and the pressure is intense. This is more than a state championship pass, or a game winning fast pitch.

Carlos looks over at Liz with the rock in his hand. She looks back at him with a worried look.

"You can do it Carlos, save my friend."

"Go for it man," Harv said.

Carlos shakes his head up and down as he bounces the rock up and down in his hand.

Crazy Lady Teresa has a cup of coffee in her hand as she prepares for the roasting of Lorraine.

"Lord, give me the strength to hit this target," Carlos silently prays.

He grips the rock firmly in his hand and concentrates on the target. He winds up, snaps his arm and flips his wrist releasing the rock – it is zooming at 90 miles per hour – *crack*! The rock smacked the side of Lady Teresa's head sending her down to the ground. She's lying there screaming in pain, "Eeee!" The coffee she is drinking flies off her hand and spills everywhere.

"Let's go Harv!"

"Oh … wow!" Harv is amazed and freezes for awhile.

"Harv! Come on! Let's go! Don't let her get that shotgun!" Carlos yells.

She is stunned enough that the boys have plenty of time to get there. She is starting to roll over to where the shotgun is. She's reaching over to grab the shotgun. Harv pounds her arm just in time – *kabang*!

"Ouch! Son of a bees wax! You rotten kid!" Teresa screams.

He smacks her on the legs a couple of times – *smack*! *smack*!

"Ouch! Eeeee!" She is stunned and can't move a muscle.

"Harv that's enough!" yelled Carlos.

"I hate her!" Harv said.

"I know, let's tie her up fast," Carlos said with the rope in his hands.

Liz is helping Lorraine. She is untying her to remove her from the flames.

"Harv, get some water to help put out that fire, I'll finish tying up this sorry sick lady."

The crazy lady is in pain, whining and squealing. Carlos is finishing the job by wrapping her feet together with some strong rope.

Liz is doing a fine job helping Lorraine calm down. She is embracing her while Harv helps get her down from the uncomfortable situation she's in. Lorraine is showing all signs of shock. She can't say anything at the moment. Her entire body is shaking – a nervous wreck.

"You're okay Lorraine – everything's going to be okay." Liz said calmly.

Lorraine's eyes are wide open looking over Liz's shoulder – as if someone's going to attack her again.

"I'll stay with Crazy Teresa. Y'all take Lorraine to the hospital emergency room and then call the police."

"Are you sure you don't want to come with us?" Liz asked.

"I wanna make sure this piece of trash doesn't get away before the police show up. Just make sure and tell them I'm here waiting."

"Okay, I love you Carlos, you did an amazing thing," Liz gives him a hug.

"Thanks Liz. I'll see y'all when ya get back."

"Okay, bye."

Harv puts Lorraine over his shoulder – one of the easiest ways to carry a person.

"Sorry Lorraine you're going have to hang in there a little longer while we get you to the car. I know you're probably tired of hanging." They all chuckle a bit.

"Yeah Lorraine, you'll have to hang out with us on the way to the car," Liz said trying to put more smiles on her face.

They all start chuckling and laughing – a relief from all of the excitement. They walk into the dark trail. The woods are so foggy that it makes it difficult to retrace the trail they used to get there.

Carlos is left behind with Crazy Lady Teresa. He preserves some of the fire so he can stay warm. He grabs some more wood and adds to the fire that burns. Carlos sits next to the warm fire, keeping his eyes on Crazy Teresa – she's a big lady and as strong as an ox.

"Why did you take Lorraine? Carlos asked.

She stares at him and doesn't say a word. After a few minutes she begins to struggle with the rope around her. She is trying to break herself loose but the rope is too strong.

"You're not getting out of that rope, that's a pretty strong rope and I double knotted it just about everywhere. Only Houdini can break loose from that."

"I'm a sick person," Teresa said.

"They say you escaped from the Oregon State Mental Hospital. Is that true?" Carlos asked.

"Please … no more questions," she said.

Crazy Teresa closed her eyes and blocked out everything. Carlos is tired but has to fight staying awake. The police will soon arrive and he will have a chance to relax a bit.

The time passed through the night – an hour had gone by. Carlos starts to doze off a little. He hears the sirens from a distance – a sigh of relief. Soon enough he hears the sound of vehicles driving up the trail. The sound gets louder and louder as they get closer to the scene.

"There they are!" the police officer said.

"You okay son?"

"Yeah I'm fine – a little cold and hungry but I'm fine," Carlos smiles.

"You're a hero. We heard the story – the newspaper wants to interview you."

Carlos had experienced interviews in the past, but nothing like this. He had to stay awake for a little while longer.

"Hey officer!" Carlos shouted.

"Yes," the policeman said.

"I'm concerned about Lorraine. How is she?"

"She's a little shook-up but I think she's going to be okay."

The officer paused for a bit to think.

"She might have to go to a few weeks of counseling to help her get over this terrible ordeal. She's young and full of life – she should come out okay."

"Thank you sir," Carlos said as he walks away.

He finds his way down the trail to the main road. Waiting for him are his parents, Pete and Isabel. The Bradfords are also there waiting.

"You okay son?" Pete asked.

"Yeah I'm fine – just a little startled by everything. It happened so fast."

"Carlos, we were so worried. Thank God you're okay. You did a brave thing tonight and I'm very proud of you," Isabel said.

"Mom, Dad, this is Mr. and Mrs. Bradford."

"We've already met them, they are very nice people," Isabel said.

"You have?" Carlos is surprised.

"Mr. Bradford has set up an appointment for us to meet Ginger. She might have a job for both of us."

"Wow, that's great Mom. I hope things work out."

"Come on, let's go," Pete said.

Carlos starts walking with his parents toward the old station wagon. He stops and turns to watch the Bradfords walk to their truck.

"Hey Mr. Bradford!"

"Yes Carlos."

"That's some birthday party you threw for your daughter. We could have done without the kidnapping though," he smiles.

They all start laughing and get into their vehicles.

Sunday morning after church, all of the people come up to Carlos and express their support on what he had done. He felt great knowing he had done something to save a good friend's life. When the family returns home, Carlos finds his way to his bedroom for a well deserved nap. He turns on the radio to listen to some pop music while he falls to sleep.

The phone rings after a short while.

"Carlos! Liz is on the phone," Lydia yells toward the attic.

Carlos stirs a bit realizing Lydia is calling for him.

"Okay! I'll be there in a sec," he answers.

He walks slowly down the steps. Lydia sets the phone down on the table.

Carlos makes his way to the phone and picks it up.

"Hello."

"Hi, how are you," Liz asked.

"Oh, I'm tired and sleepy."

"Well, when you're ready I have somewhere to take you today."

"That sounds good, how 'bout three or so?" Carlos asked.

"Great, I'll pick you up at your mansion at three."

"Ha-ha, we'll see you then," Carlos laughs sarcastically.

"You sound so cute when you're sleepy."

"Bye Liz."

Carlos walks back up to his room and takes another nap before getting ready for a big day.

Later in the day Liz drives up in her Corvette.

"Wow! Whose car is that?" Lydia asked.

"That's Liz's birthday present believe it or not," Carlos replied.

All Lydia could do is open her eyes wide and her mouth wide. She remained speechless for a bit.

Liz hops out of her car and shuts the door. Her hair shines on a sunny day. She wears a fitted light blue shirt with new fitted jeans. Around her neck is a necklace that glitters against the sun's reflection.

She knocks on the door three times and waits. Carlos opens the door.

"Nice car," Carlos said.

"Thank you."

Liz steps into a very small entry room.

"My dad's getting me a Porsche for my birthday," Lydia says.

"And then you'll wake up from your dream," Carlos laughs.

Liz smiled and didn't say much. Her smile said it all.

"You ready Carlos?" Liz asked.

"I was born ready."

"Y'all have fun in that nice Vette," Lydia said.

"Y'all have fun in that old Ford station wagon," Carlos laughs.

"Carlos that's mean," Liz said.

"You wash your car? It looks better than the other night up in the woods."

"That's an understatement."

"Where ya taking me?"

"You'll see."

They drove off with some of the neighbors staring at them. It's not often a car like that comes by this side of town. Carlos waves to them as they drive by.

After a short while Liz ends up on the road that leads to Lorraine's house.

"Hey, isn't this the way to Lorraine's house?"

"Yep."

She pulls into Lorraine's driveway. It's a big home – not as big as the Bradfords' home but awful close. They drive around a paved circular driveway and park in front of the house.

"I don't think Mrs. Fletch is gonna like this," Carlos said.

"Oh, I think she'll be flattered you're here. It was Lorraine's idea," Liz said.

The front door opens and Laura Fletch comes out to greet Carlos and Liz.

"Well hello Liz and Carlos – very nice of you to come by," Mrs. Fletch said.

"Hi Mrs. Fletch," Liz responded while Carlos said nothing standing behind Liz.

Laura looked at Liz and then she looks at Carlos for a moment.

"Carlos … before you come in to see Lorraine, I want to apologize for my negative behavior toward you the other night."

"Ma'am, there's really no need, but if you feel ya have to, apology accepted," Carlos said.

"I talked to my husband last night. If there's anything we can do for you to repay what you've done for us, please let us know. I've already written you a thank you letter – you should get it soon."

"There is one thing I would like from you Mrs. Fletch."

"You name it," she said.

"Well, this is kinda hard for me to say."

"Don't worry, it's okay. I'm all ears," Laura said.

"I would like it if you didn't judge people by their skin color. Also, don't judge people based on how much money they have. Some of us are more fortunate than others – that's life. But that doesn't mean the fortunate can't get along with the unfortunate."

"Carlos I'm sorry I made you feel bad," Laura said.

"You have a beautiful house and an amazing daughter. Obviously you're set pretty well. I've been blessed with a gift, being able to throw with amazing accuracy. This helped save your daughter's life. Does any of this make sense?" Carlos asked.

"It makes perfect sense – I never looked at it from that angle before."

Laura looked down for a bit and thought for a few moments.

"Mrs. Fletch, it's going to be okay. Can we see Lorraine now?" Liz puts her arm around her.

"Of course you can. We've set an appointment for her to get some counseling – she's afraid to go outside."

They walk inside following Laura toward Lorraine's bedroom.

"Lorraine, I miss you," Liz said as she embraces her.

"Hi Lorraine," Carlos said from a distance.

"Carlos, I can never thank you enough for saving my life. When the rock hit her I knew it had to be the Gervais quarterback. I'm so happy to know you."

"Lorraine, I'm really glad you're safe. Why are you afraid to go outside?" Carlos asked.

"I don't know, I guess because of the fear that it might happen again."

"Well, you don't have to worry anymore, they have that Crazy Teresa locked up at the Oregon State Mental Hospital."

"That doesn't help much in my mind," Lorraine looks down as she covers both eyes.

"Lorraine, if you want we can come outside with you," Liz said.

"Maybe another day, but not today," she shakes her head saying no.

"Okay, sure – maybe another day," Liz said.

They all look at Lorraine and can tell she is in sad shape. It's difficult seeing someone you care for in that situation.

"I've been getting these panic attacks. The doctor is helping me through all of this. I have these nightmares and can't sleep – I'm exhausted."

"I'm so sorry you have to go through this," Carlos said.

"I'll get through it – it'll just take time. You guys are already making me feel better. Liz, can you stay the night tonight?" Lorraine asked.

"Sure, I'll ask my mom. Carlos and I are going to Salem for a bit, after that I can come back. Harv said he's coming to see you later – he's worried about you."

"I look forward to seeing him. I owe all of you a big *thank you* for what you did for me – getting me out of that hanging mess."

"I can't believe that Carlos actually hit that crazy lady with that rock – that was pretty amazing," Liz said.

"The way he throws that football, it doesn't surprise me at all," Lorraine said.

"You can thank Liz, she found the perfect rock in the fog and wet forest. If it wasn't for her you might still be hanging down," Carlos said.

"Some of us get a second chance at life. I feel very blessed to have friends like you guys. Carlos you have changed my mom's heart to think differently about people. She feels really bad about the way she treated you last week. I hope you can find it in your heart to forgive her," Lorraine said looking at Carlos.

"She's forgiven. Tell her not to worry about it. I've been treated much worse before."

"The sad part of all this, is, why should it take something like this to change a persons view on things – especially people?" Lorraine asked.

"Maybe because you're her daughter it was that much more powerful," Liz said.

They went silent for a few moments."

"You guys go ahead and go – have fun in Salem. I'll be okay. I'll wait for Harv – I can't wait to see him."

"Okay Lorraine, get well soon."

"See ya Lorraine – take care of yourself," Carlos added.

As they leave, Harv shows up jogging to the front door.

"Hey you guys. Are you leaving already?"

"Yeah, we've been here for a little while," Liz said.

"She's really excited to see you Harv," Carlos said.

Lorraine's mom opens the front door.

"Hi Harv! Come on in she's expecting you."

"Hi Mrs. Fletch."

"She's in her bedroom upstairs – you go ahead on up. She's afraid to go outside. This ordeal really affected her."

"That's perfectly understandable," Harv said as he walks up the steps.

He enters her room and finds her staring outside of the window.

"Lorraine?" he quietly calls.

"Oh! You scared me."

"Sorry."

"It's okay. I'm so glad to see you," she walks to him and gives him a hug.

"Thank you for saving my life. You, Carlos, and Liz are my best friends ever."

Harv looks at her and smiles. There are a few moments of silence.

"How are you holding up?"

"Not too good. I can't go outside without thinking about it."

"Wow … that bad huh?"

"My parents took me to see a doctor. I have to go to counseling once a week for awhile… I'm not looking forward to that. Please don't tell anyone."

"Don't worry Lorraine, I won't – you'll get better."

There's a short pause for a moment as he looks at Lorraine. She's looking down in a very thoughtful pose.

"Liz is trying out for the basketball team. I'm sure she'll want to be your teammate," Harv said.

"I hope I'm ready to be her teammate. I'm hoping to be back at school in a week or so – hopefully I can leave the house without having so much fear by then."

"I can help you however you want me to – just let me know what you need."

"Of course Harv, thank you."

"Write down all of your classes for me and I'll pick up your homework and bring it to you everyday."

"Why?"

"That'll prevent you from getting too far behind – I mean if you're capable of doing the work."

"I suppose you're right – sure that sounds good," Lorraine said.

Harv spent the rest of the day with Lorraine. He learned that she had been traumatized severely by the terrible incident.

The following week, he's very good to her. Harv delivers her homework assignments and even stays to help. It makes Lorraine feel more at ease knowing he is there for her. It sure helps her with the healing process.

What Lorraine experienced was such a horrible shock. That type of thing does something to the human mind. She started experiencing panic attacks and developed some phobias – for example, difficulty going outside. She was also afraid of being in a forest, or sleeping in the dark. She often required a nightlight to be on all night.

Carlos continued to get together with Harv, but only to ask questions about assignments he didn't understand. Harv's attention is mostly directed at Lorraine. Carlos learned some great study habits from Harv – this allowed him to continue improving in all areas. He brought up his average to a B+. He spent countless hours of studying with Harv previous to what happened to Lorraine.

The next day at school there are all kinds of questions about what happened to Lorraine.

"Hey Liz! I heard your friend went crazy, what did you do to her?" Shawna asked.

"You know what Shawna? Mind your own business, Lorraine is fine." Liz stares her down.

"You think you're such a hot thing don't you? In my book you're a big B."

"Shawna … why don't you go crawl in a hole and stay there until the sun rises from the west?"

"What's the big deal with Lorraine? Why is she not in school?"

"You wouldn't understand Shawna. Get lost – leave me alone before I get physical with you," Liz is giving her an evil eye.

"Okay Missy … you don't have to get all crazy on me," Shawna walks away with her friends, chewing her gum louder.

It got to the point where Carlos, Liz, and Harv, did not want to talk about it anymore. Some of the students started making fun of her and laughing. Sick jokes and teasing went on for a few days. But eventually it wore itself out.

Carlos and Harv enter the gym for the first day of tryouts. All of the players started shooting baskets to get warmed up. The coaches are watching. Coach Kenneth Cleveland had transferred from another high school to come coach at Gervais.

"You have a nice shot young man – what's your name?" Coach Kenneth asked.

"Carlos Swavey, and thank ya sir."

"You have a little bit of a southern accent. Where'd you play ball at last year?"

"I'm a transfer from Texas – I played in Dimmitt, Texas."

"What position did you play?"

"Shooting guard and point guard."

The coach shakes his head up and down and continues to watch. He talks to the other coaches in a whisper. They're talking about every player that goes up for a shot.

Harv is not one of the better players – it's evident he needs some work. Carlos is looking at all of the players. He knows that Harv would be lucky to make the team. Carlos begins to think of how he can help Harv get on the team if he were to get cut.

The tryouts went on for several days and a few players were so out of shape they simply didn't return, they just gave up. There has to be several players eliminated in order to bring the roster to 12 players. Harv is, 6' 3", and height is a good thing in basketball.

After the final day of tryouts, the coach brought all of the players together.

"Okay fellas! I'm going to post up a list of all the players that'll be on the team. The list will be in my office tomorrow morning. Thank you for trying out and I look forward to a great season."

Everyone is dismissed and the coach heads to his office. He has a lot of work to do with his coaching staff. Carlos hangs around while the rest of the boys start leaving.

"You go ahead Harv I'll catch up with you in a bit."

"Alright man – see you."

Carlos jogs over to the coach's office – he opens the door.

"Carlos, how can I help you?" Coach Cleveland asked.

"Coach, can I ask you something?"

"What is it?"

"I need to know if Harv Bradford is on the team."

All of the coaches look at each other for a moment.

"Why is that so important to you?" Coach Cleveland asked.

"I know I can help him – I did it in football. I taught him the skills. He's a hard worker and learns fast. He just needs that one-on-one type instruction."

"That's the most bizarre request I've ever had in all the years I've coached – and from a student. This kind of thing usually comes from a parent," the coaches chuckle.

"Coach, you gotta give him a chance. Give me a chance to work with him."

"To be honest with you, Harv is one of the kids we all agreed to cut from the team. We had a coaches' meeting yesterday."

"Coach, please, give me two weeks. If you don't see a huge improvement, then cut him."

"Young man you're asking me to eliminate another player's opportunity to be on the team. Do you think that would be fair?"

"No sir, I don't. I just thought I'd try. Harv really wants to be on the team. He has a passion for sports."

"I'll tell you what, I admire your courage and coming to me about this – we'll put thirteen on the roster. I normally don't do this kind of thing. If I don't see any kind of improvement in two weeks, he's gone."

"You got a deal. Thank you so much coach," Carlos said with a smile.

"Now get out of here," Coach Cleveland smiles as he closes the door.

Carlos runs to the locker room. Harv is walking out of the locker room.

"Hey Harv! Wait for me I have something to tell ya."

"Okay, hurry up man – I have to go."

"Do you want to improve your basketball skills?"

"Yeah, you know it."

"I need your help with some homework. I'm having a difficult time understanding how to do a demonstration speech."

"We can do the same thing we did during football season. I have a hoop inside the shop – it's warmer than outside," Harv said.

"That sounds great – I'll be over in an hour," Carlos said.

"Okay. My mom and Liz are preparing a great meal tonight – you're welcome to join us."

Carlos feels more comfortable going to the Bradfords knowing there's no more sneaking around going on.

"Alright then, we'll see ya'll tonight," Carlos starts walking away.

After practice Carlos' muscles are sore, and walking to the Gervais Market is a good stretch for him. It takes him about 10 minutes to walk there from the high school.

"Hey Mr. Lind."

"Hi Carlos, are you going out for the basketball team?"

"Yes sir, we had tryouts today. I should know tomorrow if I'm on the team or not."

"That new coach that just arrived is supposed to be pretty good I heard," Mr. Lind said.

"Coach Cleveland? Oh yeah, unfortunately we need good players too. But a good coach is always a plus," Carlos replied.

"Well, good luck in basketball I'm sure you'll do great."

"Thanks Mr. Lind."

After work Carlos walks home with thoughts of how he can help Harv and Liz improve their basketball skills. Liz shoots a two-handed shot which is all wrong. He'll have to teach her the correct form. Harv's ball handling is very bad, but his shot is okay when he's close to the hoop. He had to come up with a plan to help both of them.

When Carlos arrives at his house, he enters with a sigh of relief that work is over. The smell of the food is something else – especially when a tired boy is hungry. Isabel is such a great cook and she is very proficient.

"That smells so good – tortillas and beans. Alright!" Carlos said.

"I thought I'd fix you one of your favorite meals tonight. If it wasn't for you we wouldn't be having a meeting with Ginger this weekend," Isabel said.

"That's great Mom. What did Dad say about that?"

"He wants to wait and see what she's gonna have us do – we don't know what we'll be doing yet."

"I talked to Ted last week and it sounds like a job that Dad will like, but I'm not sure what else it involves," Carlos said.

"Well, I'm sure your dad won't be picky – it's better than no job at all."

It's one of the roughest years the Swaveys are experiencing. Christmas is approaching and things are unpredictable right now. Food on the table is the number one priority and rent is second. There aren't too many jobs out there right now, but somehow they manage to keep their heads up.

Carlos sits at the table with the rest of the kids. He starts to eat, tearing a piece of tortilla off, and using it to grab some beans from his plate. He uses his hands – that's how most Hispanics eat tortillas and beans.

Pete pulls up. They all hear the sound of the car and then the door shuts. He enters the door with a sad look on his face.

"I'm done. They handed me a pink slip today. I'm laid off."

He walks over to the table and sits down with a very disappointing look. Everyone is speechless for a few minutes. Isabel puts her head down as she waits for a tortilla to cook on the pan.

"It's okay Pete, we have a meeting with Ginger this weekend," Isabel said.

"We'll see what happens. At least we have a month's paycheck for food and rent – hopefully that'll hold us for awhile," Pete said.

Carlos is listening but has no comments at all. He knows his family is struggling.

"This probably isn't a good time to ask for some basketball shoes huh?"

Pete looked at him with a disgusted look on his face and didn't say anything. He continues eating and ignored the question.

Life doesn't seem fair – that's just the way it is sometimes. Carlos knows what he has to do to not end up like his parents. He knows that an education is vital. Watching the Bradfords gives him hope and faith that someday he can live a comfortable life in the future. He might not become as wealthy as Ted Bradford, but he should still be able to live a comfortable life.

"I'm going over to Harv's house tonight," Carlos speaks out.

"Don't stay too long you have school tomorrow," Isabel said.

"Okay."

Carlos didn't say too much because he knows it will be late when he returns. He has a lot of work to do. He puts on his hat, coat, and gloves and hops on his bike. When he arrives at the Bradfords, Liz is waiting for him at the door. She greets him with a hug and a small kiss.

"Hi busy guy."

"Hey Liz."

"We have dinner ready if you want to join us."

"Oh … um … I forgot about this y'all. I ate with my family already. Would it be okay if I just had dessert?"

"Of course, not a problem – come on in," Liz said.

They walk to the kitchen and sit at the table.

"Hi Mrs. Bradford."

"Hi Carlos, would you like a plate?"

"Mom, he already ate – he's having dessert with us though," Liz explained.

"Oh, okay great," Elaine said.

"I'm thinking we can work on studies first after dinner. That way our food can digest before working on basketball skills," Harv said.

"Sounds like a plan to me. Is it okay if Liz comes out with us so I can work with her too?"

"Sure, I don't see why not," Harv said.

"Are you sure you want to play basketball this year Liz?" Elaine asked.

"Yes, I think I can actually help our team. I'm one of the taller girls this year," Liz said.

"Did you talk to your dad about this?" Elaine asked.

"Yes, I finally convinced him to let me go out for the team. He said as long as I maintained a 4.0 GPA, basketball is not a problem. Carlos is going to help me with basketball skills."

"Carlos, that's very nice of you," Elaine said.

"Not a problem Mrs. Bradford, your two kids have helped me bring my grades up. I think it takes more than a teacher to help one student. Teachers can only do so much."

"Mom, you don't know this but Carlos and I made a deal at the beginning of football season." Harv said.

"What kind of a deal?" Elaine asked.

"He helps me in sports and I help him in academics. You saw the results – I actually played varsity football. Not only did I play, but I scored my first touchdown. I can't describe the feeling," Harv said.

"I think you mentioned that to me before … or maybe it was your dad. What are you going to do for Carlos, Liz?"

"Give him rides in my Corvette," Liz smiles.

"Fair enough kids. Good work. It would be great if other kids at school could do what you guys have done," Elaine said.

"With personality differences it would be tough but not impossible," Liz said.

"Who's ready for dessert?" Elaine asked.

"I am," Carlos said. Everyone starts laughing.

When dinner is over, Elaine takes care of the dishes and the kids went into the family room to study. Harv and Liz both help Carlos on how to give a demonstration speech for his English class. They work on the project for an hour.

Now it's time for them to go out to the shop in the backyard. It's a pretty good size shop with a 50 ft. by 50 ft. concrete floor and a 30 ft. high ceiling. There is a basketball hoop at one end built into the wall.

"Wow! This is nice. We should make the free-throw line to begin with. It's 15 ft. from the backboard," Carlos explains.

They use black tape to create the line. When the line is completed, he starts showing Harv some basketball drills. Harv begins to work on them for about a half hour.

"Okay Liz, let's show you how to shoot the basketball the correct way. That two-handed shot ain't gonna cut it – too easy to block and very inconsistent," Carlos explains.

"That's the way I learned how to shoot. I guess when I was little the basketball was too heavy for me. Two hands made it easier for me," Liz said.

"Yeah, well someone should have bought you a smaller basketball – it's lighter."

"I guess, oh well. Maybe my dad couldn't afford to buy me one," Liz responded.

"Ha-ha!" Carlos laughs.

Carlos grabs the basketball and looks at Liz.

"Watch me shoot a couple of shots. Focus on how I'm holding the basketball."

He shoots a few shots and they all go in. Carlos has a nice touch on his shot. It's something you don't learn overnight – it takes years of practice.

"Wow, you make it looks so easy," Liz said.

"See how I spread my fingers across the ball? I use my other hand to only support the ball – it's really my right hand that does all the work."

Carlos shoots the ball one more time – it hits nothing but net.

"Wow! That looked great," Liz said.

"Now you try it," he hands the ball over to Liz.

Teaching her the basic fundamentals of shooting was going to take time. He has her stand three feet from the hoop. She begins to shoot with only one hand to start with to get the basic technique down. She does this for 15 minutes while Carlos goes back to Harv to show him some defensive techniques.

Ted Bradford shows up in a three-piece suit with shiny brown shoes. He observes the last five minutes of lessons Carlos has instructed. When he's all done he walks over to Ted.

"Hey Mr. Bradford, I like the color of your shoes."

"Thanks. It's great what you're doing with my kids. I really appreciate that."

"No problem at all. They've got a long ways to go but the first day shows promise."

"Daddy, can I give Carlos a ride home?"

"Sure, but come straight back home – it's a school night. And grab some water or juice on your way out. You need to stay hydrated."

"Thanks Mr. Bradford," Carlos said.

Liz takes Carlos home and they talk basketball and all sorts of things on the way back. They seem to focus on many positive things. They talk about how important grades are, being active in sports, and treating others with respect. In addition, they talk about helping Lorraine recover from the nightmare she went through.

When Carlos returns home he walks up the steps to get ready for bed. His dad is standing at the bottom of the steps.

"You might have to find another job now that football is over. We might need you to help out until we start working again."

"Dad, I'm playing basketball – tryouts were all week. Basketball is one of my favorite sports – I can't miss it."

"You're gonna get hurt and you won't be able to work – you're wasting your time."

"What about Mike and Lydia?"

"They're looking for a job tomorrow after school. I want you to go with them."

"I have practice!"

"Not another word from you Carlos," Pete said.

"Yes sir," Carlos continues to walk up the steps with his head down.

Carlos loves the game of basketball and is about to do whatever it takes to be on the team. This is another reason education is so important. With no education his parents had to work labor job after labor job. Carlos thought to himself, if he has a family someday he would be able to provide for them. He really knows that graduating from high school and college is something very important.

The young man thought all night about how he could earn more money, and at the same time play on the basketball team.

The next day at school, he and his friends eat lunch in the cafeteria. The weather is too miserable to walk to the Gervais Market.

"How's Lorraine doing?" Carlos asked.

"She's doing a lot better – she actually went outside by herself for the first time. She said she felt a little panicky but survived it. According to the doctor, it's going to take a long time," Harv said.

"I feel really bad for her. We can help her out when she returns to school," Carlos said.

"Are you okay Carlos? You seem a little down today," Liz said.

"I'm a little frustrated."

"Why?" Liz asked.

"My dad wants me to work more to help my family out. He just got laid off from the processing plant."

"I'm so sorry Carlos. Is there anything we can do to help?" Liz asked.

"Yeah, help me find a job or I'm not gonna be able to play basketball."

"I can talk to my dad. I'm sure he has work that can be done. He's always hiring people to do some kind of maintenance work around our house. He hires Harv from time to time.

"You'd do that for me?"

"Yes, of course."

"Thank you so much, you have no idea what that means to me."

"No problem Swavey. We got your back," Harv said.

That evening, the Bradfords were at home eating dinner, Liz didn't waste any time.

"Dad, can you do me a big favor?"

"What might that favor be, do you want a Porsche to go along with your Corvette?"

"Ha-ha! No."

"Then what is it?"

"Well, Carlos is in need of a job. His family is in a financial crisis. He won't be able to play for the basketball team unless he can help his family out. His dad is making him work to help out."

"That's terrible. What can I do?" Ted asked.

"Can you hire him to do work around here?" Liz expressed.

"I had planned on hiring a company to paint our fence. I could hire Carlos to paint it on the weekends. I can also pay him to give you and Harv basketball lessons. I've seen what he can do – he's a talented young man."

"Dad! I love you – you are amazing," Liz said.

"Take him into town and open a savings account for him if he doesn't already have one. I'll give him a $100.00 signing bonus to do work for me."

"What a great idea – I'll go with you guys tomorrow after practice," Harv said.

They are very excited to give Carlos the news the next day at school. To be wealthy is a blessing for some people. To be able to help a boy without hurting his pride is important to the Bradfords. They could have easily handed him over some money, but that would not teach anyone anything. Carlos would feel much better knowing he earned his money.

The next day at school, Liz pulled Carlos to the side of the hallway.

"I talked to my dad last night – he has a job for you and he's paying you a $100.00 signing bonus."

"Signing bonus!" Carlos reacts.

"He's a lawyer. Do you want the job?"

"Of course, what will I be doing?"

"Painting our property fence. Not the eight foot fence, the four foot fence."

"Sounds great. That'll keep me busy for a long while."

"He said you could work on the weekends."

"You have no idea how thankful I am. I can't wait to tell my dad. And I can play basketball this season, yes!" Carlos is full of joy at this point.

"My next question is, what do you want for Christmas this year?" Liz asked.

"You've already done so much for me. I would want to spend time with you doing something fun."

"That's easy and definitely doable," Liz smiles.

After a pause, Carlos looks into Liz's eyes.

"What do you want for Christmas?"

"I'll have to think about that one."

"Okay, think about it and let me know before Christmas of course." Carlos races away to his next class trying to beat the tardy bell.

The next week proved to be a busy tiring week for Carlos, Liz, Harv, and Lorraine. Lorraine is improving on overcoming the phobias she developed. Doctor visits and counseling are helping her cope with the ordeal.

It's late in December with only one week until Christmas. Liz is starting to drive Lorraine to school and all of her friends are starting to help her feel safe and comfortable.

"Lorraine, it's really nice to see you at school again. How are you?" Carlos said.

"I'm doing so much better. I'm sleeping better and I haven't had a nightmare in three days."

"That's great."

"Thanks to you guys I'm back at school again."

"Hey, what are friends for … right?" Carlos said.

"Right," Lorraine smiles.

"Are you going out for the basketball team?"

"Yeah, I need to talk to the coach."

"No need, I've taken care of that for you," Liz jumps in.

"Well … well, if it isn't Miss Crazy," Shawna steps in.

"Shawna, you better take that back," Lorraine says.

"What if I don't … is that going to send you back to the nuthouse?"

"Okay, that's it!" Lorraine shouts.

Kalin Jensen is standing next to the group of girls. One thing she doesn't mind is to see Shawna get beat up.

"Get her Lorraine! That a girl!" Kalin shouts.

She pushes Shawna down to the hall floor and jumps on top of her. She begins to slap her face – *slap*! *slap*!

"Get off me!" Shawna screams.

Harv grabs Lorraine. Carlos gets behind Shawna placing his arms around her waist to hold her back while she screams and swings her arms. She's trying to hit Lorraine.

"Easy … easy," Carlos said.

"You just wait you crazy girl," Shawna yells.

Lorraine tries to attack her again, but Harv holds her back firmly.

"Lorraine! Don't listen to her, she's the crazy one," Harv shouts.

"Errg! She gets me mad," Lorraine says.

"Let me go!" Shawna says to Carlos.

"If I let you go will you leave Lorraine alone?"

"Yes … now let me go!"

"Okay, easy now."

Shawna picks up her books off the floor and walks away with her friends. She is steaming but can't do anything.

"You're lucky Carlos is a nice guy!" Kalin yells at Shawna.

The principal is walking toward the altercation.

"Hey …what's going on here?"

"Oh, nothing sir … we were just rehearsing for a play. Then we helped Shawna pick up her books," Carlos said.

"That's very nice of you, but take it to the drama department. Now let's get to class," the principal walks away.

Basketball practices are going well, and the boy's team is set to play their first game against Woodburn High School. This league basketball game will take place before the Christmas break. Carlos is the best ball handler and shooter Gervais has ever acquired. Coach Kenneth has a good feeling about his new team. With Carlos running the point guard position and Clifford playing strong forward, they are going to be a threat in the Capital Conference.

When basketball practice ends, Harv and Liz give Lorraine a ride home.

"It's so dark outside," Lorraine said.

"It'll be okay, we're here with you," Liz said.

"I can walk you to the door when we get there," Harv added.

"You guys are so good to me, you have no idea how much I appreciate this."

"It's so strange how your brain gets affected by something so scary. I'm sure you'll be fine in time," Liz said.

"I guess they transferred Crazy Lady Teresa to a maximum security mental hospital."

"Harv, I don't think Lorraine wants to hear that name right now."

"Oh, sorry Lorraine," Harv said.

"That's okay – I know you're only trying to help."

When they arrive at Lorraine's house, her mom is waiting for her at the door. Harv walks her to the door and says goodbye.

"Thanks Harv and Liz!" she yells out.

The next evening Carlos is sitting at the dinner table with his mom and dad. Pete starts biting into his tortilla when Carlos breaks the news to him.

"Dad, I got a job."

"Good, we really need the money. Where did you get a job?" Pete asked.

"Liz's dad hired me to paint one of their fences."

"How much is he paying you?"

"I don't know I didn't ask."

"Well, let me know when you find out. I guess you can play basketball – I hope you don't get hurt."

"Our first game is tomorrow against Woodburn – you should come."

"I have to change the oil in the car – the starter also needs to be replaced. I think that's more important than a waste-of-time basketball game."

"I understand – just thought I'd invite you."

Carlos felt bad for his family's situation. He loves his parents but can never understand why coming to his game is such low priority. Isabel didn't say anything – she remained quiet and continued eating.

"Did Mike and Lydia get a job?" Carlos asked.

"They're still looking. I think a fast-food place is supposed to call Lydia," Pete said.

"Thanks for dinner Mom, it was very good."

He walks upstairs slowly. You can hear the old wooden squeaky steps that had been partially repaired with new boards and nails – *creak*! *creak*!

Things are looking up for the basketball season. Carlos has support from his parents to play. He has a girlfriend that any guy would kill to be with. Now he is going to be one of the starters for the Gervais Cougars. He falls asleep thinking of how lucky he is and in how many ways he's been blessed.

The train usually goes by about midnight. He has learned to block out the terrible sound and sleep through the noise. The woodstove burns through the night to keep the family warm. Pete always makes sure the wood is refilled to keep the fire burning all night.

The next morning there's someone pounding at the front door. Pete walks over and opens the door.

"Hi sir," Pete said.

"I need the rent money – you're two weeks behind," Dale French, the landlord, demanded.

"I'll have it for you next week for sure."

"Okay, next week. I'll be back or you can bring it over to me if you'd like."

"Yes sir Mr. French, I'll bring it over to you next week."

Pete shuts the door as he looks down at the floor in shame. He walks over and sits next to the window. He looks very worried as he stares out of the window.

"Pete, it's okay. The money we have saved for Christmas? We can use that for the rent," Isabel explained.

"Ginger said we could start our new job in January – I'll have to see what I can find until then," Pete said.

Tough times have arrived for the poor family. The pressure Pete feels is enormous. Just feeding his family from week to week is a big challenge for him. And his challenge of trying to come up with the rent money is even a bigger challenge. Pete spends the rest of the day calling some factories for employment.

Later that Friday evening, the Gervais basketball team starts boarding the bus to travel to Woodburn, Oregon, the home of the Bulldogs.

"Carlos! Come here!" Coach Kenneth yelled from afar.

The coach isn't in the bus yet and Carlos is stepping onto the bus as he hears the coach. He stops immediately, turns around, and walks over to the coach.

"Yes sir?"

"Tonight is our first game and I know you're only a freshman. But you're one of our best players and I'm asking that you take a leadership role out there tonight. Play smart and do what you've been doing in practice all week. I'm counting on your help – you'll be one of our captains this year. I've already talked to Clifford – he'll be the other captain."

"Yes sir, I'll do my best."

"Thank you. Now let's go get'm tonight."

Carlos has grown an inch over the fall. He now stands at 6' 0" tall. The two shooting guards are J.J. and Johnny Hampton. J.J. played on the football team as a wide receiver – he is quick and can shoot the basketball quite well. Johnny Hampton is the other wing – he plays basketball year-round. A thin kid that stands at 6' 1" – very basketball minded.

Cliff is playing the post position. He's a strong, 6' 4", fundamental player and a great rebounder. Playing the power forward position is Hector Gonzales. Hector is 6' 2" and has a big body for blocking out and getting rebounds – a great inside force.

The Gervais boys enter the Woodburn High School gym. The crowd noise is exciting as they walk up to the stands to watch some of the JV game. At the end of the third quarter they will all go into the locker room to get ready for a battle against the Woodburn Bulldogs.

Wooburn has a player that's 6' 6" and is headed to play NCAA Division I basketball after his senior year. Clifford will have his hands full guarding David Rice, a great shooter and very smart. If Gervais wants to win their first game of the season, they will have to stop David.

Woodburn has another player that's 6' 4", Todd Hilliard. Todd is strong and can also shoot very well inside the paint.

The girls' team is playing Woodburn at Gervais. Carlos will not be able to watch Liz but he's thinking about her and hopes she uses the skills he taught her.

In the Gervais boys' locker room, Harv is sitting there looking at the floor wondering if he'll even get in the game.

"Hang in there Harv. Even if you don't play tonight, try to learn as much as you can by watching. We can continue working on some skills – you'll improve with time," Carlos said.

"Thanks man, I hope so."

Coach Kenneth walks in the locker room.

"Okay boys, I want you to try to relax. I know they're bigger than we are. But that doesn't mean we can't win if we execute. We want to start out trapping on the press. Let's catch them by surprise. If that doesn't work we can back off. Run your plays and look for a good open shot. Keep the turnovers to a minimum. If we can do that, we have a chance to win tonight... any questions?"

The players look at each other and shake their heads indicating a no.

"Okay, let's play ball!" Coach Kenneth yells.

"Yeah! Alright!" chanted the team as they run out of the locker room.

After the warm-ups concluded, both teams walk to the center circle to get ready for the jump ball. David Rice looks serious as he faces Clifford during the jump ball. The referee tosses the ball upward and Woodburn gets the tip convincingly. They come down and Rice gets the ball immediately. All Clifford can do is put his hands up. Rice turns around and shoots the basketball over Clifford, hitting the basket off the backboard.

"Yeah! Go Bulldogs!" the Woodburn crowd yells.

Coach Kenneth looks at his assistant and shakes his head.

"If that happens again we need to call a timeout."

Carlos receives the ball on the inbound pass and dribbles down the court. He slows down as he dribbles toward the bench.

"Coach! We need to deny the ball and help on the weak side. Then we'll be able to control Rice."

"If he does that again call a timeout," Coach Kenneth answers.

"Okay sir!"

He calls the play and the Cougars execute it. The ball gets into J.J.'s hands and he drives to the bucket for two points. The small Gervais crowd gets a little excited with a few hollers. The score is, 2 – 2. Woodburn comes down and does the same thing, the ball comes to Rice and he hits another turn-around shot.

"Timeout!" Carlos yells out to the officials. The team jogs to the bench and they all circle around the coach.

The coach stands up and crosses his arms with a frustrated look.

"Okay gents. Clifford, I want you to get in front of Rice and keep him from getting that ball. Hector, when you see the lob coming to him, you help out on the weak side. Let's switch to a 2-3 zone. Hector you play the middle."

The Cougars contained Rice a little better with a zone defense, but it opened up the outside more. By half-time the score is, 30 – 25, in favor of Woodburn. Carlos has scored 15 points and David Rice has scored 20 points.

The zone defense helps keep the score close. The Bulldogs have a much bigger and stronger team than the Cougars, but sometimes that doesn't matter. It's how a team executes and limits turnovers that can make the difference.

The very first play of the second half Woodburn takes control of the ball. Gervais comes out with a very tough full court press. They trap the point guard and force him to make a long pass. Carlos intercepts the basketball and dribbles in for the easy lay-in. That narrows the gap, 30 – 27, in favor of the Bulldogs.

The Cougars are playing the Bulldogs very tough. The challenge against David Rice and company is coming down to the wire. At the end of the fourth quarter, with 50 seconds left to play, Woodburn is ahead, 60 – 59.

Carlos dribbles the ball while he calls out a play. J.J. sets a screen and Carlos drives by his defender. A Bulldog switches and stops Carlos from scoring. Carlos gives Clifford a nice bounce pass. Clifford goes up for the shot, but only to get blocked by Rice. He slams the ball against the backboard – *bam*! Woodburn's, Todd Hilliard, comes down with the big rebound. Carlos fouls and stops the clock with 10 seconds left.

Todd walks over to the free-throw line on the opposite side of the floor – the rest of the players follow him. They line up around the key. He misses the first shot and steps back for a breather. The referee hands him the ball once again. Todd takes the second shot. It hits the back part of the rim and bounces to the front part and rattles out. Hector gets the big rebound! He calls a timeout. They all jog to the bench.

"We have 9 seconds. We want to take one shot. Play the clock down. Carlos, I want you to go straight to the basket. Johnny, I want you to set a good screen for him. Okay, let's go!" Coach Cleveland demands.

Johnny passes the ball in to Carlos. He's dribbling to the left and then to the right. Johnny hustles down to set a screen, Carlos drives by the defender with determination. Carlos sees Rice, but doesn't slow down. He takes two steps and off of one leg, springs up full force and slam dunks the basketball! You can hear the rim rattle. The Gervais crowd is going crazy!

The time has run out for the Bulldogs and Gervais wins the game. No one thought Carlos could dunk the ball as a freshman. His adrenalin was pumping and the timing was so right for the dunk.

The team is walking to the locker room after celebrating and talking to a few fans. Harv catches up with Carlos.

"I didn't know you could dunk the ball!"

"I didn't either," Carlos replied.

On the way back home the team stopped to eat at a fast-food place. Carlos has some money that he saved up from working. He also has the bonus Ted Bradford gave him. He has a total of $200.00 in the bank.

He enjoys eating with the team after a victory against a tough team.

"I think we have some work to do on defense and offense, but our future is looking bright," Coach Cleveland said.

Harv did not get in the game, but he understands that he's not ready yet. He needs to improve in several areas of his game. Carlos knows he'll eventually get there, but with hard work once again.

"I can't wait to start working on some more skills again," Harv said.

"If you want I can come over everyday during the Christmas break – I don't mind helping you as much as you need."

"That would be great – I'm looking forward to it. You played a heck of a game Carlos."

"Thanks man, I'm glad we pulled off the victory."

Sports are what keep Carlos going. He really enjoys the competitiveness of it and the team environment with the guys. Not only that, but because of sports, Carlos is able to maintain good grades. Who knows where Carlos would be without sports.

Liz anxiously waits for the arrival of the boys' team bus. The girls' game ended with a loss. Liz scored 15 points and pulled down eight rebounds. She is excited to tell Carlos about her night.

The bus finally arrives and the players start stepping off the bus carrying their bags.

"Hey guys! We lost but I did well. The stuff you showed me worked."

"Very nice, what was the score?" Carlos asked.

"30 to 35, they barely beat us."

"That's okay you'll get'm next time."

"How'd you guys do?" Liz asked.

"We won. You should've seen Carlos, he had an awesome dunk to win the game at the end," Harv said.

"Congrats Carlos, you star-stud," Liz said smiling.

They all hop into Liz's Corvette and drive off. Liz pulls over in front of Carlos' house to drop him off.

"See you tomorrow Carlos," Harv said.

"We'll see ya'll."

"Bye sweetie, see you tomorrow," Liz said.

Carlos walks in his house.

"Did you win?" Pete asked.

"Yeah Dad, we did just barely. What are you doing?"

"We're struggling with math. There's this program we got into that will help us get a GED."

"Wow, that's great. But that's so unlike y'all to study with books and all."

"Well, it's a government program that pays us to study, believe it or not. We just applied for it and we got it," Pete explains.

"Very nice Dad."

Sometimes the state government provides certain programs to help low-income families that are struggling. Pete and Isabel are taking advantage of any help they can get.

It's Christmas Time

In the past Pete and Isabel would buy gifts for all the kids. They would wait until midnight, on Christmas Eve, to put them under the tree. All of the kids would be surprised in the morning.

This year that's not going to be the case, but Carlos still has hopes that it might happen again. Christmas is only a few days away and there's not much talk about it from his parents. The family is struggling financially because of the layoff from the processing plant.

The next few days Carlos spends his time helping Harv and Liz with their basketball skills. They are having plenty of fun learning all kinds of things. Dribbling between their legs and shooting the basketball with the correct form. Playing games to improve the skills makes it worth the effort.

It is finally Christmas Eve. Lydia is cooking breakfast with her mom next to her.

"I can't believe Christmas is tomorrow," Lydia said.

"Don't get too excited we don't have any money this year," Isabel said.

Carlos heard her but isn't sure if she's pretending. In the past they always bought a gift for everyone, even if it was just a little something. Back in Texas, he remembered getting fireworks and unwrapping a board game. All of the presents would be stacked under the tree with Christmas lights reflecting in shining colors.

Carlos kept thinking if he should take his money out of the bank to get presents for his family. But he shied away from that idea. He knew he needed that money to last him through the basketball season. The weather is not permitting him to do more painting on the Bradfords' fence. That extra money would have helped.

The little money that Pete has is for food, utility bills, and paying the rent. Mr. French was serious about getting his rent payment on time. It is the worst holiday season the Swaveys are beginning to experience. There are no Christmas lights up on any part of their house. The only thing decorated is the Christmas tree that Pete picked up from a tree lot.

"Nice Christmas tree, where did we pick that up?" Carlos asked.

"Your dad picked it up for two dollars down the road," Isabel answered.

"Well, I'm going to bed – I have to get to sleep so Santa can drop off my presents," Carlos said.

Pete and Isabel looked at each other with sadness.

They watched Carlos and Lydia walk away. The rest of the kids stayed up awhile longer playing a board game that they bought at a garage sale.

Carlos lies awake for a bit wondering if there will be any presents in the morning. He eventually falls asleep.

Meanwhile at the Bradford's home, Ted and Elaine drive up after returning from a Christmas party at the law firm. Their house is decorated with Christmas lights everywhere – it looks so beautiful. There are green, red, white, and blue lights lined up perfectly in different areas. Ted hires a company to decorate their house every year.

They walk in the house laughing and singing Christmas songs.

"Hi kids!"

"Hi Mom and Dad, did you have fun?" Liz asked.

"Oh yeah, but I'm glad it's over," Elaine sighs.

There is a huge Christmas tree decorated with beautiful lights in front of a big window. Presents are piled up around the tree.

"What did you guys get Carlos?" Elaine asked.

"Can't tell you, we're inviting him over tomorrow evening so he can open his presents," Liz responded.

"That's a great idea Liz, I look forward to that."

"My present to Carlos is not throwing him out of the house," Ted smiles.

"Dad!" Liz shouts.

"Just kidding," Ted laughs.

"Now you have to get him something really nice," Elaine smiles.

"I agree with Mom," Liz added.

"I'll see what I can work out," Ted said.

"I feel bad for him," Harv said.

"Why son?"

"Because I know his family is struggling financially. I can't imagine being in his position – especially at Christmas time."

"Yeah, I know what you mean," Liz said.

"Well, maybe we can cheer his family up somehow tomorrow," Elaine said.

"Hey, it's Christmas Eve. The important thing for their family is that they have each other. That's really what matters – right?

"I think you're right Daddy," Liz agrees.

"Let's all get a good night's sleep and just relax. No work tomorrow, just celebrating Christmas," Ted said.

"Okay, goodnight Mom and Dad. We're going to watch some TV first," Harv said.

The next morning, bright and early, Carlos wakes up and walks down the attic steps – *creak*! *creak*! He slowly turns the corner to the living room. The sadness he feels is unexplainable. No presents, no Christmas music, no cinnamon rolls, and no sign of Mom or Dad. He can hear the crackling sound of the fire in the woodstove. Pete had re-filled the wood during the night because it was so cold.

Carlos felt empty inside. He had never experienced a Christmas like this – with no presents. He went back upstairs and tears came out of his eyes while he covered his head under the blanket. He didn't want anyone seeing him like that – especially his parents.

The younger kids seem to be entertaining themselves with some old toys they had from before. No one seemed to be too excited this morning.

"There's no money this year but it's still Christmas and we're celebrating the birth of Christ. I have a turkey in the oven – Merry Christmas everybody!"

Isabel is trying to stay positive. Carlos knows that he still has his family and they are together. In his past experiences he's used to getting presents at Christmas time.

Once the day gets going it is easier for the family to adjust. They will survive the holidays somehow with no money.

About 11:00 a.m., Lydia opens the front door.

"Merry Christmas!"

She has two big bags full of presents.

"Where did you get all the presents?" Pete asked.

"I got a job and my boss paid me two weeks in advance."

"Wow! Thanks Lydia," Carlos said.

"Lydia, I will pay you back for all these presents," Pete said.

"No Dad, it's my gift to all of you, Merry Christmas!"

The gifts are small, but because of the special thought, it made them more meaningful. Carlos witnesses his sister's great idea – cheering up the family.

He tears the wrapping paper off of his present right away.

"Thanks for the basketball shorts Lydia, I love them," Carlos said.

He acknowledges that Lydia is the only person without a gift. It doesn't seem quite fair.

Carlos runs upstairs and grabs the gift he bought for Liz – a small bucket of M&Ms. He switches the tags and writes, "*To: Lydia*."

He runs down the creaky steps.

"Hey Lydia, Merry Christmas!" Carlos hands her the present.

"Oh, thank you Carlos."

He knew he had time to get Liz another gift before going there in the evening.

"I was gonna do the same thing, but Lydia stole my idea," Mike laughs.

"Shut up Mike! That'll be the day," Carlos said.

They all start laughing as they open their presents. Later they enjoyed a Christmas lunch. I guess sometimes that's how we can define wealthy – family spending the holidays together.

Meanwhile, back at the Bradfords, celebrating Christmas morning involves plenty of presents being opened. Liz opens some amazing gifts. A car stereo with speakers, top of the line clothes, basketball shoes, movie tickets, and so on.

"Merry Christmas! … and thanks for the presents everyone," Liz said.

Elaine is about to open a special gift from Ted. They all watch her.

"Oh my goodness, this is so special – thank you Ted."

Ted gave her a gold bracelet with diamonds. Their two kids' names were engraved with a message below from Ted. She put it on and it fit her precisely.

The thing about Christmas is that it goes by so fast once it gets here. The anticipation is so intense and the excitement is amazing. Not everyone celebrates Christmas, but for the people that do, it's always a special moment. After all, it is the celebration of Christ being born.

The evening has approached and Carlos is ready to ride his bike over to his friend's house. As he starts walking toward the door, the phone rings.

"Is that for me," Carlos asked.

"Yeah, it's Liz."

He walks over as Lydia hands him the phone.

"Hello."

"Hi famous basketball player," Liz said.

"You're too kind."

"I was wondering if I could come pick you up," Liz said.

"Yeah, sure."

Carlos turns his head and looks at Lydia.

"Liz is gonna pick me up."

"Wow, you have your own limo service and everything," Lydia smiles.

"Very funny," Carlos said.

Carlos went back upstairs to wait for his ride. He does some reading and cleaning up while he waits for Liz.

When Liz pulls up in her Corvette and parks on the side of the road, everyone looks out of the window with curiosity.

"Well, it's been fun y'all. I gotta go – see y'all later."

"Have fun Carlos, bring me something back. If they have cake bring me some," Lydia said.

"I'll think about it," he runs out of the house toward Liz.

"Who's that nice looking gal in that Corvette?"

Liz turns her head looking around.

"Where? I don't see her," she laughs.

He hops in the Corvette and they drive off.

Upon arrival Carlos is looking at Liz.

"I can't believe how beautiful you look tonight."

"What a nice thing to say. Thank you."

"And you are so lucky to live in an amazing house, and you own a Corvette. What's it like?"

"I don't know, I guess it's great. My dad spoils me."

"There's nothing wrong with that. It's amazing how we come from two different worlds."

"Yeah, I guess we do – I really like learning about your world," Liz said.

"I want ya to know that I think you are one special lady." Carlos puts his arms around her and kisses her on the cheek.

They finally arrive at Liz's house.

"Let's go inside, we have some presents for you."

"For me? Wow, y'all didn't have to do that."

"It's Christmas just enjoy it," Liz said.

He follows Liz into her house feeling really lucky to know a family of such wealth.

"Merry Christmas Carlos," Elaine said.

"Yeah, Merry Christmas!" Ted agreed.

"Merry Christmas Mr. and Mrs. Bradford and thanks for inviting me."

"You're very welcome. Thanks for showing up," Harv said.

Carlos walks over to talk basketball with Harv. Liz went to the dinning room to help Maria set up for dinner. Ted walks into the family room to watch football on his new big screen TV that he received as a Christmas present.

"I can't believe Christmas is finally here. What did you get for Christmas Carlos? Harv asked.

"Oh, just some clothes and stuff – nothing too big."

The answer he gives Harv is safe. He feels too embarrassed to say he received one present from his sister. He leaves it at that.

"What did you get Harv?"

"I got so much stuff, it's going to take me a week to organize it all. My favorite is the stereo system for my room. I love it. My parents gave it to me."

"Wow! A stereo system?"

"Yep."

"Let's go check it out," Carlos insisted.

"Okay, sure," Harv said.

They walk upstairs to see Harv's gift. Liz is helping Maria spread a tablecloth that's decorated with pictures of poinsettias and white snow. Everything matched with color coordination. The Bradfords went all out for Christmas.

"Mom, can we let Carlos open the presents we got him before dinner?"

"That's a good idea Liz."

"Hey Ted! We're thinking of having Carlos open the presents we got him before dinner," Elaine hollered.

"Sounds good to me!" Ted answered from the family room.

The boys came back downstairs after hearing the plans.

Carlos has gifts sitting in front of him – one from each member of the Bradford family.

"Open mine last Carlos," Liz said.

"Okay, I'll open the one from your mom first."

He begins to unwrap a big box. The box is fitted with a red ribbon. The wrapping paper on it shines from the reflection of the lights.

"A basketball bag! Thank you Mrs. Bradford."

"You're welcome – look inside it."

When he unzips the Gervais Cougar bag, he looks inside and finds a chocolate candy box. The candy box has a card taped to it. Carlos grabs the card and opens it. Inside the card is a $100.00 bill with a nice message written on the card.

"*It's been a real pleasure getting to know you... Merry Christmas*!"

"Wow! This is way too kind of you Mrs. Bradford – thank you very much," Carlos smiles.

"Merry Christmas!" Elaine said as she smiles.

The next present he opens is from Harv.

"I hope you like it Carlos. If you don't we can return it."

"He begins to open the present. It is in a big box with blue and gold wrapping paper.

"Y'all are the most generous people I've ever known. Thank you so much."

Harv got him a toboggan with the Cougar's colors, gloves, practice shorts, and a nice Gervais Cougar t-shirt.

"Thanks Harv! I don't know what to say."

Carlos had never received such nice gifts before.

"Carlos, before you open the present I got for you, I want you to know that I wanted to do this because it's Christmas and you are a special boy. I hope you like it and accept it."

"Sure Mr. Bradford, I understand."

Carlos starts tearing the Christmas law paper circled by a brown ribbon.

"Wow! Movies! Thanks Mr. Bradford."

"Don't forget to open the card," Ted said.

When he opens the card he sees a $500.00 check with a message on the bottom, "*Two month's rent – Merry Christmas*."

"Mr. Bradford, this is very nice of you – thank you very much."

"You're very welcome Carlos," Ted smiles.

It is very difficult for Carlos to hold the tears back, but somehow he manages to hold back.

"Okay, mine is next," Liz said.

Her gift to Carlos is wrapped in a light blue box with shiny ribbons on top. He looks at Liz and smiles at her. He tears the paper and sees a box. Inside the box he sees two Portland Trailblazers basketball tickets and a gift certificate to eat at a buffet.

"Blazer tickets! Man this is great. Thanks Liz."

"You're welcome, open the next box in there," Liz said.

"There's more?"

"Yep."

He opens a small box. It contains a men's bracelet that reads, "To a person with a great heart, Love Liz."

"I like this, thank you."

Carlos pulls out a small box that is wrapped up in newspaper.

"Liz, I just happened to have a small gift for you. I wasn't able to get a gift for the rest of your family."

"Carlos, you being here for Christmas dinner with us is like a gift to all of us," Mrs. Bradford said.

"I can't wait to open this," Liz said as she starts unwrapping her present.

"Oh wow, a necklace. It's beautiful. Thank you Carlos."

The necklace is silver with a cross that shines against the lights. Liz immediately puts it on. It fits perfect.

Liz has no idea how much trouble Carlos went through to get her another gift after he had given Lydia the one intended for her.

"It looks great on you," Carlos said.

"How did you know I liked silver?"

"I didn't, but I knew it would look great on you because of your hair and skin color."

"Well, you have great taste in style," Liz said as she smiles.

"Is anyone hungry?" Maria asked.

"I'm starved, let's eat," Ted said.

Liz is so glad that Carlos accepted the gifts that they gave him. She knows that it must be tough for him to live a poor life and then come to her house and experience a rich life. She puts the differences aside to focus on the person that he is. And if she can help in anyway, she will.

Carlos is thinking to himself how lucky he is to be spending Christmas evening at Liz's house. He is learning so many great things from being around them – things that his own parents never learned.

The talks around the Bradfords are more educated. He often asks Liz what some of the words mean. His vocabulary is pretty weak.

He looks around the house and observes all of the law books that are organized in the shelves. The only books that Carlos' dad owns are automotive books.

Yes, definitely a difference and one that he liked. This is what he wanted if he had a family some day. He knows that it's a long shot, but worth a try.

"Your dad sure has a lot of books," Carlos said.

"Yeah, I've read a good part of them," Liz answered.

"Do you read a lot for enjoyment?"

"Books are something we've always taken on vacations, or received as gifts."

"The only books around our house are school books that we get from the school. You know, for homework," Carlos said.

"With books you don't have to pay anything to go overseas."

"Huh?"

"Well, when you read about Italy or Spain, it's like you're there in your own imagination. I've learned so much and I've been to so many places by reading a book. So I guess I do enjoy reading."

"That makes perfect sense to me," Carlos responded.

"How about you Carlos?"

"I wasn't raised reading books. The only books I read are the school books I was assigned. I guess I saw books in a negative way because I looked at them as homework, and I hate homework."

"Well, don't get me wrong, I hate homework too. Why in the world do we need to do twenty problems? We grasp the concept with five problems."

"I agree with you," Carlos said.

"I recommend you start reading books that interest you. That might help. I've read some of my dad's law books. That material is so boring that if I were to read it too long I'd fall asleep. But my dad has an amazing interest in those books."

"My mom is the one that usually reads. She reads the Bible and magazines. But she never really explained the benefits of reading to me," Carlos said.

"Interesting," Liz said.

"Both my parents respect doctors, lawyers, teachers, and many others. But I never remember them explaining to us how those people became successful."

"Maybe they didn't learn things from their parents growing up either – that's definitely a thought."

"Yeah, true. Just being around you and your family, and listening to your conversations, I've learned so much."

"Well, just be careful what you learn, we're not the perfect family."

"Ha-ha! I hear you, neither are we," Carlos laughs.

"Carlos, I feel the same way you do. Being around your family has taught me an abundance of things. I wasn't aware of how fortunate I really am until I spent some time with your family. And there's no reason why I can't share my wealth to help someone. Does that make sense?"

"Yeah, it does. I think that's very thoughtful of you. Why do you think the good Lord made some families rich and some poor? That doesn't seem fair," Carlos asked.

"That's a good question. But you could also ask why did the good Lord bless you with such amazing talent in sports?"

"Yeah, it's crazy isn't it?"

"That's for sure."

While they talk and eat dinner, their plates are suddenly empty.

"Are you ready for some pie?" Liz asked.

"That sounds great. I'll take milk with mine," Carlos said.

"Okay, I'll get some out of the fridge and you go milk the cow for yours."

"What?"

"Just kidding," Liz laughs.

A Surprising Call

The Christmas break is something Carlos is enjoying a lot. Not going to school and sleeping in, what teenager wouldn't enjoy such a treat? He is also spending time with Liz and Harv. He played many games that he had never heard of with Liz's family. They introduced him to several board games and some video pong.

One evening after Carlos has just returned from basketball practice, his mom is sitting in the living room reading a magazine. She hears him come in.

"Carlos, someone called for you today."

"Who?"

"It sounded like an older man – he said he would call back later."

"Okay. I'll be upstairs in my room."

"Okay," Isabel said.

Later that night the phone rings. Lydia picks up the phone.

"Hello."

"Yes, may I speak to Carlos?"

"Sure, hold on one minute. Carlos! It's for you!"

"Coming!"

Carlos runs down the attic steps to grab the phone, he's curious to see who it is. Could it be Coach Durham from Texas? Or maybe one of the Gervais coaches? He had no clue. He grabs the phone from Lydia.

"Hello," Carlos answers the phone.

"Well hello young man. I'm Gil."

"Hello Gil, is that short for Gilbert?"

"No … just Gil. My name used to be Gilbert, but I didn't like it so I had it changed to just Gil."

"Okay Gil, what can I help you with?"

"I received an anonymous tip from someone about how well you throw the football as a freshman in high school. So a few weeks ago I decided to come watch you at the state championship game in Portland. Needless to say, I was not disappointed."

"Well that's nice to hear Gil," Carlos said.

"Anyway, I don't want to take too much of your time, but I would like to meet with you at a later time after your basketball season is over – just to talk."

"Talk about what?"

"Carlos, I'm a scout. I'm an NFL scout. I'll be keeping an eye on you for the next three or four years. You have a gift that doesn't come by too often."

"An NFL scout?"

"Yes sir, you have a great future in the NFL ahead of you son."

"I don't know what to say. It sounds really good," Carlos said.

"Well, one thing for sure is I'd like for you to keep this between you and me. Don't tell anyone. I mean, you can tell your family, but no one else. They have rules and I don't want to break any of them. I'm not trying to recruit you, but that's not saying that I won't be trying in three years. I'm just trying to look out for you and our team."

"Okay, sure. No problem."

"And when we meet, you are welcome to bring your parents and maybe even a friend, but no one else. I'll call you again after basketball season. It's been a real pleasure talking to you."

"Yeah, thanks for the call. One more thing before I let ya go."

"Yes Carlos."

"What makes you so sure I'll be able to play in the NFL?"

"Son, I haven't seen a quarterback with your kind of talent in a very long time. I've been around quarterbacks all my life. I know a gift when I see one. You're a very special young man."

"Okay sir, thank you. I look forward to meet'n with ya."

Carlos hangs up the phone and has a big smile on his face.

"Who was that?" Isabel asked.

"Some NFL scout, not sure from what team but I think that's really exciting!"

"NFL scout, what do you mean?"

"Scouts are people that search for new talent, like players they are interested in. Mom, the NFL pays big time money."

"Sounds too good to be true," Isabel walks off to the kitchen.

The rest of the day Carlos can only imagine what it would be like to play NFL football some day. He calls Liz up and talks to her for hours about the telephone call he received.

"Carlos I know that sounds great right now, but you really should think about the remaining high school years you have in front of you. If that's what you're meant to do in the future, it'll all fall into place for you. But you need to focus on your education first."

"Yeah, I fully understand that, and you're right."

"But very exciting! I fully agree with you," Liz said.

"I'll keep you updated when he calls me again, and I would really love for you to be there with me if I decide to meet with this person."

"Thanks, I'd love to be there."

Carlos was so excited about someone wanting to talk to him about the NFL for his future. He didn't know the complexity of recruiting and what was legal as far as recruiting a player right out of high school. But it didn't matter, because to him there is hope that some day he could possibly pull his family out of poverty. Naturally getting through high school is a priority for him. Getting a college education is something important to him as well. When he graduates from high school, if he stays healthy, he will have the option to play either college or professional football.

The next day Pete is replacing the air filter in the Ford station wagon.

"Hi Dad."

"What are you up to Carlos?"

"I have a question for you."

"What question?"

"When I graduate high school, what do you think I should do if I have a choice of playing professional football or college football?"

"I think that if you're offered a lot of money to play football for the NFL someday, I'd want you to take it in a second. The one thing you want to prevent is getting hurt and not ever having that opportunity again."

"That makes sense to me. I could always go back and get my education during the off-season."

"During the what?" Pete asked.

"Oh, sorry – off-season is any other season other than football."

"I see."

"Thanks for your opinion Dad," Carlos starts to walk away.

"Carlos, can you hand me that half-inch wrench?"

"Sure Dad. By the way, if I ever make it to the NFL, will you come to at least one of my games?" Carlos asked as he hands him the wrench.

"Son, if you make it to the NFL, I'll be the first one to buy a plane ticket to come watch your game – thanks for the wrench."

Carlos has everything going for him. His grades are really good and he is one of the top athletes in the state. His girlfriend is the prettiest and smartest girl at Gervais High School. His future in football is looking very bright. Carlos has been able to fit in with the Bradfords, which takes some doing.

The only thing now is for him to continue doing what he has been doing and to not give up on a college education. We don't know what the future holds and what might happen. Sports are a risk. Every time you step on the football field or the basketball court, there's always a chance of injury.

To dream and to desire gives this young man the discipline and the work ethic to never give up on following a dream that could provide for him and his family. Can a Texas transfer become a legend at Gervais High School? Time can only tell.